To Be
Continued

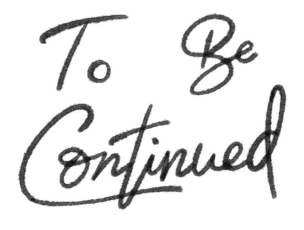

To Be Continued

NOW

BOOK TWO

GRACE WOODS

PURPLE INK
LLC
SHERIDAN, WY

To Be Continued Now

Copyright © 2023 by Grace Woods and Purple Ink LLC
All rights reserved under International and Pan-American Copyright Conventions.

Published by

PURPLE|NK
  L L C
1309 Coffeen Ave.
Sheridan, WY 82801

Library of Congress 2023909823
ISBN 979-8-9884133-6-3 (print)
ISBN 979-8-9884133-3-2 (ebook)

Author's Note:

Welcome to book two of the To Be Continued Trilogy. It's thrilling to share this racy and inspiring love story with you. Just a heads up, in book two there are brief mentions of gun violence and sexual misconduct. There's also imagination, devotion, and chemistry so hot the periodic table blushes.

You're in for a joy ride.

CHAPTER I

WHY ARE YOU HERE?

Ashley Barris locked eyes with the man sitting in the SUV parked below her living room window. Though it was dark and his face was unreadable, his eyes reflected the dim amber of the streetlight.

"Please," she whispered, though no one could hear the one-word prayer except her cat, Bamba, who was nuzzling her leg. Ashley wasn't sure if she meant *Please go* or *Please, come back into my life*. All she knew was in this moment, every nerve in her body was buzzing with unnamed want, and her blood thrummed through her, forceful, like river rapids inside her circulatory system, raging against the confines of her body.

"Luke," she whispered. His name tasted sweet in her mouth, like a favorite dessert she'd gone without for too long and now craved.

In fact, she was starving for him—a full-body hunger. After she'd left him two weeks ago, furious about his willingness to plunder the earth for corporate greed, she'd done everything she could to erase her memories of him. Just today, she'd blocked his texts and deleted him from her contacts. She'd set all but one of his gifts aside in a bag to take to the thrift store—it was too painful to have them around. She'd even stopped eating certain foods that reminded her too much of him.

But seeing Luke tonight at the Lift House Gala, breathing him in—that masculine, musky, citrusy scent—feeling his presence and, even more powerful, feeling the way her heart leapt up when she saw him, the way her breath caught in her chest, well, she was overwhelmed.

In this breathless moment, it didn't seem to matter anymore that Luke was an oil executive whose company she protested—a company that even now was one of several planning to drill in the Arctic. At this very moment, all she could remember was how beautifully her body blossomed beneath his touch, how whole she felt when they were together. *Two sides of the same coin*, he had once said to her.

No, no, no, don't do it, said her armored self as she reached into her purse, but her fingers were full of *yes* as she found his contact and pressed Call.

Luke answered in the silence before the phone even rang on her end. She heard him breathe in, a serrated pull of air, before he exhaled her name in a ragged petition for mercy. "Ashley." Her knees noodled at the need in his baritone voice—so vulnerable, so raw.

"Luke." Her heart stomped and thrashed like a bull in its bucking chute trying to escape into the arena.

In the silence that followed, they gazed at each other through the glass, through the darkness. Ashley opened the window and felt the hot air rush in; Houston summer nights offered little respite from the heat. She could hear his Chevy wasn't running, and a smile almost found her lips. Luke knew how idling car engines infuriated her.

"John's gone," he gritted.

From where he was sitting, Luke would have seen John Truman, her date from the gala, drive away just moments after her living room light turned on. The statement was Luke's way of asking *why* John had left. As if she would have asked him in.

Did he really think she would see someone else so soon after she'd left *him*?

"He's gone," she echoed.

"Thank god."

She could barely see into the dark car, but she could make out his hand pushing through his hair to massage the top of his head. It made her long to run her fingers through that black silk again, to feel the light spring in the curls as she tugged. He exhaled long and slow.

"Luke, why are you here?"

"I had to see you, Ashley. I miss you. I miss your smile. I miss your soft hands in my hands. I miss your laugh. I miss you telling me to get out of the shower already. I miss your terrible puns and your science geek way of seeing the world. I miss the smell of you and the warmth of you in bed beside me and hearing you speak Spanish on the phone with your mentee. I miss everything about you. And then when I saw you at the gala with John, I…" His voice broke. "I heard what he said to you. How he's hoping for *something real, something beautiful, something lasting* with you." The words sounded ripped from his throat.

Ashley's mouth was dry. No words would come.

"Is that what you want, Ashley? John?"

"Luke—" Her voice was thick with warning.

"Are you sleeping with him?"

"Stop it. No."

Despite her sharp tone, Luke's answering sigh was saturated with relief. "Good." He inhaled a tortured, ragged breath. "Tonight, watching you two together, it was ripping me apart, wondering if you—"

Ashley remembered the look on Luke's face, how he'd recoiled. He had so much strength, but in that tender moment when he'd overheard John confessing his attraction to her, she'd seen how vulnerable Luke was, too.

"Say something." His tone was needy and low. "I need to hear your voice, Ashley. Say something."

"Thank you for coming tonight." She kept her tone slightly formal, cloaking it in an audible armor for her own protection. "To the gala, I mean. I was surprised to see you, but I'm grateful you supported the Lift House. It's so important for the teens."

There was a brief pause in which she heard only the quiet song of Luke's breath and her own beating heart, an intimate duet. Ashley was astonished by how deeply their connection was communicated in that silence. Finally, he spoke. "I want you to say, *Come upstairs.* I want you to say, *Let's talk.* I want you to say we have a chance."

She felt a caving in her chest. "I'm not going to say that, Luke."

"Then I'll say it. Can I come up? Let's talk." He stepped out of the car into the lamplight, still looking up at her window. The streetlamp washed him in an amber glow, and she took in his strong arms straining against his rumpled dress shirt, his fit waist and long legs. Even when he was standing still, she could sense a wild energy that paced through him, as if he were trying not to charge her building and run up the stairs to meet her. Electricity tangled through the nerves along her spine, firing like lightning into her limbs.

Ashley wanted to say yes. She was tired of protecting herself. Tired of pretending she wasn't utterly devoted to this man. Tired of the war in her—how could she adore his heart and mind but hate his actions? Exhausted, she felt her resistance to his urging start to weaken.

One. Two. Three. Four. Feeling out of control, she'd subconsciously begun to count streetlamps on the block. She shook her head. "Better not come up."

"Then you come down." In the lamplight, she could see his face—unmasked, hopeful, eager. Could he see her expressions as well?

She paused, and he capitalized on her hesitation. "Okay. Not tonight. But tomorrow. Tomorrow morning, I'd like to cash in two hours of my Spanish lessons." Luke had bought ten hours of Spanish instruction from Ashley in the gala's silent auction—and had paid an exorbitant price. "It was slightly underhanded, I suppose, for me to buy those lessons, but it gave me hope, Ashley, hope that you would see me and remember, remember who I am, who *we* are. And we carry our hope with us—"

"—until it *becomes* us." Ashley couldn't help but finish Luke's sentence. It was a phrase that his beloved childhood nanny, Rena, had often used when he was a child. After meeting Rena, Ashley had started to use the phrase, too—even had thought it during her speech at the gala. Funny, the things that become glue between two people, like a common lexicon. It both hurt and healed her to fall into this easy connection between them.

Luke made a purr of satisfaction deep in his throat when she spoke the familiar words. "Yes, Ashley. And look what we've *become*. I learned so much about you tonight when you delivered your speech about how you'd run away from home and became a resident at Lift House. The more I know of your story, the more I'm astonished by you. I know my work bothers you, but I'm not a villain. It's not that simple, Ashley. There's more to my story, too. Let me share it with you?"

Ashley inhaled, but she didn't say anything. Was she really considering letting him in again?

"Go with me to the museum tomorrow? I'll pick you up."

Ashley looked up to the sky, where she couldn't see the stars shining through the glow of the city. *So much hidden light.*

"I'll meet you there."

"Really?" His surprise made her smile.

*"Por supuesto que sí."** *Oh, I'll give you Spanish lessons*, she thought with a smirk, a plan unfolding in her mind. But the smirk became steely as she thought of other lessons she'd hoped she could instill upon him—like how fragile the earth's ecosystems are and how important it was for him to change the focus of his family's empire from oil to renewables. "I'll meet you there at noon."

"Good night, then, Ashley. Dream of me?" He held up a hand toward her window, as if from the distance he was cradling her face, then climbed into his Chevy, and the SUV roared to life. She winced.

Sí, she whispered, though the phone call had ended. *I absolutely will dream of you.* Just last night, she'd dreamed of ecstatic lovemaking, her dream body recalling with ease just how good it was between them. With a sigh, she pressed her forehead to the glass and watched the Chevy's red taillights disappear. It would be a long time before sleep would find her, not until after she let her fingers do what they were longing to do, Luke's name floating from her lips.

⸻

Ashley woke the next morning to a room full of sunshine and the bright ping of an incoming text. 8:06? How had she slept in like that? She rolled over and picked up the phone.

John: Hey beautiful. Meet for lunch?

Ashley sighed and leaned back into her pillows.

Ashley: Sorry, I have plans

John: Cancel them

Ashley: Can't

John: Let me pick you up for dinner?

---

* Yes, of course.

Ashley: Sorry

John: Rain check?

Ashley stared out into the brightest of mornings, not a cloud in all of Texas. Would the day come when she would want to make good on that rain check?

John was a wonderful man, a handsome, generous, kind, and smart man. And they were compatible in so many ways, both invested in education, community service, and protecting the environment. Sure, she'd thought about what it might be like between them, though he'd been strictly off-limits when he was the principal at her school. He was amazing. And he was interested in her.

But he's not Luke.

And there it was. Her heart was planted and rooted in another garden. No matter how hard she had tried to push Luke away, disheartened as she was by his involvement with fossil fuels and his commitment to perpetuate global dependence on oil, she was still drawn to Luke.

You can't change a man, her mom had said, *but you can find new ways to meet him.*

How her mom had so much wisdom about men was beyond her. Ashley's dad had disappeared from their lives when Ashley was four; Ashley hadn't seen him since. And as far as she knew, her mom had never dated after that. Still, her mom's wisdom echoed true. *You can find new ways to meet him.*

As much as she told herself she was meeting Luke today to honor her commitment to the Spanish lessons, she knew that was a lie. She was meeting him today because, painful as it was, her heart and her body completely belonged to him.

Nothing's changed, said her brain. *You're just setting yourself up for heartbreak again.*

Ashley sighed.

John: ??

you there??

There would be a time to talk more honestly with John about her feelings—once she figured them out herself.

Ashley: yeah.

Rain check, please?

CHAPTER 2

LUKE WAS ALREADY WAITING outside the museum when Ashley walked up the stairs to the giant marble building. Ashley paused mid-step to take him in—his raven hair slicked back on top, dark, loose curls hanging down past his ears. His sharp jawline. His blue eyes already locked on hers. Even at rest, his full lips were always set toward a smile, a sweet predisposition. At the moment, he was smiling broadly, as if her appearance was the best gift he could ever receive. Nothing reserved about it.

Seeing his smile, Ashley felt as if each cell of her had just grown wings, and all at once, they fluttered.

Doomed.

He was dressed in a light gray T-shirt that hugged his fit torso, leaving little to the imagination, and the short sleeves showed off his well-defined arms. Ashley blushed, her body warming as she remembered how good it felt to be wrapped in those arms. His jeans hung low on his waist, showing off his flat midriff. She remembered tracing her fingers down the dark line from his belly button to his— *Oh.* Catching herself in the memory of exploring his body made her instantly self-conscious and awkward. Suddenly, walking up the museum stairs felt as if she were walking in a carnival fun house full of moving floors and deceptive mirrors, and she was not quite able to figure out how to put her foot onto the next step.

Luke closed the gap with long, easy strides, stopping on the step above her. At six foot one, he was over half a foot taller than she was, but the added height of the step made her tilt her head even more to look him in the eye.

"You look breathtaking," he murmured, causing a sweet tremor to ripple through her chest. Ashley looked down at the navy cotton sundress she had chosen, simple and humble, light and comfortable. He didn't follow her gaze, keeping his eyes locked to her face. "The dress is lovely on you, but that's not what I'm talking about. *You* are beautiful, Ashley."

Her heart thudded hard against her ribs. While one part of her told her to not succumb to his flirtation, another part whispered, *Game on.*

Ashley looked at him innocently. "*¿Te refieres a las ojeras debajo de mis ojos?*"*

Luke raised an eyebrow, clearly not understanding what she'd said, but his grin responded to her tone, which had come out slightly flirtier than she'd expected.

"I see the Spanish lesson's begun." He reached up as if to pull a strand of honey-brown hair back from her face, but he stopped himself. Her cheek felt the absence of his fingers. "How did you sleep?"

"*No dormí.*"**

"You said you couldn't sleep, right?"

Ashley nodded, raising an eyebrow in approval. Of course, his French would help him decode some of what she said—that and living in Texas most of his life, where he would have been surrounded by Spanish.

---

* You mean the dark circles under my eyes?
** I didn't sleep.

"I hope you were awake thinking about *me*." His voice lowered, and his eyes flashed. "Perhaps you knew I was dreaming about you. All. Night."

Double doomed. Her breath emerged in shallow pants. Her heart was so defenseless around him, yet her values still had their dukes up.

"*Desearía que hubieras estado soñando en cómo salvar el planeta. Eso sería muy sexy.*"* She fluttered her eyelashes and threw her most beguiling smile his way.

"I heard the word *sexy*. That sounded good."

She chuckled in a *you-missed-the-best-part-of-what-I-said* way.

"You do know that Spanish lessons usually involve helping your student *understand* the language, right?"

"*Correcto.*"** She grinned at him smugly. "Okay, Luke. Lesson one. Repeat after me. *La perforación petrolera en el Ártico es peligrosa y debe detenerse.*"***

Luke repeated the words in short phrases, and though his pronunciation made him sound like the gringo he was, he was careful and clear in his echoing of her speech about not drilling in the Arctic. The words on his lips made her smile.

"What did I say?" he asked.

"You said, 'I like learning new things.'"

"Lucky for you, I am already a fool and don't mind being used for your"—he shrugged a shoulder—"amusement."

A blush bloomed in her chest. "*Bueno.*"****

"Come on." He angled his head toward the front door. "There's something I've been looking forward to showing you."

---

* I wish you had been dreaming about how to save the planet. That would be very sexy.
** Right.
*** Oil drilling in the Arctic is dangerous and should be stopped.
**** Good.

Ashley followed Luke in, and they walked past the ticket line to the main entrance. Luke flashed a membership card at the guard, who gave Luke a happy salute, and they were both ushered in. Ashley wrinkled her brow, and he smiled at her confusion.

"They know me here."

She followed him through the main atrium toward the back exhibition halls. Past a black allosaurus skeleton. Past a saber-tooth tiger that growled when kids fed it coins. It had been many years since she'd been in the museum—perhaps the beginning of college when she was earning her degree in environmental science with a minor in chemistry.

Ashley felt a little giddy, and it wasn't all due to being near Luke. It was also the place. She stopped and stood a moment to take it all in. Luke paused beside her and gave her a questioning look. She was so overcome with nostalgia she forgot all about the game she'd been playing, speaking to him only in Spanish.

"It's just—I remember the first time I came here. I was in fifth grade on a school field trip, one of my first trips into the opulence of the city, and I remember thinking this giant marble building was the closest thing to heaven I could imagine." She opened both hands, as if holding the memory. "There's so much knowledge here. So much to explore. I wonder why I don't come here more often?"

"What exhibit was your favorite?"

"Oh, the rocks. I loved the rocks."

Luke smiled a secret smile. "Gems and Minerals. My favorite, too. Let's go there now."

When they got to the exhibit entrance, Ashley looked up and startled at the placard there. The Jeremiah James Dalton Gems and Minerals Hall.

"Wait." She touched Luke's shoulder and immediately pulled her hand back, stunned by the electricity. "Is this where you wanted to bring me?"

Luke grinned.

An older woman docent walked up to them, smiling broadly. "Welcome, Mr. Dalton. Nice to see you again. It's been a while. The rocks have missed you."

"Hi, Marcy." He gave her a generous, genuine smile. "Let me introduce you to my friend Ashley. Ashley, Marcy." The two women shook hands. "Ashley hasn't seen the exhibit for a long time, I think, but once upon a time, it was her favorite."

"Oh, it's many people's favorite." She nodded. "Certainly mine. And widely considered the finest collection in the world, rare specimens gathered from mines and private collections around the globe over the past century and a half. In fact—"

As the docent and Luke chatted a moment about recent additions to the exhibit, it occurred to Ashley that Luke showing off his family's museum wing could be construed as pompous. As if she cared about his dirty oil money. But there was something so childlike and authentic about his excitement in being here and something so humble about the way he interacted with the docent—not just polite, but excited, both geeking out as they discussed hexagonal crystal systems and "precipitation events in ascending hydrothermal solutions." Her own inner geek perked her ears. Luke's eyes sparkled as he listened to the docent. He was so alive it made her come to life, and she realized in this moment she was seeing the best side of him—the enthusiastic, curious, most human side of him.

"Come on." Luke broke her reverie, respectfully not touching her but gesturing her into the exhibit.

They wandered through the night-dark halls, the only light coming from the cases, illuminating the stones. Ashley loved

thinking about the chemical compositions and how they result-
ed in the most extraordinary colors and shapes. Though she'd
just been laid off during budget cuts two weeks ago, her years
of teaching high school chemistry gave her a strong academic
background to understand what she was seeing.

But Luke's interest in rocks went way beyond academic discipline. His degree had been in geology, but as they looked at
long green gypsum crystals and the curiously perfect dark cube
of pyrite and the unusual golden flakes of wulfenite, Luke de-
scribed to her the stories about the places the minerals had been
found and stories about the miners who had found them. He
related, too, the energies associated with most of the different
gems and minerals. "Just because the energy is ineffable doesn't
mean it isn't real," he said.

She stood for a while in front of a striking red crystalline
specimen.

"The rhodochrosite crystals are rare," Luke murmured, his
mouth close to her ear. "Look at the perfect, prismatic cleavage,
almost all at right angles."

Was it the nearness of him, the tease of his scent without
his touch, or the dark forests in his voice that gave her the shivers? Ashley closed her eyes as her whole body focused on the
warmth of his breath on her ear, her neck.

"Look at it," Luke purred. Her eyes fluttered open. "Imagine
the metamorphic forces that made it. Sometimes, when I watch
you come, Ashley"—his voice deepened—"when I watch you
come, it feels like this: a revelation of explosion, a beauty born
out of contact with magma, a bright crimson release forged
from unrelenting heat."

And then he walked away, focusing his attention on the next
window full of stones, leaving her wanting, almost gasping, gaping at the rhodochrosite that was now a visual metaphor for the

earth-shattering bliss she'd experienced with him in their love-making. Her whole body ached with the loss of his presence.

Now who's playing with whom?

When her heart rate slowed and her breathing calmed, Ashley moved to stand beside him. He was staring at a crystallized gold structure. "*Te gustan las rocas.*"*

Luke ignored that she was playing a game with him and lifted a hand toward the case, keeping his gaze focused on the glittering mass. "Isn't it marvelous? Look what the earth can make. Look what it gives us. With heat. Pressure. Time. This."

He gazed at it intently, admiringly. "When I was a boy, I would come here and stare at these rocks for hours. I fell in love with them, with the earth. That early curiosity became a doorway for me with my work—the thrill of learning more and more about the earth's building blocks. All rocks have energy stored in them. All rocks have stories. All of them, including oil, are expressions of how the earth shares its remarkable gifts with us."

Ashley stared at the gold crystals rising, almost in the shape of a dragon.

"I wish my great-great-grandfather could see this: this crystalline gold, this room with his name on it, his legacy. This exhibit began as his private collection. He struggled as a wildcatter, but he had dreams. He had dreams of becoming wealthy, *not only* so he could be rich, *but also* so he could share his wealth. As you know, his motto that's been passed down through our family is *not only, but also.*"

"Not only, but also," Ashley echoed. She remembered well the first time Luke had told her about this motto. It was during their first open discussion about his company promoting fossil fuels versus renewables.

---

* You like rocks.

"My great-great-grandfather said you need to pay attention to the soil, to give the land respect. That's how he started Dalton Oil." He turned to face her, and though the room was dark, his eyes glittered, as if they were blue tourmalines that belonged here in the hall of gems.

"I want to give the land respect, Ashley. That's what brought me into the work I do. That and, well…" He took a deep breath. "Everyone knew *my brother* was destined to be the one who followed Dad into the family business. He chose to read books about geology and mining, even at age eleven. Dad was over the moon."

Ashley let out a soft sigh as two young kids ran past them, playing chase through the exhibit, and their mother called after them to walk.

In the silence, as they waited for the family to pass, Ashley remembered the day in Memorial Park when Luke had first told her about how his brother, Jimmy, had been killed in a terrible accident when the boys were ten and twelve. They'd been playing chase with their sister, Elaine, when Luke had found a gun in their parents' closet, and in a moment of childish exuberance and play, Luke had fatally shot his older brother.

Ashley and Luke moved to a quieter corner of the hall, and he continued to share his story. "After Jimmy died, I did everything I could to step into his shoes, to make good on his life. I didn't really know I was doing it until a therapist pointed it out. How I had started to collect monkeys because that was *his* favorite animal. How I had learned to make jokes because *he* was the funny one. I would rather read a book than watch a football game, but to this day, I watch football games with my father because Jimmy would. And I stepped into the family business *because Jimmy would have*. So, you see, working for our family's business is not just a job for me." He took a deep breath. "It's how I fill the hole where my brother would be if I hadn't picked up that gun. But I couldn't do my job, Ashley, if I didn't also believe that in some ways, I am being of service to the world."

For a while, they just stood there in the dim, breathing into the loss that was still so present for Luke.

"Sometimes when I come here, I think I can feel my great-great-grandfather, can feel the love he had for me before I was born. I can feel that he would love me and forgive me, even after what I did. It's weird, right, to feel the love and forgiveness of someone you never knew?"

Ashley thought right away of her father. Could she feel her father loved her? Or did she just feel the *wanting* to be loved by him?

"You're a good man, Luke." She gave his hand a squeeze, then reluctantly, she moved to pull her hand from his, but he didn't let her, and she gave in to how good it felt to be touching, her whole body attuning to his as heliotropic flowers attune to the sun. She could tell he felt it, too, a connection that had longing in it, but even more than that, a connection that resonated with *belonging*. His eyes sought hers.

"I'm not worthy of you, Ashley, but I want to be. Being without you these weeks has been hell. Something is shifting in me. I have thought so much about things you've said. I want to be good enough for you."

Something in Ashley clicked. "It was you, wasn't it?"

Luke gave her a blank look.

"It was you who gave the anonymous one-million-dollar donation last night."

He shook his head. "No."

So humble. "You don't need to be modest about it."

"It wasn't me."

Of course he wants to stay anonymous. So in keeping with his character. Ashley feigned belief. "Well, *whoever* it is, I just want to say thank you to *that person*. It was generous and will make such a big difference to the homeless teens."

Luke shrugged and pulled her a little closer by the hand. "I did, however, spend five thousand dollars on Spanish lessons, and so far, all I've learned to say is *I'm a good learner*. What else do you have for me?" His voice was dark and suggestive, and Ashley's body immediately responded, softening, melting, her heart pulsing.

"What do you want to learn, Luke?"

"How about, *I'm hungry*?"

"*Tengo hambre.*"

"*Tengo hambre*," he echoed.

"Good." She rewarded him with a smile.

"How about, *May I take you to lunch?*"

"*¿Puedo llevarte a almorzar?*"

He dutifully repeated the Spanish phrase, then gave her a pointed look. "And now you say, *Yes*."

"*Y ahora dices sí.*"

"What did you just say?"

Ashley raised an eyebrow. "*And now you say yes.*"

"Sassy girl." He leaned down closer to whisper in her ear. "How do you say, *Later I'm hoping you'll let me eat you*."

Ashley blushed. "*Te mostraré cómo se hacen realmente esos cristales rojos*,"* she said, referring to the rhodochrosite exhibit they'd seen before.

"Now what did you say?"

"I said, *Let's go find a café*."

---

* I'll show you how those red crystals are really made.

CHAPTER 3

"I COULDN'T HAVE DONE what you did last night." Luke shook his head in admiration. "Telling your story to a whole room full of people? That was powerful." The glint in Luke's blue eyes looked something like pride, and Ashley felt her whole being orient to him, as if he were her true north.

They were sitting under a red umbrella at a small round table on the museum's patio, eating salads and drinking iced tea. Their glasses were sweating in the mid-July heat, and Ashley was grateful for the cool and bitter drink. Everything about her was running hot right now.

Sit tall.

"Honestly, I didn't think I could get up there last night either." Ashley had been the keynote speaker at the event, sharing how her work as a mentor for Lift House had evolved out of her being a resident. Though she didn't have a fear of public speaking like Luke did, she'd still felt nervous, even though she'd been longing for that moment for years.

"You didn't seem nervous."

"But I was." Ashley squirmed inside. What she didn't want to tell Luke was she'd gotten a lot of strength from him being there—from seeing his face in the crowd. While she stood on-stage, she'd felt as if she were speaking only to him, and it had given her the confidence she needed.

"There's so much more I want to know about you." He leaned closer. "I know the woman you are now—strong and determined and generous. I want to know *everything* about how you got to be that way. I want to know more about what drives you. About the days in the life of Ashley as a girl, Ashley as a teen. Ashley in college."

Ashley smiled and shook her head. "You always make me feel as if you really want to hear about my life."

"I *do*. I want to know everything about you." His voice got soft. "Even about why you left me. I can't change who I am, Ashley, but I can change how we connect."

His words were full of double meaning, infused with urgency and devotion, and they warmed her, melting her reserve like ice in the sun. For all their challenges, there was no doubt in her mind this man cared for her deeply, truly. "I want to ask you a million things first. But *first* first, will you tell me more about the story you told last night? Why did you need to leave home?"

Ashley leaned back in her chair. "Oh, Luke. It's old history." She sighed, and then, to her surprise, she shuddered. "And it's still hard to talk about."

"You don't have to tell me."

"I want to. Thank you for asking. It wasn't easy to bring it up last night. In fact, I told Mom not to come to the event because I didn't want my speech to stir anything up in her, but I think it might help me to talk about it." She took a hesitant breath.

"Where to start. Mom had breast cancer. I was almost seventeen. Jewel was thirteen. We were both in school, and Mom needed someone to be there at home to help her—mainly, I suppose, to get her to and from the hospital for her chemo and radiation appointments."

Luke nodded, his eyes locked on hers.

"Mom was so weak. I guess that was the first time I understood how human she was. Before that, she'd always seemed so strong. Superhuman, really. They said she'd recover, but the treatments made her weak, sick, depressed, and, well, small." Ashley put both hands up to rub her temples as she spoke, and Luke gave her the space she needed to collect her thoughts.

"So, Mom asked her brother, Spencer, to come live with us and help her. He didn't have a job, so it worked out for him. Mom couldn't see what a creep he was. 'My brother's a saint,' she would say." Her face twisted with the memory.

"Did he hurt you, Ashley?" Ashley watched Luke's hands form into fists. An attempt to contain his anger?

It occurred to her she'd never really seen Luke angry, and she almost laughed, struck by some strange relief that sixteen years after the horrific event, she finally had a protector. Though she couldn't imagine Luke hurting anyone, his indignation was a salve for the painful memories.

"He didn't hurt me. At least not physically." She felt her own fists start to clench. "A few times, I saw him in the doorway of my room staring at me when he thought I was sleeping. I didn't know what to do about it, so I pretended I was asleep. Great survival tactic, right, play dead? Tonic immobility doesn't really work—just ask the truly dead opossums. But a week later, while I was taking a shower, my uncle came into the bathroom and stared at me through the glass shower door and started…" Her heart picked up speed. "He started jacking off in the doorway. I told him I would scream, but he put his finger to his lips and said, 'You don't want to bother your mother, do you? She couldn't handle it right now.' And I knew he was right. She was so weak. So, I…"

She closed her eyes, just as she'd done when she was sixteen. As if by closing her eyes, she could make it go away. She tried not to replay in her memory the thick grunts he'd made as he came, the viscous shadow of shame covering her again.

"I closed my eyes and turned my body toward the wall. He laughed at me and told me to turn around so he could see me. But I wouldn't. He told me I owed him. That he needed *favors* for taking care of my mom." She could taste the bile of sixteen years ago rise again in her throat.

"Did he touch you?" Luke whispered.

She shook her head. "I left. That day. I went to the family of one of Jewel's friends nearby and asked if she could stay with them for a while. I made up some excuse. I told my mom I was staying at a friend's house, too, but neither of my two close friends could let me stay with them. One had an alcoholic father, and the other had her grandparents already living with them. I had a friend who was living at Lift House already. I knew where it was, so I just showed up there. And they took me in."

"So, your mom had no idea."

"That's how sick she was, Luke. She was so out of it with pain and the effects of the treatment she just nodded when I told her we were giving our uncle more room so he'd be more comfortable in our small house. And I called her every night to check on her, so she didn't know any better."

"And then what happened?"

"I eventually told one of the counselors at Lift about what my uncle had done. We had lots of counseling there—group, individual. It took me weeks to tell them, partly because I was ashamed and felt like the whole thing was my fault. And partly because I knew Mom needed his help. I knew she needed him to drive her to her appointments so she could get better. I didn't have my license yet."

"What a horrible thing to handle."

"Yeah, well, when I finally got brave enough to tell them what happened, Lift reported the creep to CPS and found a volunteer who helped Mom with the driving. And Jewel and I moved back in. It was so simple once I asked for help, I felt stupid for not telling them sooner what was really going on."

"Not stupid. Totally understandable."

"That was when I learned I have a tendency to not talk about conflict." She chuckled. "I obviously don't have a problem about speaking up when it comes to helping *other* people or the *earth*—but when it comes to my personal life, saying nothing and running away are patterns." Ashley looked at Luke, realization dawning in her. "And maybe I still have a lot of work to do on that front."

Luke's eyes sparkled. "Perhaps I can help with that." He pulled a little wooden elephant out of his pocket and put it on the table between them. Ashley smiled, remembering the other talks they'd had with this very same elephant-in-the-room token between them. "What do you want to meet head-on, Ashley?"

Ashley spent a full minute in silence being wrestled by his question. What was she most afraid to meet head-on with Luke? It was clear her body craved him, ached for him, screamed for him. It was clear her heart belonged to him. It was clear he was devoted to her. But was that enough? Could longing and connection overcome her fury and repulsion about his work? Could she ever move forward with their relationship when he was moving forward with fossil fuels? How had she managed to reconcile a love affair with an oil executive? "Okay." She picked up the elephant and blew out a big breath. She wanted more than talk. She wanted action. "Take me to your office."

⁓

Luke had not wanted to bring Ashley to his office. For all his willingness to talk and listen, he seemed very reluctant to take her to the heart of operations, Dalton Oil, the building where she had spent many hours protesting on the sidewalks, the architectural symbol for why Ashley had left him.

But here they were in the shiny elevator, riding to the top floor. Ashley's heart was a renegade metronome, thumping erratically against her chest. After a decade of chanting on the sidewalk outside, here she was behind enemy lines. She'd stiffened at that thought. Was Luke really her enemy? All those years with her protest sign in her hand, it had *seemed* that simple. Dalton was the enemy. She was the good guy. Dalton was wrong. She was right. But now, standing beside Luke Dalton—thoughtful, generous Luke Dalton—everything felt much more complicated.

Luke was rigid beside her, not at all the jovial man he'd been at the museum. She knew what he most wanted for this day was for them to reconnect, to see all the reasons they belonged together. But what *she* most needed was to face what had torn them apart.

The doors opened to an ocean of cubicles. Ashley stepped into the room. "Take me to your office." Her voice was steely, but she was shaking inside. Luke was silent as he led her through the partitions. Though there were no people, TV screens flickered everywhere. *Five, six, seven, eight,* she counted the screens in her head.

They passed through an elegant reception area with a sleek desk and a series of square glass chandeliers that cast a cool light into the modern space.

"And this way." Luke guided her around the corner to a wall of frosted glass. He scanned a fob, and a glass door opened into a spacious room. The shades on the floor-to-ceiling windows rose and let in sunlight and the shining Houston skyline.

"Wow." She walked to the windows and took in the world below. She hadn't thought a view would move her, but something about this new vantage of the city she had lived in all her life stirred her.

Luke was giving her generous space. He stood at the edge of the room, watching her as she took in his domain. As she moved slowly, cautiously, she reminded herself of her cat, Bamba, the first time the cat had come to her apartment—tentative but curious.

The room itself was spare—a dark brown stone floor, glossy and smooth. Two long couches, boxy and modern. A loosely woven rug. A low glass coffee table with nothing on it but the crystal monkey she had bought for Luke in London. At the time she bought it, she hadn't known his monkey collection was an homage to his brother. Seeing it there caused a lump to form in her throat, and she swallowed at the memory of their trip to Europe, a time both beautiful and bitter.

At the far end of the room was a dark wooden desk, asymmetrical and clean. The only two things on it were a computer screen and a glass photo frame. She walked closer and saw it held two photos—one was a photo of Luke, his sister Elaine, and his brother Jimmy when they were kids, all wearing swimsuits, all holding inner tubes up to frame their faces. The other photo was of her, a profile. She hadn't known he was taking the picture at the time—her golden hair was blowing in the wind, the Swiss Alps rising behind her. She was smiling, her face relaxed and carefree.

They'd been so happy.

She glanced up to find Luke looking at her. His open expression shocked her. It was hope.

Who knew that being with her in his office would make him so vulnerable? She was awed that this was his response—not defensiveness, not bravado, but a willingness to be exposed.

In this moment, he was so much more than Luke the oil executive who presided over the future of energy. This was the man who gave her wings—who had taught her to ski and wished on stars with her and supported her when she started her own nonprofit. This was the man who gave her his time—walked dogs with her and made her father's enchiladas and taught her to meditate. This was the man who ignited her body, who made it feel as if the sun had melted into her veins, the man who made her shiver and pant, the man who both created an overwhelming ache in her and who satisfied that ache, the man who claimed her in the most surprising ways, who made every cell of her throb and hum. This was the man who brought out her best self—the part that was a mystery even to her, the man who woke something dormant in her and breathed it into life.

This was the man she *loved*. She knew it. Though they had never spoken the word to each other, the truth of their love spread through her, a warm current of certainty. *Oh my god. I love him.* She was gobsmacked by the realization.

She didn't know how they would make things work between them, but she knew they had to. They *had* to.

She couldn't change him. She'd already learned that. But she could, what, learn from him? Or at the very least, she could let their struggles make them stronger. Could she?

Love is an invitation for us to see beyond our own convictions. That's what her mother had said after she and Luke had returned from Europe.

Love was also terrifying. *You lose the men you love*, said a familiar inner voice. *Your father, your ex-husband. Why should this be different?*

But there in Luke's opulent office, the headquarters of all she stood against, she felt her guard and her fear crumble, not in a metaphoric way but in a fully embodied way, as if in a single instant, she was shedding a thousand layers of shoulds and should nots and insecurity and loss and was left trembling and strangely new. And in this naked moment, she felt something rising in her: courage.

And curiosity. An inner voice whispered, *Let's bring it on.*

Ashley gave a little nod, as if signaling to herself she was on board, and she smiled a secret, wicked smile.

Luke tilted his head. "What are you thinking?"

She lifted her chin and raised an eyebrow. *En garde*, said her inner voice, as if a fencing match were about to begin.

Ashley made her way around the edge of the long dark desk, trailing her fingers along its polished grain, letting her hips sway. "I'm thinking there's a lot I could accomplish in this office."

Luke watched her, his blue eyes darkening as he tried to read her. His confusion somehow made her more playful.

She sat in the swivel chair and gave it a slow spin, a queen surveying her new kingdom. "Hmm."

She reached into her purse, pulled out her phone, and pretended to speak into it.

"Hello, Energy Secretary Regis? You remember that plan we had for drilling oil in the Arctic? We've reconsidered and would like to spend that full budget on remediation for past drilling disasters." She paused, as if listening to the man on the other line. "I knew you wouldn't like it, but the decision is final."

She smiled sweetly and pretended to hang up.

Luke watched her quizzically, and she gave a little shimmy as if she were just getting settled into her new chair.

She put the phone to her ear again, her eyes sparkling as she spoke. "Hello, advisory board? Yes, that's right. I am *sure* we want to transition everything into renewables." She gave a delighted laugh. "Oh, I knew you would agree." She set the phone on the desk.

Luke started to chuckle, and she watched as the grin on his face spread through the rest of his body, his whole frame relaxing.

She picked up the phone again. "Hello, engineering department?"

"Hello."

Luke had pulled his phone out of his pocket and was holding it to his ear.

"I want you to put all our engineers and researchers into developing better energy storage for solar power."

"You're in luck." His eyes flashed, and she felt an exquisite pang of lust flicker through her, her heartbeat quivering like an orange candle flame.

Yes, I believe I am.

"I'm the lead engineer, and it would be my pleasure to demonstrate for you some of the advancements we're making."

Luke's voice was full of double entendre, and he pronounced the words *pleasure* and *advancements* with a mischievous lilt. Ashley stared into his eyes as she listened, their playful act fueling her arousal. Unconsciously, she crossed her legs to give herself just the tiniest bit of friction. The move didn't go unnoticed by Luke.

"If I may come to your office, Madam CEO?"

Her lips parted. "Mm-hmm." She gave a single nod. Though she was sitting in the chair of power, it was clear who had taken the advantage. He approached the desk and put his phone down. His eyes sizzled with blue fire.

"Is that a yes?" His gaze alone caused a coiling sensation low in her belly.

"Yes." She knew the question was loaded, knew exactly what she was saying yes to. *Adventures in creative pleasure.* Ashley put down her phone.

"Nice to meet you," he rasped, reaching across the desk to shake her hand. She slipped her hand into his and shook it firmly. The contact sparked an instantaneous heat, as if he were transmitting a thousand tiny lightning bolts. Surely, she was glowing.

"Nice to meet you." She tried to pull her hand from his, but Luke didn't let go.

"I understand you're interested in improving the lithium-ion battery." Despite the businesslike words, his voice was low and predatory, full of hunger.

"You understand correctly."

He slowly released her hand and let his fingers play across her palm with provocative lightness before removing his touch. Her skin felt scalded by him, her nerves scorched by her own thoughts.

"There are four things we're addressing right now. One: decreasing size. Two: finding alternatives for scarce electrode materials. Three: decreasing cost. And four: improving battery life through self-healing mechanisms."

"Impressive." And lust drugged as her body was, she *was* impressed. Luke clearly had been doing his homework on how to improve Li-ion batteries. In fact, it was a powerful turn-on. This man never stopped surprising her. His brain was every bit as sexy as the muscles that rippled across his back. His synapses made her heart race just as much as the flex of his thighs. She stared at him, helplessly entranced. Electrodes may not be every woman's love language, but they were hers. "Tell me more."

"Actually…" His strong shoulders flexed beneath his shirt as he shrugged. "I'd like to show you." He prowled around the desk to where she sat in her chair. He was a tall man, but now, close to her, it was as if even this spacious office were too small for him. Ashley stared at his hips, the way his jeans fit flat against his trim stomach, how the denim stretched across his muscular thighs, and she felt an agonizing flip in her own belly as she saw the hard ridge of his erection pressing against his jeans. Involuntarily, she licked her lips. He raised an eyebrow, clearly pleased by her reaction.

"Let's imagine your body is the battery." He walked to the back of the chair. "It's designed to receive energy from another source. Like this." He placed his hands on her shoulders, gently massaging her skin. Heat radiated through her everywhere he touched. She felt her skin flush. Oh, yes, she could imagine he was transmitting his energy.

Then both of his hands traveled down her upper arms, down her forearms, arriving at her hands. Everywhere he touched became raw, sensitive, charged. *Go lower, please, lower.* Need suffused her blood and, to her embarrassment, made her whimper softly.

Luke leaned down to whisper in her ear, "Imagine I'm the inverter and my hands the cables that transfer that energy. Can you feel it?" He steadily kneaded her, his hands so strong, his touch firm and possessive.

When she didn't answer, he stopped moving, waiting for her answer.

"Yes." Her voice sounded breathless, needy.

"Good." She could hear his smile in his deep voice. Luke was loving this, and oh, in this moment, how desperately she wanted to please him.

His hands again began their transfer of energy, but they moved to her waist, and he pressed his thumbs against her rib cage, tracing the bones through the fabric of her dress in long, rhythmic strokes, pulling against her sides with his fingers. She absorbed the intoxicating rush of him—the clean male scent of him, the heat in his touch, the frayed tide of his breath as he nuzzled his lips against her neck. Her head lolled heavily to the side as he dragged his soft lips across her skin.

She wanted to touch him, to run her fingers through his hair, to pull his lips to hers, but she was essentially pinned into the chair, her arms beneath his as he continued his erotic exploration of her midriff, leisurely working his way higher toward her breasts.

"It can be a long, slow process, charging the battery," he murmured against her skin. His hands moved underneath the soft curves of her breasts to cradle their tender weight through the thin cotton. She arched her back as with one hand he captured a taut nipple between his fingers and rolled it, tugged at it, teased it into a stiffened peak, sending darts of sharp pleasure through her.

Ashley felt the world collapse into this very moment. Nothing mattered but the wild fluttering inside her chest, the glorious urgency she felt blossoming in her sex. Despite her tipsy bewilderment, she also felt strikingly clear—*I belong with Luke.* The thought made her gasp as he nibbled her ear.

"The lithium-ion battery depends on electrochemical phenomena." Luke slid one hand down to her bare thigh and inched it beneath the loose hem of her dress toward her dark heat. "That's what allows it to both receive and provide energy…" His fingers snuck between the tight clasp of her thighs to press against the soft, damp cotton between her legs. "Energy on demand."

Ashley gasped. He tickled a finger against the soaking layer of cloth, and her whole body shuddered. She wanted him to own her. She tried, unsuccessfully, to force the breathlessness from her voice. "Tell me more."

"Oh, yes, I will." In one quick movement, he spun the chair around to face him, dropped to his knees, and cupped the back of her head to pull her mouth in to meet his.

Oh, she'd craved this. The hot, open, fierce worship of his kiss. Luke's lips ravished hers as he nipped and bit, his mouth insistent and lavish, as if he had an unlimited reserve of pleasure to offer her. She felt the wicked tip of his tongue teasing, searching for her response, and Ashley returned the kisses with fervor, with an insatiable hunger for this man. She wanted to climb into him, to be wholly merged with him.

With one hand, Luke stroked her neck, his fingertips inconceivably gentle yet intense as midsummer sunlight, tracing sensual, sinuous paths on her skin. She opened beneath his touch the way morning glories unfurl given light, given warmth.

The other hand he slipped to her top knee. Luke broke the kiss and whispered against her mouth, "Uncross." She complied, her limbs willing but slow as if drugged. His gaze moved to the hem of her dress, and his hand urged her legs further apart. "Open for me."

Ashley slowly opened her legs, surprised at how almost shy she felt to have him give his attention so fully to this most intimate part of her body. She wanted him to look up. Instead, she watched his gaze sharpen as the spreading forced the fabric to ride up her thighs, giving him a glimpse of her dark purple panties.

A low moan escaped him, and he looked at her, his darkened eyes searching hers for some subtle confirmation that the color was sending him a message.

That morning, Ashley had agonized over the choice. She knew wearing purple there meant she had committed already to wanting to be with him again. When Luke saw the color, she knew it would signal to him *yes, please, more. Purple* was their pleasure word, the opposite of a safe word.

Ashley met Luke's eyes and nodded, and she marveled as his face softened. He gazed at her with such tenderness, such devotion, such awe, she felt the prick of tears. And then, it was like watching kindling become an inferno. The full force of his passion rose in him, and he lowered his head to her inner thighs, his forearms stretching her knees wider, his tongue and teeth and lips leaving a fevered trail as he moved up her thighs with deliberate purpose, his hands smoothing up and down her legs.

Ashley's heart thudded in her chest, and she dug her fingers into his lustrous dark hair, pulling through the loose curls, thrilling in its silkiness, grazing his scalp with her nails.

As Luke's lips came closer to her center, she pushed her hips forward to meet him, to offer him easier access, and he chuckled against her skin. "You, my dear, are receiving right now—only receiving." He lifted his head briefly as with both hands he tore the thin cotton between him and her secret flesh. The rip as he sundered the cloth shocked and thrilled Ashley. Then he held her firmly in place, pinning her to the chair, both hands spread wide on her upper thighs, framing her naked sex. She gasped as she felt all her inhibitions melt, and she offered herself to his gaze in total surrender, legs splayed, biding her breath in anticipation of the imminent plunder she craved.

Luke growled with approval. "Yes. This. Oh, your beauty." And he dove in to ravish her satiny folds with long, lush strokes of his tongue.

Heat burst through her, as if she had opened the darkest parts of herself to the morning sun, and it radiated warmth and brilliance and shine into her every cell, fueling her, energizing her, saturating her with luminance. Oh, that slide of his tongue, like flame, and she reveled in the sweet torture as he expertly swirled around the sensitive bud of her clit, then stoked it with his tongue tip, teasing her, inflaming her, igniting her, a rhythm of heat, a cadence of light.

Her inner muscles clenched around the emptiness where she longed for him to enter her, and desperate, her hips bucked up to meet his tongue, but he held her down and lightly blew on her clit as if fanning her into a blaze.

"Please," she begged. "Luke, I'm so close."

As if he were made to grant her delight on demand, he pressed his tongue flat against her and slipped two fingers into her silkiness, angling them expertly to nudge her tenderest spot. He pumped them slowly once, twice, three times, then gave her clit the barest of flicks with his tongue, setting into motion a spontaneous conflagration, her whole body shaking with almost violent fulfillment, bliss spreading and coruscating through her as Luke gently continued to coax tremors of paradise through her body, her slick walls rippling around him.

Luke. Luke. Luke. His name was a one-word mantra sparking through her blood. It was only after some moments she realized she was moaning it aloud.

When at last she sank into the chair, spent, Luke lifted his head and leaned back on his heels to stare at her with wonder, as if he had never tasted anything so wonderful before, his lips and chin shining from her juices. He wiped his face with his hand and grinned. "Electrolytes."

Ashley shook her head and laughed. "Only you, Luke. You know, of course, that electrolytes in batteries are solid."

"Yours seem to be liquid. And I bet you can guess what your electrode is." Amusement sparkled in his eyes.

Ashley raised her eyebrows. "There are supposed to be two electrodes…"

"Stickler. But I bet I can find another."

Only with Luke had she ever experienced sex that was as playful as it was passionate. That he could be making jokes about battery function after giving her an earth-shattering orgasm—that was Luke. Not another soul like him in the world. But her own passion was driving her now as she leaned toward him to grab for his belt.

He caught both her wrists and pulled her from the chair into a controlled fall on top of him. As she tumbled down, with a quick twist of his body, he transferred her back to the cool stone floor and pressed himself on top of her.

"Luke, I want to please you." She struggled against his weight.

"In good time, Madam CEO." He settled into her open legs. "But we are nowhere near done with this demonstration."

CHAPTER 4

A SHLEY STARED UP AT Luke, her eyes blurring with lust as he pressed his hard cock against her softness. She resented his jeans between them, wanting his nakedness, wanting his thrusts.

"Are you pouting, madam?" he teased.

"I want to touch you, Luke."

"Not yet. Let's talk self-healing polymers."

"What?" Her hands moved to his belt, but he carefully removed them and pinned them on either side of her head.

"Receiving, remember? Let's get a full charge before we turn back the flow."

Ashley rolled her eyes, and Luke leaned down to kiss her, hovering just above her with a dreamlike smile. His lips were featherlight, teasing, a brush with holiness. She wanted more and raised her head to deepen the kiss, but he lifted his head just out of reach.

"So, the research department has been taking some inspiration from living organisms." Again, he gently met her lips with his; this time, his tongue slipped into her mouth, and she tasted herself on his breath. She trembled beneath him, and he laughed as if reading her mind. "Mmm," he groaned, giving her permission to be curious about the taste.

And then his mouth was away from hers, planting intimate kisses on the scar on her forehead that she'd had since she could remember. "We're studying how damaged body parts heal." He released one of her wrists so he could trace the scar lightly with his fingers. "They're teaching us how to reverse damage after it occurs."

Ashley stared at his lips as they moved, and she laughed lightly. "Is that so, Mr. Lead Engineer?" This was so Luke—exciting her brain with reversible chemical bonds while opening her heart and arousing her body at the same time. She had to bring her whole self to their sex. Even now, as he intimated knowledge about hydrogen bonding, her inner walls were clenching, unclenching, and her clit was pulsing like a little red alarm bell.

"Aren't you going to ask me how we get these materials into the battery?"

She shook her head.

"I'm going to show you." He gave her a wicked grin, cupped his hand around her crotch, and lifted her in a surprisingly effortless swoop, setting her on the edge of his desk.

"Okay. How do the materials get in?"

He slowly spread her legs. "Injection. Into the electrolytes."

Ashley gave a slight groan, but she liked where she knew this was going. She leaned back on her hands, watching Luke, fascinated as his long, elegant fingers methodically removed his belt and undid his jeans. Heat raced through her veins as he slipped down the denim and briefs and stepped out of them. His hard, impressive cock stood in full salute in front of the V on his lower abdomen.

Her breasts felt heavy, their bunched tips aching. Oh, she wanted this. She wanted to rip off his shirt, to bury her face in his chest, to sink her teeth into his tender skin, but she forced herself not to move.

Luke smiled, alert to her body's response. "Yes." His voice was low, seductive. He rubbed his thumb against her lower lip, then trailed it down between her breasts till he arrived again at the hem of her dress. He gathered the fabric and slowly, slowly lifted it up her legs to reveal her swollen lips. He pulled his fingers through the dampness and painted her cream onto his cock, giving himself one long pull, then another.

Ashley could feel her wetness dripping down her thighs. She didn't know if she were more thrilled or horrified to have her juices baptize Luke's desk.

Has he ever done this with anyone else?

A quick twinge of jealousy stabbed through her, imagining some previous lover—his ex-girlfriend Savannah, perhaps—perched on this desk. She shook the thought out of her head and tried to focus only on the moment.

Luke made that easy—he lifted one of her knees to the side, resting her foot on the top of the desk, opening her petals wide for his eyes to devour. She felt exposed, vulnerable, and then he lifted the other leg, effectively splaying her dark entrance. She felt wanton and wicked and totally desired.

Luke's eyes were hooded with lust, his thick cock practically leaping in his hand. "You're so ready for me," he murmured huskily. He stepped forward to notch himself at her glistening opening, moving his satiny tip through her slickness, rubbing it against her aching clit. She'd just come with his tongue so beautifully, and already she wanted him so much again. The body was such a strange, greedy thing.

Ashley loved this moment, this moment right before their bodies became one. She loved the anticipation as much as it tortured her. Her back arched, and she pressed her hips forward to offer more of herself to him, but Luke, again, used his hands to pin her in place, and then, with a strong driving force, he shunted his long, thick cock deep into her, burying himself in her warmth, filling her with electrifying heat, thrilling her nerves into ecstatic synaptic song.

Ashley cried out—in pleasure, in union, in submission, in surrender. He felt so good inside her, stretching her, satisfying her, making her whole. For a moment, neither of them moved their hips, stunned by the steady voltage humming between them. Their chests and shoulders heaved, trying to keep up with their tattered breaths. Ashley opened her eyes to gaze up at Luke's face, a look of rapture washing his features.

And then he slowly pistoned his cock into her, rhythmically serving her, exquisitely massaging her, filling her with profound pleasure. She watched his chest muscles flex beneath his shirt, then let her eyes move to where their bodies joined, mesmerized by the glistening length of him as it appeared and disappeared again and again inside her.

And then he was devouring her neck with his mouth, his tongue swirling, teeth nipping, lips tugging at her skin. Ashley whimpered, thrilling in his possession of her, her body a tautly strung bow, arching, straining toward release. Sweat trickled down her side. "Luke."

He was fierce now, incendiary, his thrusts demanding as he plunged into her again and again in a feral, almost frantic plundering. Ashley's breath came in torn fragments timed with his lunges, and she twisted and writhed, her body working to accommodate his movements. "Take me," he commanded. "Take. Me. Take. Me."

As if all she needed were his invitation, Ashley stopped trying to control how she met him and felt her body completely surrender to him, utterly receptive, a flag that knows how to move only when given life by the wind.

"That's it." His encouragement came in grunts. "Let it come to you. Let me give this to you." Ashley followed a soul-deep summons to yield, and then, almost instantaneously, she shattered around him, instantly ablaze, a surplus of bliss exploding through her, a luminous tremoring that rippled until she knew herself as radiant current, as pure energy.

"Yes." Luke continued to caress her with his hard length, gently stroking himself inside her as she came and came. Her body was still flying, weightless and whirling, and the whole time she reeled, Luke was kissing her neck, pressing soft whispered yesses into her skin with his lips, and they stayed like this until her body stopped its trembling.

"Oh." Ashley collapsed back on the desk, her knees still splayed, Luke still hard inside her. She watched his muscled thighs flex as he struggled to hold back his own pleasure. "The switch flips now, yes?" she asked him, still panting. Ashley pushed up onto her elbows and shot him a wicked smile. Mustering all the command she could, she directed him, "Your turn. Now, sit in my chair."

Luke's mouth curved into a smile that both emboldened her and left her breathless. He slipped out of her and stepped back to his chair, his cock angling straight up as he sat.

"Lock the chair so it won't move."

As Luke adjusted the chair, his eyes never left Ashley, who was standing now, removing her dress. His hand slowly worked his erection as he watched her.

"This is how it works, right?" She pulled the thin blue fabric over her head, dropping it to the floor and giving her long honey-brown waves a toss. Was she crazy? Wearing only her heeled sandals and purple lace bra in Luke's office. Who could come in? No one, right? The risk of it, the vulnerability of standing naked in this unfamiliar place, sent a cascade of shivers down her spine and somehow enforced her boldness—her arousal, too. She took a step closer to Luke. "Once the battery is fully charged, the electricity flows the other way. Are you ready?" She could hardly believe he'd kept himself from coming inside her.

Luke nodded, his eyes widening with desire as she straddled him, resting her feet and shins outside his thighs, spread wide for him. His hands gripped her waist to lift her and help her settle on his cock. Once she felt him at her entrance, she lowered herself slowly, slowly, sinking onto him with excruciating control, sheathing him in her warmth. His whole body trembled as his head fell back, and when she'd finally seated herself on him fully, they gasped in unison. He lifted his head, eyelids heavy with pleasure, and her hair cascaded forward, creating a golden curtain around their faces. She ground her hips forward and back, relishing how full she felt, how connected to him. Still ripe with her discovery, she marveled at it again: she *loved* this man.

Perhaps Luke could read the look on her face because she watched his blue eyes turn molten, heard his urgency deepen in the way he groaned, felt his need for her grow like wildfire. With a low growl that birthed a thousand goose bumps on her arms, Luke used his hands to slide her body up and down his shaft. She almost teased him about needing to let her do the work, but he was aroused beyond stopping, and all she wanted now was to please him, to feel his warmth surging into her, to watch his face as he came undone. Sweat shone on his brow, and he relaxed his hold on her waist. He was panting, drugged with pleasure.

Ashley leaned back, changing the angle so his cock could slide into her even more. As she rode him, she felt her walls greedily pulling him in, felt the rapid patter of her heart, the exquisite fullness where his hard length sank into her again and again as if he couldn't get in her deep enough. They found a rhythm, thrusting faster and faster, reveling in the sensual friction, the rising charge. Her body continued to open for him, to stretch for him, to draw him in—and she marveled to think she had almost lost him. How could she have lived without having him inside her again? "Luke," she moaned, her voice thick and fueled with an almost desperate passion. As if on her command, his body went rigid beneath her, and she thrilled as he threw back his head and roared, his body shaking in ecstatic surrender.

Ashley marveled at how beautiful he was in this totally animal, vulnerable state; it flooded her with satisfaction. This remarkable man, she needed him. She *needed* him. His pleasure gave her so much pleasure. She leaned her torso into him and nuzzled his chin and neck with her head as his cock continued to pulse inside her.

For a moment, they just held each other, and she floated on Luke's chest as it rose and fell. Almost without realizing it, she synchronized her breathing to his as they had weeks ago in Luke's meditation room.

The world was only breath.

Luke was the first to speak. "Thank you." There was a tenderness, an honesty in his voice that almost broke her, and Ashley, stunned by it, felt too raw, too vulnerable, and found herself reaching for levity.

"Good thing it's a Sunday," she whispered into his neck. "You were loud enough to shake the whole building." She planted an open-mouthed kiss on his skin and savored the salt on her tongue. "It might be hard to convince your secretary those cries were in response to rechargeable batteries."

Luke's laugh was so natural it made her laugh, too. It slipped through her as if she were trying to hold a waterfall—a beauty that can only be experienced, not captured.

"I've missed you, Ashley." He stroked his hand through her hair.

"I've missed you, Luke."

"You'd make a hell of a CEO."

She laughed. "You give a mighty fine engineering demonstration."

He stilled his hand in her hair. "Ashley, I want you to know that we really are moving ahead with our research for cleaner energy technologies, even more so now than three weeks ago. I certainly hadn't imagined telling you about it this way, but… the opportunity to show you about it was too good to pass up." His hand moved down her shoulder to explore the curve of her waist, her hip. She felt goose bumps rise on her skin wherever his touch had been. "I want you to know that I hear you. If I fail, I'll try to fail up, like in FIXX."

Ashley smiled at his reference to the educational video game she'd developed in which kids worked together to clean up environmental disasters and were rewarded for their resilience. It was the centerpiece of the STEAMEA (Science, Technology, Engineering, Art, Math, Environmental Activism) nonprofit that she'd started with Luke's help.

Luke whispered, "I want you to come into my life again. It's like I've been underwater the last few weeks without you. I miss every part of you. Please, Ashley. I want you close to me."

"That's what I want, too, Luke."

"Say you've missed me again. I want to hear it."

Ashley marveled at how this accomplished, handsome man who appeared so confident was also so remarkably vulnerable. She knew how hard it was for him to show her his vulnerability, and she saw now how he needed to see openness from her, too.

"I've missed you, Luke."

"Oh, thank you for saying so." He nuzzled his nose into her hair and breathed her in, then wrapped both arms around her and held her lightly, held her as if she were a cloud that could disappear through his arms if he squeezed too tightly. He rained soft kisses onto her head, as if he could not believe his great fortune. "I don't want my work to come between us. Ever. I know you'll be pissed about the company sometimes. But Ashley, I am not afraid of hard conversations. I am only afraid of losing you again."

"It's hard to separate you from your work, Luke."

"It's hard to separate from *you*, Ashley."

For a long moment, they said nothing. Ashley breathed in Luke's good, musky scent. She had to try to make this work with him. Why did life have to be so complex?

"Ashley, look at me." She lifted her head and felt his eyes search her for confirmation. "I believe that what we have between us is stronger than what happens outside of us. I will prove it to you, Ashley, every day. I believe in *us*."

Us. The word covered them like a soft, warm blanket.

Ashley's feet were starting to fall asleep, and she squirmed a bit. Luke laughed. "Let's clean up." He lifted her from his lap as if she weighed the same as a leaf. Standing naked in his office, the brazen CEO she'd pretended to be was gone, and she felt suddenly shy and self-conscious.

Luke took one last look at her and grinned. "I will never see this desk the same way." He patted the back of the chair. "And this chair." He shook his head in wonder. And her self-consciousness evaporated.

She followed him to a bathroom that was hidden behind one of the panels behind his desk. As she got dressed, she noticed Luke staring at her, a wry look on his face.

"Will you unblock my number now?" His voice was both sheepish and insistent.

Ashley blushed, then nodded. "How did you know?"

"Pretty sure you would have responded to the text I sent you this morning if it had gone through." He grinned wickedly.

Instantly, she wondered what she'd missed.

"I ask because I want to send you a text about going to dinner with me tonight."

"I'm going to Mom's tonight."

"Tomorrow?"

"Tomorrow works."

"Yes!" Luke gave a fist pump like he'd just won the lottery.

His puppylike enthusiasm was contagious, and she felt the urge to giggle. In this moment, still aglow in sex-dazzled bliss, she could almost believe everything would work between them, that love could overcome their obstacles.

"Any restaurant in town," he said. "Just name it."

"I'll text you."

"I've missed your texts."

Luke offered her his palm, and they walked out of his office holding hands—so different from the awkward way they'd entered. Ashley still felt uncomfortable on the trading floor, still hated the TVs with their talking heads, and yet she felt so at home in this moment with the man who oversaw them. *Power to the paradox.*

As they waited for the elevator, they heard a squeak down the hall—a wheel on a cart being pushed by a female custodian. She was petite, slender, her graying hair pulled back. From a distance, it looked just like Ashley's own mother, who had worked as a housekeeper by day, waitress by night, as she raised two girls on her own.

A rush of gratitude and appreciation flooded Ashley as she watched the woman move the mop across the floor.

That's what we do. We clean it up. She felt part of a lineage of women who took what was messy and made it spotless again. She thought of her work with environmental activism—first as a protester and now with her work with STEAMEA. And she said a silent thank-you to the woman in the hall.

It takes us all.

"Sooo." Luke's voice brought her back to the moment. "Does today really count as my Spanish lesson?"

Ashley giggled. "*Tal vez no.*"*

---

* Maybe not.

"I don't know what you said, but I can tell you that I do like my teacher. A lot. Even if she didn't teach me much Spanish today." His eyes glittered with mischief.

"*Pero me enseñaste algo muy importante, querido*,"* she said, eyes dancing.

Luke stared at her blankly, not comprehending.

That I love you.

The truth still stunned her, and the vulnerability she felt around it frightened her. What if Luke, like her father and her ex-husband, left her? And so, she held the secret lightly in her heart, like a butterfly cupped between two hands, knowing it was something meant to be shared but not yet finding the strength to let it be free.

---

* But you taught me something very important, my dear.

CHAPTER 5

"**T**HE BOARD SHOULD BE informed of any claims made against the nonprofit and when threats of lawsuits arise."

Ashley yawned and realized she'd read the same sentence three times. She picked up her phone and texted Luke.

Ashley: Verdadero @ 6:02?
Best guac in town

She returned her attention to the stack of books on how to best run a nonprofit. She'd checked them out of the library, thinking she could use more tips on how to better move her organization forward. Since her high school had laid her off in early May due to budget cuts and since she'd learned she didn't get her dream position teaching in Peru, making STEAMEA financially viable had become top priority. But at the moment, reading about risk management and insurance held no appeal. All she could think of was Luke.

Luke: I've heard it's spec-taco-ler

Ashley: Oooh. I like when you taco dirty to me

Luke: Taco walk on the wild side?

Ashley: I'm nacho usual date
In queso you're wondering...

Luke: I'll order us a bottle of jala-peño grigio

Ashley was working out a pun for *enchilada* when she got a FaceTime request from John. *Oosh.*

"Hi, John." Her stomach sank. She'd been dreading this conversation.

"Hi, Ashley. You look like you want me to come pick you up for dinner."

Ashley tried not to roll her eyes. She was not used to this flirty side of him being aimed at her, and it made her uncomfortable. She covered her awkwardness with a little laugh.

"I was thinking, tonight we could go out somewhere quieter, just us—"

"John," she interrupted. "I feel like I need to be clear. I'm only interested in friendship."

He gave a wry smile. "I worried I was pushing it too soon after things were over with Luke. It's just I didn't want to—"

"It's not really over with Luke."

John's flinch was so quick she would have missed it if she'd blinked. He smiled then and nodded.

Ashley flushed. "I *thought* things were over, but…" She let her voice taper off. "Maybe I was wrong to ask you to come with me to the gala." She winced, closed her eyes. "I didn't mean to lead you on, John."

John's chuckle was humble and warm. "No. Ashley. It was great. I'm glad I was there to see you. I am proud of you—bummed, of course, that you're not free—but I'm not at all embarrassed about what I said the other night. I meant every word."

I'd love to kiss you. She remembered the dark and hungry look in his face, how her body had responded to him with a flutter of desire she didn't necessarily want to feel. And though she'd told him no…

John gave a self-deprecating chuckle. "It was my honor to be your date for such a special occasion."

John. Always so thoughtful, so honest. Ashley felt terrible, as if she were the boot that had trampled a beautiful wildflower.

"Thank you, John. You are very special to me." She hated the way the words sounded. Though the sentiment was true, it sounded empty. She should just get off now.

"I've gotta go," John said abruptly.

"I'm sorry, John."

"I'll see you at the next board meeting." John, like Luke, served on her STEAMEA board. Would it be weird when they met again?

"See you."

Ashley sat with the phone in her hand, staring at the books. Ping. Another text came in. She saw she'd missed five messages from Luke.

Luke: I value our relation-chip
        Ashley? Where'd you go?
        Did you crash and burrn-ito?
        Did I get too cheesy?
        See you tonight. 6:02

It wasn't the amorous dinner conversation she might have envisioned, but Ashley was passionate as she filled Luke in on the last STEAMEA board meeting he had missed, apparently because he was in Mexico and not because he was avoiding her. "And the programmers showed screenshots of crucial game scenes in FIXX, so the board members could see the oil spill students will be cleaning up and what kinds of tools their teams could use."

Though she was talking his ear off, Luke seemed genuinely interested in Ashley's reports about the game she'd devised. She flashed on her ex-husband, Mark, who had often quickly lost interest in whatever it was she was talking about.

"Sounds as if FIXX is ahead of schedule."

Ashley nodded. "In fact, we can play it soon."

"A toast." Luke raised his mojito. "To FIXX. And to the brilliant woman who dreamed it up."

"And to the handsome, thoughtful, *wicked* man who helped make it possible." Ashley recalled with a blush how Luke had blindfolded her when he'd first shown her the prototype for FIXX—and how much she'd enjoyed that.

Ashley and Luke clinked glasses and stared into each other's eyes as they drank. The loud restaurant wasn't exactly romantic, but Ashley felt a frisson of heat tear through her anyway when the edge of Luke's lips curled up as he continued to stare at her. She never ceased to be startled by the effect Luke had on her, how the slightest smile could make the hairs on her nape tingle.

"You are so incredible." His voice was lower, softer, and it moved across her skin like a caress, a near whisper that somehow became the only voice audible in the clamor of Verdadero.

The contemplative angle of his head made his ebony hair fall across his forehead, and she longed to reach over the table and move it, any excuse, really, to touch him here in this public place. Just across the table, he was too far away, and after their reconciliation yesterday, she was craving closeness, wanting confirmation of their connection. A strange and beautiful ache fluttered inside her, stealing her breath—a many-winged awareness of just how much Luke had infused her every atom since they'd first met four months ago. It seemed laughable now that she thought she could leave him when he was so clearly an inextricable part of her.

"Luke, I—"

—*love you.* Was she really just about to blurt that out? The weight of the words terrified her. Every man she had ever loved had abandoned her. Her father had left her when she was four. Her ex-husband had used and betrayed her.

"Yes?" Luke leaned in.

"I was just thinking about the game, and—" Luke frowned and reached into his coat pocket.

"Sorry," he said, pulling out his phone. "I've been ignoring my phone, but someone is obviously trying to reach me." He looked at the screen. "Elaine? If it were anyone but my sister…" His thought trailed off as he answered. "Hello?"

Ashley took a sip of her mojito and watched Luke's face transform from playful to pained.

"I understand." He nodded. "I'll come right away."

A knot tied itself into her gut. *What's wrong?* She sought his saddened expression for answers.

"It's my Rena." Just saying her name, his eyes filled with love for the woman who had been more of a mother to him than his own fragile parent. "She's dying."

———

"My Rena." Luke whispered the words when he saw the slender Black woman lying in the big four-poster bed. Wearing a white flannel night dress, she looked peaceful, her face completely relaxed.

Her eyes opened slowly, and seeing Luke, she offered a weak smile. "*Quoi ça dit, cher?*"*

"Oh, my Rena." He approached her slowly, reverently. Ashley stayed in the bedroom doorway with Rena's daughter, tears stinging her eyes.

Rena turned over a hand, offering Luke her palm. He sat in a chair by the bed and took her hand in his, gazing at her, stroking her wrist gently with his thumb.

"I'm dying, *cher.*"

He nodded. He started to say something, but he choked.

---

* What's up, dear?

"Lukey." Her thin voice was an admonishment and a blessing. "*Mon pauvre.** I'll always be nearby. Just in the other room."

Luke's face broke into grief, big tears spilling down his cheeks. "Yes." His voice was soft, unbearably sad. "Yes."

"I'll be with your brother there, *cher*, just around the corner. And what a beautiful room it is. So close, so close to you, always."

"Yes." Luke didn't even try to wipe the tears, just let them fall.

Rena took a deep breath and closed her eyes. "Tell me about Ashley." Ashley startled, hearing her name.

"She's here now."

Rena responded with a smile, but she didn't open her eyes. "*Ça c'est bon. C'est bon.*** I knew she would come back. You were so worried, but I know love when I smell it. You will be happy with that one, *cher.*"

Luke sat with Rena for a long, long time, watching her drift back into sleep, listening to her breath, staring at her face as if to learn it one last time by heart.

"I love you, my Rena," he whispered and kissed her cheek.

Ashley drove Luke back to his penthouse across town and held him through the night as he cried.

———

"I think she was holding on just so she could say goodbye to you." Ashley squeezed Luke's hand, and he squeezed hers back.

Luke swallowed and took a deep breath. "I miss her so much already."

They were walking dogs from the Happy Go Lucky Open Door Shelter, a no-kill facility that Luke had founded. Though Luke usually walked the dogs only on Saturdays, he'd taken off work today to process Rena's death. When he had asked Ashley

---

* Poor little thing
** That's good.

to join him in walking the dogs, she had canceled her tutoring appointments.

Mostly they walked in silence, but Ashley could tell the calming effect the dogs had on Luke. He bent down to give King Kong a loving scratch while they waited to cross the street. "Such a good dog," he crooned. Dogs brought out the best in him— she'd seen it before. A tenderness, a sweetness, a boyishness.

"Tell me something you remember about Rena from your childhood."

Luke reached for her free hand and held it in his for a while as they walked, his expression contemplative.

"After Jimmy died, I didn't speak for a year. And when I did, I had a stutter." He took a deep breath.

Ashley had so many questions, but she waited for him to begin again.

"I guess it happens sometimes with emotional trauma. The stuttering lasted for a few years. I was teased at school, of course. Kids are cruel. And I was weird enough already."

Ashley had heard the stutter return when Luke had spoken at the London conference—he was terrified of public speaking. Though he had loved being onstage in high school plays, getting up in front of a crowd as himself was anathema to him.

Rena had told her once when they were alone about Luke's stutter, and she was glad to hear about it from Luke himself now. She knew it represented a difficult chapter in his life. It was hard to imagine that eloquent, pun-loving, velvet-voiced Luke had ever been anything but perfectly articulate, and it made Ashley's heart ache for the young boy who had been through so much.

"Of course, my parents hired the best speech therapists, but nothing helped. So, I talked less and less. Except with my Rena. When I would come home from boarding school for Christmas or summer, I would sit in the kitchen with her while she cooked.

She would speak very slowly with me and never made me feel ashamed of using my voice."

Though he didn't say it, Ashley heard the implication that other important adults in his life didn't offer him the same respect.

"And one day while she was making bread, she asked me to read to her from my favorite book. I was fifteen, and I didn't want to, but she insisted."

"Let me guess." Ashley knew he'd loved philosophy books as a young teen—that he referred to those men as his "uncles," his adopted family, and they had been quite real to him. "Uncle Marcus."

The smile Luke gave her melted her knees. "You know me," he drawled, staring at her as if she were a marvel. How could she forget? Luke had given her a copy of Marcus Aurelius's *Meditations* translated by Gregory Hays and then ravaged her on every surface in his penthouse—had licked and teased and pounded her into orgasmic oblivion—all while reciting Stoic philosophy. Ashley couldn't help the shiver of longing that shuddered through, her remembering how he'd arranged her on his thick white rug and made love to her as if the world were ending and they were duty-bound to wring as much pleasure from that moment as they could. The thought of him reading the same passages to Rena made Ashley laugh.

He continued. "It was the first time I didn't stutter. Every day that summer, she asked me to read to her. And by the end of the summer, so long as I wasn't too nervous, I could speak normally again."

"What a gift she gave you—the gift of her attention."

"And her patience. It was my Rena, always my Rena, who was strong for me. Who encouraged me. Who pushed me. She never let me give up on things that really mattered. Like fighting for you."

Ashley glanced up at him suspiciously. "You talked with her about us?"

He flashed her a sly grin that made her want to bite his lush lips. "Every Friday morning at nine. Among other things we talked about."

"Really."

"She called our lunch meetings *dream gumbo*—always fifteen minutes—and we'd talk about our hopes and dreams with each other."

"What a great ritual." It thrilled and terrified her that Luke's dreams revolved in some way around her.

"It's helped shape everything for me. What is that look on your face? What are you thinking?"

"How lucky you were to have Rena. Like I was to have Tica." Tica had been Ashley's neighbor, and the Peruvian immigrant had helped to raise her while her own mother was working multiple jobs to support Ashley and her sister, Jewel. And it was Tica who had trained to be a teacher, who had encouraged Ashley to become a teacher. In fact, playing "student" with Tica had been her favorite childhood game. She'd been a serious, studious girl, and Tica had encouraged her passion for learning and teaching.

"Speaking of dreams, how are you doing now with not going to *why-uh*—" He stalled, then started again. "*Why-uh*—?"

"Huayllabamba?"

"Yes."

Ashley laughed at Luke's attempted pronunciation of the small town where Tica had grown up, but inwardly, she winced. Though it had been almost a month since the rejection from the visiting teacher program, it still hurt. Her dreams of teaching in Huayllabamba were based on wanting to honor Tica and help students in that community just as Tica had helped her. She'd been dreaming of it for a decade—ever since she'd become a teacher. And she'd been turned down multiple years in a row by

the program that offered teaching positions there to US teachers. Perhaps it was foolish to have her heart set on this one program, but she'd had tingles when she'd first read about it. She just
knew it was the right program. She wasn't the kind of person to
get tingles. There was something about that place, something
drawing her beyond her commitment to honor her old mentor.

"It's still hard," she admitted. "Although at the moment, I
also can't imagine that I'd be leaving you in a few weeks."

Luke rewarded her with a big hug, pulling her into his arms
right there in the middle of the sidewalk. Though each of them
had a dog pulling on a leash, he held her tight to him, his powerful arms stabilizing them in the middle of the city.

"*You* are my dream, Ashley."

———

Eight hours later, Ashley was still thinking about the way Luke
had said those words, *You are my dream*. Though she was at her
monthly book club gathering, sitting on the couch in her friend
Jamila's house, surrounded by some of her favorite women on
the planet, she was replaying again and again the look on his
face when he'd said it—sincere, focused, hopeful. Just three days
ago, she'd been trying to convince herself she never wanted to
talk to him again. Tonight, she felt as if her body had been taken
over by a circus—her head was spinning, her stomach was doing giddy flip-flops, and she was grinning like a clown.

"Something tells me you're not thinking about *The Thorn
Birds*." Her friend Meg came and sat beside her.

"Why would you say that?"

"Because of that I've-got-the-best-secret-in-the-world look
on your face. So. Do you?"

Ashley took the glass of wine Meg was offering her and
flashed her a noncommittal smile.

"Oh, so you do." Meg raised her glass and clinked it. "Who's the lucky guy?"

"Who said it was a guy?"

"So, it *is* a guy. Wait, Luke? Are you two back together?"
Ashley nodded and bit her lip.

"Girl, that is the *best* news. You looked fucked as a plucked duck these last couple weeks. And the look on your face now…"

The reunion with Luke still felt too new, too precious to share, as if talking about it might dilute its power the way talking about a dream sometimes made even the most brilliant dream feel flat. Eager to distract the conversation from herself, Ashley asked, "What did *you* think of *The Thorn Birds*?" Though it was a much older book, they'd chosen it for their annual long read.

"Honestly, I felt pissed. Why didn't Ralph just leave the priesthood and marry Meggie? She loved him. He loved her. It was that easy. Why wouldn't he just give in to being himself?"

Why wouldn't he just give in to being himself? It was a question Ashley had asked herself about Luke many times. Like Ralph, though for very different reasons, Luke was unable to believe he deserved sexual pleasure and intimacy.

Of course, she understood why Luke felt the need to fantasize during sex. But she had to admit that sometimes, like Meggie in *The Thorn Birds*, she wished the man she loved could get over his obstacles and just show up as his truest self. If only he could see how worthy he was. She longed to help him discover that, but, as she once read in a self-help book about healing from her divorce, that kind of discovery was an "inside job."

What would it be like to make love to Luke as Luke? And, as correlative, what would it be like to have him meet her completely as herself? She almost felt guilty thinking it—especially when the sex was so good. But some part of her longed for their sex to be born out of total authenticity. It had been bothering her right before they broke up, and here it was again, rearing its head. Their sex was crazy amazing. But she wanted something unwaveringly *true*.

"Ashley!" Meg was trying to get her attention again. "Oh my god. Are you thinking about sex?"

"What?" How could Meg tell? "I mean, actually, I was. Sort of."

"And you even admitted it! I am so proud of you! And from the look on your face, you were thinking about bone-melting, life-changing, unrestrained sex with Luke, yes?"

Meg was, of all her friends, the most sexually adventurous and curious. But Ashley didn't want to divulge her private sex life, so she re-steered the conversation to sex in books. "Well, I was thinking about how refreshing it was in *The Thorn Birds* that Colleen McCullough's sex scenes weren't all written in the same cookie-cutter fashion as most contemporary romance."

"What do you mean?"

"You know how in all the romance books these days, all the guys ever seem to be able to say during sex is *fuuuuuuck*. Like the woman takes off her shirt, and he sees her breasts, and he says *fuuuuuuck*, or he's about to orgasm and he says—"

"*Fuuuuuuck*," Meg grunted in her best climaxing male voice.

Ashley laughed. "Yeah, exactly. As if that is the only thing a guy can ever say when he's aroused. I mean really. That's the best the writers can come up with? It's Neanderthal."

"Believe me," Meg said with a knowing nod, "I've hooked up with many superhot Neanderthals, and most of them can think of something to say to turn me on besides *fuck*."

"Or the other thing I was so glad not to read in this book is how in every erotic scene these days, the guy has to say, *You're so wet*."

Meg laughed. "*Fuuuuuuck. You're so wet*." Ashley was giggling now in earnest.

Jamila, who had been listening in on the conversation, came over and added, "Even if that's what they're thinking, most of them aren't saying it."

Meg continued. "And the *other* thing the guy has to say in every sex scene is when he first slips into her, he always says—"

"*You're so tight!*" all three of them chorused in gruff, highly aroused male impersonations and then dissolved into extreme giggles, punctuated with periodic groans of *Fuuuuuuck*, which only made them laugh harder.

If they had tried to explain it, no one else would have understood. Ashley wiped her tearstained cheeks, only to cry more each time the tears had dried. *It's so damn good to have friends.* She didn't even notice as all the tension of the last few weeks fell away.

———

Luke had asked Ashley to come over after book club. Riding up the sleek private elevator to Luke's penthouse on the forty-first floor, Ashley was surprised to find her heart racing. *Fifteen. Sixteen. Seventeen.* With only two buttons on the steel walls, she'd resorted to counting her own heartbeats as they thudded inside her chest. *Nervous?* Perhaps because it had been several weeks since she'd been here last? Or was it because the energetic rush of getting back together had kept her body in a state of perpetual giddiness for days—even through the heartache of losing Rena.

Stepping into Luke's penthouse, Ashley took a deep breath, remembering the first time she'd stepped in here, how shocked she'd been by the spaciousness, the elegance. The floor-to-ceiling windows in the living room had disoriented her—made it feel as if she were in a room that was floating above the Houston skyline. Quiet music was playing tonight, the strains of classical guitar resonated in the cathedral-ceilinged room, and the music somehow softened the room's modern lines. The scent of candles reminded her of the night Luke had invited her into his meditation room and they'd experienced a wildly intimate communion without even touching.

Ashley felt her shoulders relax, felt the smile rising on her face as she moved toward where she guessed Luke would be sitting in the open living space near his bedroom, and was surprised to hear voices coming from the kitchen.

"I know Rena was so important to you, Lukey."

Savannah. Ashley came around the corner to find Luke and his ex-lover in the kitchen. Luke was devouring a slice of chocolate cake.

"Why, Ashley," Savannah cooed, "what a nice surprise." Though her words were honeyed, the expression on her face was saccharine.

Get the hell away from my man.

Ashley forced her lips into a smile as she sized up the attractive blonde woman who had once vowed to her she would get Luke back. Savannah was wearing a turquoise top that casually hung off one shoulder, showing just enough of her generous cleavage to be provocative. Her tight skirt accentuated her figure, and her silky hair was tossed into a sexy bedhead froth— the kind of look that took an hour to achieve. In short, she was ravishing, and despite Luke's repeated assurances that he felt nothing but friendship for his former lover, Ashley felt the sting of insecurity. Savannah was the kind of woman men fantasize about. Plus, she was wealthy, intelligent, and charming—when she wanted to be. Ashley considered her own cotton skirt and blouse from the sale rack at the department store where her sister worked and felt dowdy standing next to Savannah—as if Savannah were a perfectly cut diamond and she was a chunk of quartz.

"Hi, Savannah. Hi, Luke." Ashley stopped where she stood, her hackles up high.

Luke immediately walked over to her and pulled her into one arm, balancing his plate with the other. "Chocolate," he said, holding the plate a little away from her, an apology in his voice.

"It's Lukey's favorite," Savannah crooned. "Isn't it, Lukey? He's always loved to eat my cake."

The tasteless double entendre made Ashley's lip curl. *Seriously?* Savannah had at one point acted like a friend to her—had even friended Ashley on Facebook. Then just a few weeks ago in London, she'd shown her inner badger—ugly, possessive, and dangerous. *Perhaps that's not fair to the badger.* Badgers aren't malicious, just mean. Savannah defined malicious—she delighted in being spiteful and malevolent. And beautiful. Ashley had never met anyone like her. She had thought the evil queen was a stereotype made up by Disney. But Savannah had taken evil queen to a whole new level—she had even succeeded in turning Luke's grown-up daughter, Corinna, against Ashley. If Savannah's brand of beautiful malice didn't have such a direct effect on her life, she might laugh about it. But having Savannah here in Luke's kitchen felt like a threat. Ashley knew the woman would stop at nothing to get Luke back.

Down, girl, Ashley said to her own inner badger. *We need to keep the peace. This woman isn't going away.* Though Luke and Savannah had broken up over a couple years ago, their families had been friends for decades. And Luke and Savannah still worked together. At least Savannah worked in the London office.

"I'm so glad I'll be working here in Houston again." Savannah's Texas accent was so thick she practically sang the proclamation.

No fucking way. "How nice."

"I *loved* London, but there's no place like home and *family*." Savannah gazed at Luke deliberately. "Of course, I will miss our Rena—what a wonderful woman she was. But we'll get through this loss together. I am always here for you."

"Thanks, Savannah." Luke seemed to take her comment at face value. Could Luke really be so oblivious to her interest? Or was he just ignoring it?

"Well, Ashley," Savannah drawled, "good luck with your little, um, *nonprofit*, what's it called, STEMA?"

"STEE-me-ah," Luke interjected. "It's really taking off."

"Oh, wonderful." Savannah tossed around a hand, somehow both honoring Luke's voice and dismissing the organization in one gesture. "Well, Lukey, I'll see you at the office tomorrow. I'll let myself out. I know the way."

"I'll walk you to the elevator." Luke gave Ashley a quick squeeze before releasing her to walk Savannah out.

"Thank you." Savannah lifted her chin and flashed him a winning smile. "Bye, Ashley," she called over her shoulder, turning back to give her rival a wicked wink that Luke couldn't see.

Ashley tried to keep her lip from curling into an involuntary snarl as she watched them walk away and disappear behind a corner. It killed her not seeing them for a few moments. *Oh, for X-ray vision.* Not that she didn't trust Luke. It was the honey badger she didn't trust.

Chapter 6

Forcing her attention away from Luke and his ex-girl-friend, Ashley turned and looked across Luke's dimly lit living room to the Houston skyline. If she softened her gaze, the city lights glowed like millions of tiny candles. The flickering soothed her somewhat, helped ground her and launch her at the same time.

When Luke reentered the room, he nodded to Ashley that he was going to take the rest of the uneaten cake to the kitchen.

She followed him and leaned against the door, smiling at him as he sipped a bit of whiskey and offered his glass to her. She declined. Though she'd promised herself she wouldn't say anything about Savannah—Luke had enough to deal with emotionally without adding her jealousy to his burden—apparently, her mouth didn't get the memo to be silent. "Seems kind of late for Savannah to drop off a cake."

Luke's eyes crinkled in understanding as he offered her a tired smile. "Ashley," he murmured. "You have nothing to worry about."

He walked to her with open arms, and she stepped into them, grateful for the way he cocooned her with his warmth, his masculine grace. God, it felt good to be held by him. Ashley leaned into his frame, relishing how protected she felt. Such a strange feeling for her—she prized how independent she was.

Even as she savored the muscled planes of his chest with her cheek, she kicked her needy self. Here he was comforting her when she should be comforting him.

"That feels good," he said as she wrapped her arms around him, too, and held him tightly back. "I know Savannah meant well coming over, but even a few minutes of her chatter wore me out. Today's been rough. I feel like part of me is missing."

For a moment, they just stood there, holding each other, slightly swaying to the quiet music of their breath. Luke hummed into her hair, not a tune really, more a vibration that she felt all through her, and it reminded Ashley of the singing bowls he used in his meditation room—a place she knew Savannah had never been, a thought that calmed her jealousy. She melted into Luke even more and felt the waves of his voice reverberate through her, easing and opening her.

Intuitively, Ashley matched her inhales with his, their bodies attuning in primal rhythm. It was subtle and powerful, a startling intimacy, raw and unwalled—as if they were inside each other. With each inhale, they moved slightly apart, and with each exhale came closer together. They rode a few minutes in this boat made of breath, a private skiff for only two. Ashley didn't notice as the rest of the world disappeared, only noticed how completely united they were.

She had the feeling they were standing at the edge of the universe—as if they were at the threshold of some great discovery, some astonishing encounter with something elusive, something boundless. In this quiet embrace, she felt both completely satisfied and at the same time flooded with a sense of potential.

"My Rena was always the one who believed in me," Luke said, his voice a threadbare whisper, more vulnerable than she had ever heard him before. As if all his masks were off. As if, standing here in the circle of her arms, he was safe enough to drop all his facades, all his walls. "She was my mother figure.

While my own mom seemed to disappear when I needed her most, my Rena was there with me. She always told me I could do anything. That I had the power of the sun and the moon and the dark in me. I want to live up to being the good man she thought I could be."

Ashley swallowed any words that might try to placate or promise. Instead, she let heartache stand with them, marveling at how it held them both with absolute tenderness.

Intuitively, she led him by the hand to the living room and stood with him beside the window, both of them bathed in the glow of the city lights. Outside, everything was moving—cars, trucks, planes. And though they were standing still, inside herself, she felt movement, too, a deepening shift. As if the foundation she and Luke shared was changing. Could Luke feel all this, too? In the window, she could see his reflection, the city lights sparkling through the shape of him. She shivered with a rush of powerful, unnamable emotion, and as it passed through her, it left a feeling of spaciousness.

Keeping her eyes on the pane, she stepped slightly behind him, nestling her body into the solid warmth of his back. She reached up a hand to touch his face. Luke watched her intently in the window as she traced the outline of his jaw, the light in his eyes almost brighter than the lights outside.

"Look at you," she said, her voice a gentle command. "Look at you, Luke." She cradled his face with both hands from behind. "You are such a good man." In the reflection, his eyes followed her hands as they very slowly flowed down his strong neck, smoothed across his powerful shoulders, grazed gently down the sleeves of his cotton shirt, skimming the hard muscles of his upper arms. "I see who you are inside." She tucked her hands under his arms and leisurely felt her way along his ribs to his superbly toned torso, reveling in the pounding in his chest she could feel through her palms. "I know your big heart.

All the goodness." She swirled her fingertips over his heart in slow spirals, steeping them both in an awareness of his body and the pulse coursing through it. "Can you know the goodness and strength in you, too, Luke? Can you see you the way I see you? The way Rena saw you? Can you know your incredible, vulnerable self?"

Luke met Ashley's gaze in the window, and she was instantly mesmerized by the full force of their connection. With their eyes locked, Ashley's fingers continued to slide across his chest, massaging intentional concentric circles, pressing into the taut musculature below his shirt. A tortured sigh escaped Luke's lips, the sound of profound release, the sound of a decades-old cage crumbling to dust. She saw it in his eyes, a melting, a startled willingness, an uncertainty, a hint of fear.

"Ashley?" He said it as if he were recognizing her for the first time, as if her name were a path he was deciding to follow. He turned in her arms to face her, his blue eyes seeking hers as if they were a lifeline. With both hands, he explored her face. His fingers were featherlight, traveling across her hairline, her temples, her cheekbones, her ears. Her skin was so sensitive everywhere he touched came newly alive, and everywhere he didn't touch felt prickly and deprived.

She couldn't have taken her eyes from him if she tried. She felt totally exposed, as if Luke were seeing right into the core of her as she had been doing with him. She felt him giving her all of himself. A soft purr escaped her lips, a small sound of arousal, and she shuddered as she tried to breathe more deeply, her body somehow too small for her lungs.

At the edge of her consciousness, she noticed the classical guitar still playing in the background, a minor key, wistful and reaching, and the aching melody laced in and around them, weaving them nearer and nearer, their bodies straining toward each other.

Inside her, she felt a tightening, as if a silver lasso had wrapped around her heart and the rope was being pulled taut, tugging her toward Luke. She was captive, willing, caught in an inevitable connection. The intensity of sensation made her breath come in short, shallow pants.

Luke's face hovered closer, and she felt herself leaning toward him in equal measure, meeting his deliberate, reverential pace. When at last their lips touched, the kiss was the lightest possible kiss, a gossamer kiss, their mouths floating against each other, a luminous, breath-stealing brush with bliss. Luke lifted his head slowly, as if he were worshipping at the temple of her, his gaze laced with awe, as if he had no idea what came next but had given himself completely over to being right here, right now with her. Ashley lifted her hands to his shoulders and stared into the incandescent blue of his eyes.

The strangest wonder rose in Ashley as she realized Luke had never kissed her lips before without first slipping into some kind of role. In fact, she believed, he had never kissed *anyone* without first imagining himself as someone else.

He stared at her with such ardor, his expression slightly stunned. "Ashley?" Though her name came out as a whisper-soft question, there was a sincerity in his tone, too, that took her breath away, infusing the room with the intoxicating perfume of vulnerability.

Ashley's throat tightened even as her heart flung its doors wide open. Instead of speaking, unsure of her voice or even what she might say, she gave a slight nod, as if honoring they were in new territory together. She shivered as his eyes burned with hope.

Their hands found each other's hands, and Ashley was aware of letting Luke lead her in this unrehearsed, unknowable dance. She mirrored him as fingertip to fingertip, palm to palm, they met in erotic softness, creating a steeple of flesh and air between them. She trembled in delicate agony. Her body longed for release from the sensual tension coursing through her, and simultaneously, she was aware she never wanted the longing to end.

As if she had willed it, Luke's face leaned closer to hers, one side in shadow, the other in light, and Ashley waited, waited, waited, craving him with a smoldering desperation and devotion that rewrote any ideas she had about what passion might be.

This time, when at last their mouths joined again, his mouth was soft and hot, tasting of whiskey and midnight. Ashley moaned into his mouth as he cradled her head with his hands in her hair and shifted his lips across hers, as if sampling her for the first time. It was intimate and almost innocent, unlike any other kiss they had shared. With the tip of his tongue, he surveyed the landscape of her lips and teeth, and she trembled as he explored the silken chamber of her mouth with sensual curiosity, as if discovering a treasure chest of beauty and tenderness and vulnerability.

Need clawed inside Ashley, a scraping in the pit of her stomach, a glorious sundering, a magnificent frustration, a ravening, shimmering, gnawing demand. She longed to deepen the kiss, to crush her body into his, to give in to the urgency growing in her, pulsing in her, but she was determined to follow his lead in this lovemaking, determined to let him take the time he needed, and she thrilled in his deliberate exploration, even as it tortured her.

Slowly, the pressure of his mouth increased as his lips pressed against hers in exhilarating union, and his tongue delved deeper into the wet heat of her. Starved for him, she matched his slow, fevered intensity. *I'm yours*, she told him with the way she opened beneath him. *You are the one I want.* Though Luke's lips moved languidly, as if drugged with new pleasure, Ashley's pulse hammered, frantic and wild. This man, this resplendent, intelligent, desirable man was giving her everything she wanted, only her greedy body was clamoring *faster, harder, more.*

She groaned as she felt the ten thousand sparks leaping between them turn to chaos, to blaze, to wildfire that threatened to consume her. Luke must have felt it, too. He pulled his fingers through the downy length of her hair and gently tugged, opening her to him even more, and then he groaned into her as if the magnificence of the kiss had burned him. He stepped away.

A helpless whimper escaped from her throat, her lips instantly bereft, her nerve endings in every part of her raw. "Luke?" She let out a quivering breath. Was it too much? Too quickly? Was it too difficult to meet her this way, with no armor, no mask, no cover, no fantasy? His blue eyes were lust-darkened, the color of the Houston sky before a giant storm.

Panting roughly, Luke put one of his large hands in the center of her chest and pressed it to her heated skin just above and between the swell of her breasts. He took in the heaving of her chest, the clamorous hammering of her heart. They stood there in silence, staring at each other, and eventually, their breathing began to regulate.

"I want it to last forever tonight," he murmured thickly, his gaze devout. "I have never…I have never simply made love before." The naked sincerity in his voice unraveled her.

Though Ashley had dreamed about meeting Luke without any pretense, wondered what it would be like for him to meet her completely vulnerably, nothing had prepared her for how wildly vulnerable it would make *her*, how she, too, would need to be unswervingly authentic and present. It was stark and so rich at the same time. In this moment, loving Luke was both the terrifying thrill of the high-wire act *and* the security of the net—she had never felt so scared and so safe at the same time. *Not only, but also.*

He removed his hand from her chest and held it out to her, palm up. Ashley slipped her hand in his and silently walked with him through his penthouse to his bedroom. There, he took two lighters from a drawer and handed one to her. Together, they lit a couple dozen candles in glass jars until they flickered from every shelf and table in the room and the air smelled of burning candles, sweet and thick. As the light grew, so did the desire heating in Ashley's blood, rising in her like a tide until she felt as if she were drowning in want. She could feel how her own wetness gathered now between her legs, how her sex had swollen without even being touched, how exquisite and almost painful the small throb in her clit flared, pulsing like a beacon.

She turned to look at Luke, only to find he was already watching her from a few feet away, his smile full of animal hunger and abundant wonder and something unnamable and beautiful, as if he were going to devour her completely, fervently, enthusiastically, with excruciating leisure. Her legs weakened. The look on his face and the promises it made were almost more pleasure than she could bear, and her lower belly flip-flopped and wrestled with her yearning. *Oh sweet, delicious anguish.*

Luke undid the top button on his shirt. She undid the top button on hers. Their eyes never left each other, locked in an intimate optical embrace. A knot of pleasure tightened in her abdomen. He undid the next button; she undid the next. With every breath, she inhaled the scent of summer, the scent of honey, the scent of bees humming in their hives.

In unison, they finished opening their shirts, peeling them off, letting them drop to the floor. She admired the powerful planes of his chest and the rows of hard muscles beneath. In unison, he undid his jeans, she unzipped her skirt. They let them fall to the floor.

Standing there with only tiny scraps of clothing to cover their nudity, Ashley could see the head of Luke's cock escaping

the top of his waistband, the long hard shape of his ridge pressing against the tight black fabric. She wanted to cup it, to stroke
it, to kneel in front of him and pull his length deep into her
mouth and suck him hard until he stiffened even more and jerked and spent in her mouth.

But she didn't move. She waited for him. Her nipples strained
against her bra, tender, too sensitive. She realized she was visi-
bly trembling.

Luke's eyes softened. "Are you cold?" His voice was roughened by want, increasing her shivers.

She shook her head. He smiled.

Luke stepped out of his briefs, his erection rising between
them, the skin tight and smooth and veined. She unhooked her
bra, felt the cool air prickle against the dark tips of her breasts,
felt the change in their weight once freed. Her panties slipped
off with the hook of a finger, and she stepped out of them into
her nakedness.

With just a few steps, they met each other in the middle,
her breasts meeting the warmth of his chest, their hips joining
like magnets. With their hands pressing into each other's backs,
they molded their bodies into each other, moving ever so slightly, faintly grinding, seeking tender friction, her intimate folds
riding against his leg, his cock brushing against her belly. Luke
bowed his forehead to hers, and in a velvety sigh, he whispered,
"Yes."

That one-word mantra rang through her thoughts, rushed
through her blood, and rubbed its sweet essence into her certainty that things between her and Luke were deeply, mysteriously, irrevocably transforming.

Luke guided her arms up to clasp around his neck, then
reached down to cup the round cheeks of her ass and pull her
up to his waist, her legs folding around his sculpted back. They
swayed like that for a moment in the middle of the room. Ashley

reveled in his strength, the pleasure of being held, especially when her own legs had been wobbly as tulip stems, barely holding up her own weight. She felt as if she were floating above him, her hands playing in the dark locks at the base of his neck. Ashley nuzzled her cheek against the shadowy stubble on his jaw.

"Ashley, my Ashley, my beautiful Ashley," he whispered, raining endearments on her as he walked to the bed and delivered her to the middle of the mattress, then climbed onto the bed with her, the cream comforter soft beneath her, the mattress bending with his weight. "Every part of you is beautiful."

The words made her feel treasured, valued, more than enough, just as she was.

Luke sat beside her, his legs straight out in front of him, and then he turned his body to lift her onto him, twisting her to sit on his lap until she was facing him, her silken flesh touching the base of his shaft. *So close, so close.*

"There," he murmured. "There."

Luke bent his head to take one of her breasts into his ardent mouth, and she moaned as the wet heat enclosed her sensitive crest. He stroked the nipple with his tongue in unhurried circles, such a satisfying tease. A strangled cry lodged in her throat and sought escape. She wanted him to nip, to bite. Moved by a primal wantonness, she arched her back in supplication, offering herself to him, but with the shift of her body, she felt the underside of his hard shaft press maddeningly against her slick furrow. She wanted him inside her, ached to feel his thick arousal filling her.

"Please," she whimpered.

Luke lifted his head and kissed a trail of velvety, open-mouthed caresses up her neck. "Yes, sweetness, yes," he murmured. "We will give each other everything."

He put his hands on her waist and lifted her higher until she was dangling right above his cock, his thick head nesting firmly against her soaking entrance. And then she was being lowered, slowly, slowly, as he breached her warmth. Her heart hammered wildly as his erection slipped hotly into her, fraction by fraction, stretching her, dilating her, and she sighed in ecstatic, trembling relief.

The whole time he slid his shaft deeper into her silkiness, Ashley watched Luke's face as it opened in erotic satisfaction, his mouth widening, his eyes unfocusing, his whole body tensed like a spring, and she felt her body tightening around him.

When at last her rounded cheeks met his thighs, Luke released her waist and leaned back on his arms. With her knees bent, she, too, leaned back, staring at the place where their bodies were joined. She could see the taut skin of his cock each time he pulled out and how eagerly her snug body received him, pulling him in, pulsing around him, seeking an even deeper penetration.

For a moment, neither of them moved, both so close to the precipice of orgasm neither of them wanting the pleasure to stop. Involuntarily, Ashley squeezed his cock with her inner walls, and Luke shuddered. "Oh. Ashley," he grunted, trying to lift his hips.

Ashley realized in this position she had almost total control of the angle, the depth, the speed of the thrusts. Luke had established such sweet unhurried motion in this lovemaking, and she fought with the part of herself that wanted to ride him hard. Instead, she rocked gently, riveted by the changes in Luke's expression with each minute shift of her body. She leaned back farther and, to her surprise, felt the magnificent pressure increase on that heavenly inner spot of her. Her eyes widened, and slowly, she moved to rub his cock against that pleasure point. Her breathing became increasingly labored as she ground toward her own gratification. Oh, the sweet torture, and she felt her body begin to deliciously clamp—

"Ashley, my love, stop."

She stopped, her lungs heaving, every part of her screaming *move, move*.

"I want it to last."

Ashley whimpered, and Luke smiled at her with agony and devotion. As she waited for the raging tides of her arousal to subside, Luke stared deeply into her eyes, and she saw in that fathomless blue something she'd never before seen during their sex—an open sky, an unguarded startling intimacy. She gasped.

Luke nodded, as if he knew what she saw, affirming the honest miracle of the moment. Gently, he lifted his hips, encouraging her to begin a rhythm again, and she eagerly slid her body over his hard, satiny length in long, liquid glides. She loved seeing him enter her again and again. Savage growls formed deep in his throat, low and primitive, the dark timbre of an ancient drum, arousing her, awakening her, her senses all fully charged. There was no time. There was no world. There was only this slow, rocking, erotic rhythm. There was only this hardness stroking inside her. This quivering softness. This raw music of union. This very here.

The throbbing in her clit echoed through her whole body, a delirious pleasure of strain and thrust, grasp and release, yet she forced herself to breathe slowly in time with Luke, to link her movements to their breath. She had never felt so wholly present in sex—so deliciously stretched both physically and emotionally, completely immersed in her partner, herself. The revelation made tears collect in her eyes and trickle slowly down the sides of her face, as if there was too much beauty to contain and it was now leaking out of her.

Luke groaned, and she felt him stiffen inside her. He was close.

She leaned back again and began surging, massaging her G-spot with his glorious cock until the beginning of her own orgasm began to take her. Its dark waves lapped at her, rising in her, carrying her toward a shimmering climax.

Luke's face glowed in the candlelight, shining with sweat. "Ashley," he rasped, "come with me." His hand gently coasted up her inner thigh, then sought out her delicate bundle of nerves. With the slightest touch of his thumb, she shattered into glittering waves, pleasure crashing all around her, a drowning, an all-consuming, rippling bliss. She heard Luke calling her name as he, too, shuddered, felt the flood of warmth as his thick cream filled her.

And all the while, through the haze of ecstasy, Luke and Ashley had gazed at each other, sharing a dazzling intimacy that defied language, a love spoken by eyelash and iris and blink and stare.

Luke offered her his hand, and he pulled her exhausted body over his. Ashley draped her nakedness on top of him, nuzzling her face into his chest, their bodies still connected. She rode on the rise and fall of his torso as he breathed and felt so completely at home—at home in her body, at home with his body. Luke wrapped both his arms around her and held her tight, cocooning her in the afterglow.

"Ashley," he whispered into her hair, kissing the top of her head. His voice trembled a little, but his arms were steel, cradling her in rock-solid firmness, as if he were trying to tether his soul to hers forever. "I love you."

"Luke?" She tried to push up to see his face, but he held her securely against him.

"I didn't know I could feel this way, Ashley. I didn't know it was possible. I thought maybe I was too broken to love someone like this, but you've opened me. You've shown me how I was still holding myself back and letting that be my life. I'm scared, Ashley; I'm afraid of hurting you somehow, but I am also so sure I love you, and it's too powerful to hold it in, too powerful to pretend it isn't real. I don't know what happens next, but I know I love you. I love you so much, and I will do everything I can, *everything,* to make you a happy woman." He gave her a squeeze, enfolding her in warm conviction. "And someday, though I have done terrible things, someday I hope you can love me, too." His words fell on her like a rain of rose petals, fragrant and soft.

"Luke." Ashley pushed herself up against his body to investigate the dark blue pools of his eyes. She wanted to slip into them and stay forever. "Luke, I love you, too. I was too afraid to tell you." He gave her a confused look. "Or maybe it's that I was afraid to admit it to myself. I've been so hurt before. But you—you are so good to me, so generous, so funny, so real, so completely the man I love. It is so easy to love you, Luke." She checked herself, thinking of his work. "Well, except when it isn't." He chuckled. "But even then, even when I am furious with you, even when I can't reconcile the things you do, even then I love you."

"You *love* me?" Disbelief blossomed on his candlelit face.

She gave him a giddy grin. "I'll say it as many times as you want to hear it, Luke. I love you."

He stared at her with wonder and lifted a hand to touch her cheek with a near ferocious tenderness. "I'm afraid you'll disappear."

"I'm right here, Luke," she whispered, snuggling her body closer into his. "I'm right here." And she closed her eyes and melted into him, stunned by how good it felt to be nestled in his arms.

Even in this moment of ultimate bliss, Ashley had never been so aware of how risky it was to give away one's heart. And yet there was nothing she could do but give it. She fell asleep feeling more whole than she'd ever felt before.

CHAPTER 7

"HEY, SLEEPYHEAD."
Ashley was vaguely aware of the scent of fresh-brewed coffee and the bedroom being filled with light as the electric blackout shades began to rise.

"Mmm." She opened one eye and saw Luke in his bathrobe, setting a mug on the bedside table closest to her.

"Can you smell what I brought *espresso-ly* for you."

"It's too early for punning." She pulled a gauzy cream sheet over her head, relishing how soft it was, how warm.

"It's not early, *brew-tiful*. It's already 7:02."

"What?" She poked her head out from under the covers. Luke had probably been up for hours already and would be leaving soon for work. "Why didn't you wake me up?"

"I *am* waking you up." He let his robe drop to the floor, revealing his nakedness, sleek and powerful. She was mesmerized by his powerful thighs—the way his muscles flexed into new planes as he walked toward her in the bed. A smile spread across her face as she remembered the night before—sensual, mind-melting hours of making love, real love, with Luke.

"What is that look on your face?" he asked mischievously, slipping beneath the covers, curling his hard body into hers. "And how do I put it on there more often?"

"I was just thinking about last night."

Luke rolled her onto her side and molded his hard body against her backside.

"Did we really—" Ashley paused.

"Make beautiful love all night?" A shimmer of pleasure tingled through Ashley's skin. He rested his hand against the jut of her hip bone, then levered his hard cock into the smooth crease of her ass, the heat of him immediately arousing her. Ashley felt her cheeks flush and her pulse begin to race.

"And do you think we could—"

"Find pleasure in each other's naked bodies again right now?" He nibbled on her ear and sent a thousand tingles rushing down her spine.

Ashley responded by rocking herself into him, thrilling at the gasp he made as she writhed her round bottom against him, marveling at the hot sparks his moan set off inside her. She rolled on her back and looked up at him. "Kiss me." She was aware of a powerful feeling that rose in her—the feeling that Luke would do anything for her. It was coupled with a terrifying vulnerability—knowing she would do anything for him.

"Yes, ma'am." Luke drawled in a leisurely Texan twang she so seldom heard from him. Perhaps his years in school on the East Coast had tempered his Southern accent, but he sure could lay it on for effect when he chose to. His head bent over hers, the midnight waves of his hair falling into a curtain around their faces. Their breaths mingled, and their mouths found each other in open anticipation, moving with erotic softness. His stubble chafed a little at her upper lip, but there was nothing that would stop her from completely giving in to the heaven of his kiss.

Luke had not yet showered, and she inhaled his warm, salty male scent—it fueled her passion, and she arched her back. He rolled onto her, pinning her to the mattress with his hard, lean body as he continued to ravage her mouth with increasing pressure. He tasted of coffee and cinnamon and urgency. She moaned as he left her lips only to lavish kisses in a silken path down her throat, exploring her, finding the points that made her melt.

Yes. It was as if Luke was just discovering the part of him that was able to meet her sexually without hiding, and it was clear he found enjoyment in simply kissing her—as if kissing were not a prelude to something else but an end in itself.

Though of course, way led on to way, and it was after eight before Ashley was aware again of the time.

"Luke!" She startled in his arms, realizing she must have dozed off again in post-climactic bliss. Her eyes widened in panic. "You'll be late."

Luke was facing her on the pillow, staring at her dreamily, as if he had been watching her a long time.

"Luke, you are late for work!"

"I called in earlier and said I was working from home and would come in late." His lips slid into a seductive smile. "It's a perk of being a boss."

Ashley relaxed again into the sheets, relishing their softness. Like everything else in Luke's penthouse, they were the highest quality. And she realized with some dismay there really was a big difference between his sheets and hers. Strange how the smallest things sometimes reminded her of how big the differences were in their lives.

"Hey." He stroked her cheek. "There's something I need; I think it's in the top drawer over there. Would you grab it for me?"

"Sure, what is it?" She stretched and rolled out of bed, walking naked across Luke's bedroom. She felt confident and sexy in her body—a feeling she hadn't had in years, maybe never.

She reached the top drawer and opened it. "Empty." She gave him a querying glance.

"Must be the next drawer down," he said with a shrug.

"Empty."

"Oh, next drawer down?"

"Empty. What exactly are you looking for, Luke?"

"Must be in the bottom drawer."

Ashley pulled the drawer open with her toes and noted a single sheet of paper floating in the bottom with her name on it. She shot Luke a curious look. He smiled innocently back.

She bent down to pick it up and brought it back to the bed without reading it.

"Aren't you going to see what it says?"

"Yes." She snuggled in and looked at Luke's distinctive right-slanted cursive.

Your clothes belong here. And so do you. Move in with me.

She looked up into Luke's eyes, humbled by the hope and love she saw dancing there. "I have never felt so whole, Ashley, as I do when I'm with you. I want to wake up to you every morning. I want to sleep with you in my arms every night. I want to hear you singing in the kitchen and eavesdrop while you tutor just so I can hear your voice. I want to bring you coffee with just a hint of sugar and make the bed together and see your books on the shelves with my books. Move in with me, Ashley. This will be *our* home. Say yes."

There are moments when time seems to be pinned in place—when we are aware of the invitation to leap and find ourselves in a new and wondrous world. And what is it that keeps us from leaping? A fear of free-falling, losing our bearings? A fear of not belonging in the new place?

Ashley could barely keep track of all the thoughts swirling in her. Her body, charged with positivity, was pulsing *Yes! Yes! Yes!* Her heart beat wildly against her chest, urging her to leap. But she had always lived more by her brain, her cautious, practical, logistical brain that had saved her and steered her well again and again. *You two are too different*, it said. *You're going to get hurt*, it said. *Men always abandon you*, it said. It said, *Wait. Wait. Wait.*

Was now the time to listen to her brain? Or to trust her feelings? Luke, for all his hang-ups about worthiness, was still so much more able to access his feelings and take emotional risks than she was. He had always been the one most willing to move their relationship forward into new places. Was that something he had to teach her? Was it time to leap with him over some unseen edge? Blood pumped in her ears, and tears threatened to spill out her eyes, though she didn't know why.

Luke sensed her hesitation and gave her hand an understanding squeeze. "I know it's a big choice. You don't have to tell me—"

"Yes."

Luke tilted his head as if trying to read her. "It's okay to take your time. I don't want you to—"

"Yes."

"Yes?" Luke looked into her eyes, disbelieving.

"Yes!" Each time she said the word, she could feel her own excitement and certainty grow. She was free-falling but without fear—such a glorious rush. As if she could fall and fall and fall with total trust that Luke would catch her no matter what. "Yes."

"Oh, Ashley, thank god you didn't take your time. I don't know how I would have made it another second without knowing your answer. You make me the happiest man in the Milky Way galaxy." She laughed as he made a hot necklace of open-mouthed kisses that curved around the front of her neck.

"I think every single atom in my body is dancing," he murmured into her skin.

"That's seven octillion atoms," she said on a gasp as he nipped behind her ear.

Luke lifted above her to look into her eyes. "You made that word up."

"Would I lie to you?" Her eyes flashed. "It's a seven with twenty-seven zeroes after it. And that's how many atoms you have in your body. Give or take."

Luke nuzzled his face back into her neck. "You have no idea how it turns me on when you talk science and math to me." He pressed his hard cock against her thigh as if to prove it. "How soon can you have your stuff in here?"

"Um…" All language left her head as he coasted his hands across the cool skin of her stomach and then massaged over her mound. His mouth possessed hers with long erotic strokes of his tongue until her brain puddled and she felt intoxicated with sensation.

"How about tonight?" he murmured in her ear, his voice dark velvet.

"Tonight?" Ashley laughed, thinking of the impossibility, but her body arched against him, saying yes to anything he'd ask of her. She ran her hands through his dark mane, pulling his head up so she could see the blue burn of his eyes, but what she saw was so much more astonishing than fire; she saw peace— two glassy oceans with fathomless depth. For a slender moment, she waded into the tenderness, certainty, and vulnerability she found in his gaze. Any uncertainty she had been feeling receded.

Luke lapsed into a winsome grin. "Tonight might be too far away."

Ashley shook her head on the pillow. "Luke, I can't move in that fast."

"I think you can," he said, moving his lips to the sensitive peak of her breast. "Perhaps you could use some incentive." He slipped a leg between her thighs to open her. Her most secret place clenched instinctively, and she pressed herself into his thigh, pulsing against him.

"But…" she began, and then she found her mouth covered with his. It was a long time before she said anything but *yes*.

———

Ashley sat on her living room floor between two piles—one named *keep*, one named *give away*. How could she have accumulated so much *stuff*? An easel, a back scratcher, an ice-cream maker she had bought for school because the district couldn't afford it, and she'd wanted it for fun experiments. *Won't be needing that anymore.*

She sprawled out on the floor between the two piles and stared up at the ceiling, marveling at how quickly her life had changed. In the last few months, she'd lost her job with the school. She'd started a nonprofit that actually paid her to create online programming about environmental activism for kids. She'd fallen in love with one of the most handsome, sensual men in all of Houston—in the world! And he'd fallen in love with her. And now they'd be living together.

Bamba, her cat, came and sat on her lap, then began to purr and knead her paws into Ashley's stomach.

"Oh, you. I will come visit you all the time." Because Luke was allergic to cats, Bamba would move in with Jewel, who had always coveted Bamba. "You'll be happy with my sister. But I'll miss you." Ashley smoothed her hand over the cat's back, and it rolled its spine to receive the touch. "We've been through so much together, little cat. We made it past Mark and that nasty divorce. We found this little place. We got a job at the school. How many nights did we sit here alone, snuggled up with books? Who would have ever thought I would fall in love?"

Bamba purred and pushed her face into Ashley's hand, encouraging her to keep petting. "And he's wonderful, Bamba. He makes me so happy."

She smiled as she thought about the message she'd left for him this morning. They'd decided not to shower together because…temptation, but she'd left him a message in the steam on the glass shower walls.

I love you. To be continued.

Oh, how she had loved the resonant sound of his laughter when he'd read the secret message.

"He really loves me, Bamba. You understand, right?"

The cat saw a fly in the corner and pushed off Ashley's stomach like it was a launching pad. "Oof." Ashley laughed. That was the thing about cats. They could only take so much sentimentality.

But Ashley was feeling deep currents of nostalgia. This tiny apartment had been great for her. She remembered the day she'd moved in and how much fun she'd had arranging the closets and cleaning the whole unit until it sparkled. And the best thing about the apartment—it had been *hers*. All hers. But she felt a happy shiver, remembering the way Luke had said *ours*. She had wanted to pay him rent, but he wouldn't hear of it. "No, darlin'," he'd drawled. "Why would you pay me for what is *ours*?"

Her lease wasn't up for a few more months, but Luke had refused to let that be a reason for her to not move in right away, so she was making plans to sublease the apartment.

This whole day had felt surreal. Driving home from Luke's penthouse, she had stared at the other people in their cars driving to wherever they were going. For them, perhaps, it was just another Wednesday. But for her, everything had changed. She had a new home.

Home. The word both thrilled and terrified her. At her mother's house, she'd always felt the absence of her father. At her apartment with her ex-husband, she'd been betrayed. Here, in her little apartment, she'd felt self-sufficient and capable but often lonely. But with Luke? Everything seemed possible, including finding *home*.

Delight rose in her, great waves of happiness crashing in her until she could no longer be still. Small as her apartment was, it would be a week before she would be done here, sorting and cleaning things out, packing things up, but suddenly, she couldn't be done with it soon enough. "C'mon, girl, let's get back on it." She stood. She'd be tutoring students in a couple of hours, and she wanted to make some headway.

Ashley licked her lips, noting they were still bruised from hours of kissing. The memory of last night inspired a low flutter below her rib cage, a sweet clenching in her gut. *Dang.* She missed him. *Now.*

But it wasn't just his talented lips she was missing. It was more about the promise in his eyes this morning—that oceanic calm, that sense of fathomless possibility.

We're going to be together. The words entered her like a revelation. *Together.*

Ashley's phone dinged, and she checked her texts.

Luke: Need to go overnight to west Texas for work. Sorry!!
          She texted him a photo of the piles.

Ashley: No problem—look what I'll be doing tonight

Luke: Can't have you in my arms soon enough. Meet me
          tomorrow night after work? I have a secret plan

A giddy joy rushed through her. *Secret plan?* Luke was a planner—even more so than she was, and yet he loved surprises, both giving and receiving them. He was a glorious enigma.

Ashley: I'm in

Luke: Call me later so I can make you feel good. I'll tuck you and
          Harry in with a little bedtime story

Ashley snorted, actually *snorted*, at Luke's reference to the dildo her sister had bought for her when she and Luke had broken up. She couldn't believe she'd told him. She couldn't believe he'd brought it back up.

Luke: I promise it will end happily

She sent him a gif of a woman jumping for joy. That's what it felt like inside of her—as if someone inside her who believed in happy endings was jumping for freaking joy. It felt so foreign. And wonderful.

Ashley sighed, then checked her email. A note from Global Dynamic Classroom?

> *July 18*
>
> *Dear Ms. Barris,*
> *You have submitted several applications over the years to teach with La Mente Abierta in Huayllabamba, Peru, and we appreciate your enthusiasm for our program and for this particular school. Although your application for this year was initially declined, the position recently reopened, and we hope you will say yes. We apologize for the short notice. As you know…*

Ashley's eyes blurred as she scanned the rest of the letter.

> *Extra stipend to help take care of her belongings… Airline tickets needed to be purchased immediately…know within a week…in the classroom August 15 when our students return from their winter break…*

She slumped down on the couch and let the phone fall to the cushion beside her. *Now?* Anguish squeezed her. She couldn't go to Peru. Not now, when she had finally found happiness with Luke. Not now, when he had just asked her to move in and she'd said yes. Not now, when he had told her that he loved her and she'd told him she loved him, too. *Not now.* Not when she was just embarking on a new chapter. She searched for an inner yes, but in this moment, her heart hammered a steady beat of *no, no, no.* Her adrenaline raced, and she felt a turbulent swell of unease surge through her.

Ashley closed her eyes and fought down a sob. How could this letter she'd wanted so desperately only months ago now distress her so? So much had changed since she'd applied for the job teaching in Peru. She couldn't say yes to it now. It wasn't just that her life had changed—her *dreams* had changed.

For a long time, she sat there, collapsed on herself. It seemed so long ago that this letter was what she wanted most to receive— the invitation to go to Tica's birthplace and take her mentor's ashes to the little sacred chapel on the mountainside as Tica had wished. It seemed so long ago she dreamed of being with the people in Huayllabamba and teaching in the school where Tica would have taught, helping the community there the way Tica had helped her here in Houston.

When at last she opened her eyes, there on the coffee table in front of her was the only fancy picture book she owned, *Lure of the Rural,* a collection of images of the Peruvian countryside. She stared at the green mountains, the terraced hillside, the sheer cliffs, and she was filled with the most poignant ache. For two decades, she had fantasized about living in this landscape.

"*Luke.*" She touched her lips and closed her eyes. *Oh, Luke.* So much was at stake.

She could hear Tica's voice in her head. *Fortune and olives are alike,* she would say. *Sometimes you have none. And sometimes too much.*

The next day, Ashley pulled up to her mother's small home. Like all the other houses in the neighborhood, it needed attention— needed new paint, a new roof, a new walkway. But her mother was proud of this place—she'd worked hard to pay it off. And though Ashley harbored many difficult memories from here, all her recollections of her mother involved love.

Parking the car, she felt her gaze drawn to the neighboring house where Tica had lived and felt a rush of gratitude. She remembered sitting at the old wooden round table in Tica's home when she was a girl and eating *rocoto relleno*—spicy stuffed peppers—and drinking hot chocolate and listening to Tica talk about the high mountains where she had grown up. How the temperature was so moderate compared to Houston and the corn kernels were the biggest in the world. How the townsfolk would dance through the streets, and they could change the weather through prayer and by simply blowing at the clouds. How much Tica had loved the smell of roasting corn and the sound of laughter late at night in the streets. And how she longed to go back, but she was tethered to the United States by her four sons and their children and her husband. Plus, Tica had left her hometown on difficult terms—no one in her family or the town had understood why she would leave the Quechua village of Huayllabamba. Her own parents had felt so betrayed they had told her not to return. She'd never seen them again.

And Tica would hold Ashley's slender young hands in her work-roughened palms and smile. "Jesus gave me and my Cusi four beautiful boys. And when I prayed for a daughter, he gave me you. It just took many years for my prayer to come true."

When Tica was growing up, she had dreamed she would become a teacher in her village. When her husband had decided they should leave the village just a few months after they'd married, Tica had followed him to Cusco, where he worked as a carpenter. Despite her parents' admonition, she'd dreamed of returning to Huayllabamba, but instead, she and Cusi had moved to America. Ashley knew some part of her still imagined what it would be like to be a teacher in her home village. "Instead of

a classroom of many, I have a classroom of six," she would tell
Ashley, laughing at her joke as she gestured to her own four
sons, Ashley, and Jewel.

Because of Tica's attention, and because of the devotion of
her own mother, Ashley had grown up with a strong sense of
self. How lucky she was to have such remarkable women role
models—resilient, loving, nurturing, capable women who had
ferociously supported her. It was part of why she, too, was a
mentor now for Emilia, a rising senior in high school who also
wanted to become a teacher.

A profound swell of gratitude surged in her, thinking of how
different her life would be without her mom and Tica's constant
daily presence. But the gratitude was accompanied by a terrible
tug. She felt torn, pulled apart by life, aware that now, for the
first time, she had a real chance to make good on her promises
to herself and her beloved mentor. But the sacrifices it involved
were too big.

"I am going back for you someday," Ashley said aloud, staring at Tica's door, thinking of how many times she had said
those exact words to Tica. "Someday, I will be the teacher and
role model for the girls in your village that you were for me."

Ashley stood a moment on her mom's doorstep before
knocking, lost in thought about Peru. What was she going to
do?

She was startled by a knock on the door—her mother
knocking from the inside, trying to get Ashley's attention. Ashley smiled at her mother and waved brightly as her mom undid
the multiple locks.

"There's my sweet Ashling," her mom said, calling her by her
nickname, a blend of *Ashley* and *darling*. Her mom pulled her
into her arms. "I'm so glad you're here."

Ashley held her mother tight for a long time, noting how thin
her mother had become. She'd been quite sick with pneumonia

and had almost died, and it made Ashley even more eager to spend as much time with her as she could.

Could I really leave her now for four months? Alarm bells went off in her head.

"Hi, Mom. I brought you some cookies." She reached into the canvas bag on her shoulder and pulled out a small tin of homemade lemon shortbread.

"You're trying to fatten me up, aren't you, love. Well, I could use it." Her mom tugged at the loose elastic around the waist of her sweatpants.

Ashley and her mom shared tea and cookies, and Ashley listened as her mom talked about doctor visits and wanting to visit her sister Jane in her hometown and juggling her bills, but Ashley was distracted by thoughts of Peru. And Luke. It was as if there were a tornado in her head, swirling, tearing everything up, making it impossible to focus.

"Something's up, darling. What is it?"

"Oh nothing, Mom, just tired." It was true she was tired. But Ashley wondered at her reluctance to share with her mother about either Luke's invitation to move in or the acceptance letter from Peru.

"Is everything good with Luke?"

"Oh yes, everything's great, Mom," she said, her voice a bit too bright. *In fact, Luke is more committed to me than ever and willing to be vulnerable, and I am so full-body chafed from mind-blowing sex two days ago it hurts to move today. And he asked me to move in, and I said yes. And then I was invited to leave him and go to Peru. I'm being torn apart by everything I ever wanted all happening at once.* "Really great."

Her mom gave her a disbelieving look. "Well, you look tired. I never was any good at getting you to sleep more when you lived at home, and I sure can't do anything about it now, but you need rest, love. Your body's not a machine."

"Yes, Mom. Thank you." Though she didn't roll her eyes, somehow, the eye roll made it into her voice. Her hair fell into her face, and she pushed it back behind her ear. She felt a sharp pang of melancholy, thinking how often Luke pulled her hair back for her, a sweet, intimate, daily gesture. He was so good to her, so gentle.

Her mom's voice softened. "Whatever it is you are struggling with, Ashling"—she held up a hand—"and you don't have to tell me what it is, it is the struggle that gives our lives meaning."

Ashley tried again not to roll her eyes. Her mom saw and gave a small shrug.

"There was a time, sweetheart, when I thought it was my job as your mother to make sure that you didn't have to struggle. But being your mother and watching you grow from challenges has taught me how important it is to let you be wrestled by life." She gave a small smile. "Still, it's hard to see you struggling. If it's money, I can—"

"No, Mom. Not money. I'm fine."

"Good." Her mother nodded, accepting Ashley's assurance. "Then whatever it is, remember, you can only take one step at a time. And then another."

"But what if I want to take two steps at the same time in different directions?"

Ashley's mother nodded and was quiet. "Then, my love, before you take the next step, you stand very, very still. Then you let the next step choose you."

CHAPTER 8

AS THEY DROVE THROUGH the streets of Houston in Luke's Chevy, Ashley couldn't help but notice his playlist played one romantic song after another, including recent covers of "Every Little Thing She Does Is Magic," "Love Me Like a River Does," "Kiss on My List," and "All the Way."

"Where are we going?" Ashley asked, laughing as Luke continued to speak to her only in pig Latin.

"Oo-tay a-ay ery-vay ecial-spay ace-play."

"For a vice president, you sure are a goofball."

"Ep-yay."

"What has you in such a great mood?" Ashley asked. Though Luke looked the part of the powerful executive, dressed as he was in a charcoal suit, crisp white shirt, and silver tie, he was acting anything but polished and cool. He was giggly and foolish and fun.

"Must be the socks." He grinned and lifted a pant leg to show her his bright purple socks with the words *Life is grape!* swirling through grape clusters.

"Did you buy yourself those socks?"

He nodded.

She laughed and shook her head. "They're really *raisin* the bar on puns. Ha ha. But you gotta admit, you're goofy today."

"I'm in love." He beamed at her before returning his gaze to the end of rush-hour traffic, his smile so genuine she couldn't help but smile, too.

Luke put his big hand on her lap and kneaded his long, strong fingers into her thigh. So much was in that touch—it was possessive, comfortable, playful, sensual, and loving.

Ashley smiled and closed her eyes and simply received it all—his goofiness, his strength, his love. *How could I be this lucky?* It felt so good, almost unreasonably so. When in her life had she ever felt so beloved? And yet she felt uneasy.

She hadn't mentioned to him the invitation to Peru. It felt too, too what? Like a dirty secret. Because some part of her had started to consider it. Some part of her desperately wanted to go, insisting it was not only possible, it was essential. It had been her dream for so long—one that had fallen apart before. Of course, she couldn't just let it go. Would she really need to sacrifice this dream for a man? It was only four months. Not even a half a year. *That's not long.* She exhaled deeply. *I need to fulfill my dream.* But how would Luke feel? This was a delicate time in their relationship. Would he feel betrayed? Abandoned? Would he wait for her? If it was love, their relationship could withstand it, right? Or would he stray? Savannah would do everything in her power to win him back, that was a given. Maybe he'd come down to Peru and visit her?

Just talk to him about it.

You might lose him if you do.

You might lose him if you don't.

"You seem a little quiet." Luke gave her leg a gentle squeeze. "Everything okay with your mom?"

"Yeah, Mom's great."

"Anything else you want to talk about? Like where we might be going?"

"Where are we going?" Ashley was grateful for the subject change.

"Don't you wish you knew?" he taunted in a singsong lilt.

"You tease!" Ashley lightly punched his shoulder, then told herself to be present with Luke. She created a black box in her mind, stuffed Peru in it, and closed it, telling herself she could open it later. It was a trick she had taught herself as a girl. Most of the time, it worked.

"I'll give you a hint. It rhymes with *looks for.*"

"Ummm. I give up."

"You didn't even try."

"Okay. Stooksmore."

"That's not even a word."

"How about rook more. Shook bore. Book fl—. Bookstore!"

"That's my girl."

"Really?"

"So, a couple days ago was our four-month anniversary—"

"Actually, it was exactly a week ago."

"But who's counting?"

Ashley blushed at that. Of course she was counting. Numbers were her thing. And it was so sweet Luke was counting the days, too.

"Anyway," Luke continued, "on our four-month anniversary, I came to the bookstore alone because you weren't yet talking to me. I sat on the floor right where you were sitting in the middle of the self-help section when I met you, and I got all teary-eyed, and I told myself, *Luke, you are going to win that girl back. You are going to bring her the best version of yourself. And then you are never going to let her go.*"

"I'm sorry, Luke." Her voice was barely a whisper.

"Oh, I'm not, love. I'm not sorry. You leaving me helped me understand just how important you are to me. It shook me up. It helped me refocus at work—I can see how some of the things you were saying were right—there are more ways I can effect positive change in the energy industry and include environmental protection in our decisions, though I will be fighting my father and the board on it every step of the way. But most importantly, it helped me refocus my life on what is most important. Which is you."

Ashley breathed in deeply, feeling the intensity of Luke's love for her. It was wonderful. And overwhelming. And everything she had always dreamed of for a partnership. Every cell in her vibrated with how completely she loved him. She put a *lock* on that Peru box and shoved it way, way, way down. How could she ever let that old dream get in the way of this vital, living, astonishing reality of a man who loved her as she had always dreamed of being loved?

Luke parked his Chevy in the parking lot, and before he'd turned off the engine, he leaned over the center console to pull her in for a sweet, lingering kiss—it was soft and gentle, his lips light and playful against hers. It was so new, this sensation, of kissing him with no fantasy involved—just Luke and Ashley and their raw, unguarded feelings. After a few moments, it was clear he meant to pull away, but Ashley slid an arm around his neck, then threaded her fingers into the dark, silken strands and tugged, keeping her lips pressed to his. She couldn't let him go. Instead, she intensified the kiss, crushing him to her. She *needed* his touch right now. Needed his kiss to tether her to the moment, to make him more real, to solidify their love somehow, to join her more wholly to him.

Her kisses were fierce, almost frantic, as if she were riding torrents of desire. She bit and nipped and tugged at his lips as a deluge of love, lust, fear, and longing crashed through her. She wanted to flood him, surround him, consume him. Luke met her with equal intensity, his hands stroking her cheeks, his mouth opening for her explorations. He tasted like mint and male and Luke.

She wanted him so much her whole body ached. His breath had frayed into shallow gasps as he opened and offered her the deeper exchange she was looking for. He was so willing to meet her, to respond to her, to show up completely for this kiss, and it humbled her. Thrilled her. Made her feel both powerful and unguarded at the same time.

Heat pulsed through her, red lava in her veins, and she broke the kiss to drag her lips across the stubble of his jaw, the scruff of his neck, thrilling in the salty taste of him.

With her free hand, she pressed her fingers into his chest and fisted them into his shirt, twisting the fabric in her hand. A low growl escaped her as she felt Luke begin to pull at the hem of her shirt to—

Honk! The sound of a car horn and a short squeal of brakes reminded Ashley they were in a parking lot where, apparently, there had just about been an accident. She marveled at how easily Luke made her forget the world was any bigger than just the two of them. She gave him a sheepish grin and straightened her disheveled clothes and hair, but one look at Luke's face told her he had gotten just as lost in that kiss as she had.

"I don't ever want to stop kissing you," Luke murmured, shaking his head, a wild happiness in his eyes. He reached to cup her face with both of his hands. "Now, where were we?"

⁓

"Oh, Bamba, I love that man so much."

Ashley sat on the couch with her cat snuggled deep into her lap. Last night, Luke had been wonderful. And it was killing her. Her heart tightened, thinking of how he had spoiled her with joy—she had never laughed more, had never felt so alive. As if colors were brighter and the strawberries they'd eaten were sweeter and music they'd heard was more upbeat and life was, oh, just *more alive.*

And yet she was miserable. Now that she wasn't physically present with Luke, she couldn't stop thinking about Peru. She wanted to go. No matter how far down she pushed down that box, it was not gone. No matter how happy she was with Luke, no matter how desperate she was to keep things between them on track, she couldn't deny that part of her resented declining the invitation.

Was it really an either/or scenario? Luke would understand if she left for four months, right?

Four months was nothing in the scheme of a lifetime. She closed her eyes and thought about the night before. After going to a concert, they had made happy love for hours—a totally new experience for her—sex filled with laughter and teasing and playfulness. This morning, Ashley's cheeks were sorer from laughing than from being chafed from kissing.

But it wasn't just the skin of her that felt marked by Luke's loving—it was her insides that felt marked. As if each time he touched her, he left the whorl of his fingerprints on her essence. She felt his presence pulsing through her. It was beautiful and deeply disconcerting. She never wanted the feeling to end, didn't want anything to get in its way. Ironically, the more certain she felt about their love, the more she feared she might lose him— that he might leave her. It was hard to shake that old deep-seated fear, even when Luke was so affirming.

In fact, knowing her fear, Luke had custom-designed a cotton apron for her to wear, as he said, "in *our* home." It had a big lettuce graphic on it that said *Romaine Calm, I'll Never Leaf You.* They had made breakfast together wearing only their aprons. She laughed out loud again, thinking of him standing mostly naked in front of the fridge, the muscled contours of his back, his strong sculpted legs.

The irony, of course, was that she was now considering leaving *him*—temporarily, of course. But so much could change in four months.

Now, sitting on the couch, Bamba on her lap, she surveyed her torn-up apartment and felt overwhelmed by the half-filled boxes everywhere. The disarray deeply unnerved her, perhaps because it mirrored her inner unsettledness. A host of dark-winged uncertainties flew like bats inside her.

"Why would I leave Luke?" she said to the cat as it bonked its nose lightly against her hand. "Four months feels like a lifetime away from him, especially now when we are just starting to make a life together. Things are so good, Bamba, so I can't leave now. I can't."

The cat nuzzled deeper, closed her eyes, and began to purr. The message seemed to be, *When things are great where you are, why would you leave? You have love—and you can guard it, grow it, live it, and that is the greatest dream of all.* Ashley rubbed between the cat's eyes.

She announced to the empty room, "I'm going to pack, and I'm going to move in with the man I love, and I am going to say *yes* to happiness together with Luke. *Yes* to *us.*" She replayed a moment of last night when Luke had whispered to every part of her body, *You are so beautiful.* She took a fortifying breath, moved the cat off her lap, walked to her shelves, and continued packing.

"Oh." And there, on the shelf she'd just walked to as if pulled by a magnet, was a photo of Tica and the small box containing her ashes. Ashley laughed and shook her head. *Of course.* With all the packing she had to do, she had subconsciously walked right to this spot in her apartment. "Oh, Tica, there you are."

She took the picture from the shelf, then stared at the face of the woman who had helped her so much, who had inspired her to be a teacher.

"Tica. I promised."

———

Ashley put her hand on Luke's thigh and felt his strong quad flex beneath the fabric of his pants. *Yes.* It felt like a tether to the moment, a tether she desperately needed. She dragged her curious fingers up the hard flesh of his inner leg, ending her exploration just before the point where his legs met. But she knew by the way his breath slightly hitched that he was getting aroused beside her. She smiled a secret smile.

"I'll have the crème brûlée," said the woman seated across from her, looking up from her menu at the waiter. Her dress must have cost a thousand dollars, Ashley thought. It was strange a woman like this was her newest dinner companion.

"And I'll have the tiramisu," said the other woman in the well-cut navy silk suit.

"And I'll have a bite of whatever *she* is having," Luke said to the waiter, flashing a hungry smile toward Ashley.

"Hmm," Ashley mused. "We'll have the trio of biscotti, please."

Though the words that came out of her mouth sounded like plain language, inside her was a chaotic symphony, a booming opus that went back and forth between ecstatic soaring notes and a foreboding tremolo. She'd been stewing that afternoon as she packed, worrying about her decision about Peru, when Luke had called her with the great news: He had set up a special dinner for that night with two potential donors. And he'd arranged for them to meet at Alexander's Bistro—the site of their first real date, when Luke had ordered that champagne that—

"And we'd like a bottle of the Taittinger 'Brut La Francaise,'" Luke was saying. He looked to Ashley. "Approximately six million bubbles' worth."

Ashley blushed, knowing he was teasing her. Four months ago, she'd tried to estimate the number of bubbles per seven-hundred-fifty-milliliter bottle. Luke remembered details about their conversations the way other men remembered stats for their favorite football teams. Ashley shook her head, beaming at him. Luke responded by grabbing her hand beneath the table and pulling it up his very hard cock straining against his pants. The other women were still busy chatting with the server, changing their order, and Ashley did her best to appear unaffected, though she did give him a hard squeeze and a long stroke with her fingertips before returning her hand to her own lap. Her own body tingled with sexual curiosity.

"Because we need to celebrate!" Luke said, reengaging the other two people at the table, basically fueling their enthusiasm for Ashley's project with his own. He was *beaming* with excitement. He was a great board president. And with these two new donors he'd brought on board, the nonprofit now had enough contributions to create greater visibility, employ two more software IT professionals, and market more widely for the next two years.

Everyone's eyes were bright. Ashley looked at the new funders, then at Luke. She was so grateful for him, so in love.

Luke's connections had been such a boon for the nonprofit organization. Because of him, so many kids would be able to independently learn more about science, technology, engineering, arts, and math—and how to apply their knowledge to environmental action. Susan was the wife of an oil tycoon, and Lee was a financial consultant who worked for a large investment banking firm. Though they were from social circles that were far away from hers, Ashley was feeling less intimidated by powerful and wealthy people all the time. In fact, while she had made the pitch for her program, their interest had buoyed her confidence even more.

"A toast," Luke said after the server had poured their glasses. "To the wonderful mastermind behind STEAMEA. And to all the ways it will help make the world a better place."

"Hear! Hear!" they all said as they clinked glasses.

"And to each of you, who are making it happen," Ashley rejoined. And as they clinked again, Ashley looked each person in the eye and said, "Thank you," to them, her eyes lingering last on Luke's. The dry champagne sparkled on her tongue, and as they ate dessert and Luke played footsie with her beneath the table, Ashley marveled at how perfect the moment was. Almost.

When a little inner voice said, *You don't deserve this*, she felt her chest tighten. She locked the voice into her inner black box and took another sip of champagne.

———

"Here." Luke opened his hands and wiggled his fingers as Ashley kicked off her heels and leaned back into Luke's sofa. He plopped down beside her. "Let me rub your feet."

"You are too good to be true." But the offer was for real. Ashley leaned back, closed her eyes.

"What a triumph tonight, Ashley. You were amazing."

"Thanks." She moaned lightly as he pressed his thumbs into her arches.

"Sooooo, now that I have you all alone and you're getting more comfortable, do you want to tell me what's going on?"

Ashley opened an eye.

"It seems like you have a heavy load on your mind. Is it something I did? Are we going too fast?"

"Uh-uh." Ashley shook her head and sank deeper into the cushions, reveling in his touch. It was both therapeutic and erotic at the same time.

"Well, whatever is bothering you, I think I have something that might just pick you up."

"Luke, what more could you do? Dinner with new donors, a foot rub…" Ashley's litany of gratitudes trailed off into a soft moan as he pulled on her toes.

"Well." Luke took one hand away from her feet, and she whimpered in protest. "I think what I have in this envelope might just be the cherry on top. I was going to wait to give this to you, but I don't have the discipline." He gave his head a giddy shake. "Here."

She opened her eyes. He handed her an unmarked white business envelope.

His eyes danced, and his smile crept up his face playfully. "It's not for another month, but…"

Ashley opened the envelope and pulled out a travel itinerary. Two tickets to Peru. In September. And a hotel in Urubamba, the closest major town to Huayllabamba.

Ashley's chest tightened. Guilt churned in her stomach. *Holy shit.* A hot tear slipped down Ashley's cheek. Luke was so thoughtful, so generous, so sweet, and she—

"Surprise!" He gave both her feet a squeeze and beamed at her. "It was so much fun researching the Sacred Valley. What a beautiful, history-rich place. And I couldn't wait to surprise you, knowing how much you want to be there—and I want to be there with you. All those mountains and the glaciers, an ancient Incan citadel. No wonder you—" Luke's expression went from frisky to confused. "Wait, are those happy tears?"

Ashley looked up at Luke and bit her lip, her brow furrowing. She hated this moment. Hated herself. Hated what she was about to tell him and the hurt it would undoubtedly cause. He was looking at her with such wide-eyed love, his heart so big, so full, so generous—and she was about to sink a dagger into it.

Her voice was a small, ashamed whisper. "I'll already be there."

"What?"

She was going to be sick. Her mouth went completely dry. This was not how she'd planned on telling Luke about this. She'd planned out the best, logical way to bring it up so that it had the least emotional impact. And this was a disaster. Suddenly, her choice seemed selfish, and the way she hadn't told him yet felt like a betrayal. "I'll already be in Peru. I took the job."

"What?" he whispered.

"Today." Ashley grimaced.

Luke put both hands up to his forehead and rubbed at the tension forming there. He exhaled big. "I see. When were you going to tell me?"

"Tonight?" A flood of conflicting emotions surged through her, and she struggled to make sense of them. "But not like this. I'm messing this up. I was surprised by the dinner, and I—"

"You planned all along on telling me *after* you made your decision to leave?" The anguish scrawled on his face made it feel as if worms were crawling all over her skin, and she hated that she had put him in this position. "When did you find out you got the job?"

"Two days ago."

"And you didn't want to tell me they got smart and accepted you?" His voice was low, stained with hurt.

It might have been easier to handle if he'd been yelling at her, angry and shouting. But the quiet misery absolutely undid her. "Oh, Luke. I did this all wrong. I just—I was afraid. At first, I thought I'd just say no to the offer. The timing is all wrong, what with me moving in and with how close we are…" She choked, wondering just how much she'd just jeopardized that closeness. "I mean, I wanted to say no, but there are reasons I need to say yes, and when I realized that, I was afraid that if I went to Peru for four months, it would hurt us, and you would stray, and I didn't have the courage to t—"

A harsh laugh escaped Luke's throat as he stared at her, incredulous, shaking his head. "Wait. Ashley, wait. You were afraid I would leave *you*? *You're* the one leaving, right?"

Ashley shook her head. "I know I'm not making sense, but…" What had she been thinking? After all these years of trying to heal from the pain of abandonment from her father, her husband, had she become the abandoner? It seemed so obvious that she was acting on past fears. *I have really, really messed this up.* She wanted to do it over. She wanted a second chance. How had she handled this so completely wrong? "Luke—" she began.

"I need a second. Just a second." Luke stared at the tickets beside her, as if seeing the gap between what he'd imagined they represented and what was really happening. He closed his eyes and took a deep breath. And then another. And then another. When he opened them again, they were clear and pained. He put both hands on his chest, as if he were holding his heart in. "Ashley. I'm trying to process a lot of feelings. I've never felt so—" He looked as if he were trying to speak, but no words would come. He rubbed both hands over his face, swallowed, then tried again. "I…I… *Shit.* I…I want so much to be happy for you. You got the job!" His expression was so earnest and so pained. "You got the job you dreamed of. You *got* it. And yet, instead of being happy for you, all I can feel is devastated. I am so hurt, so confused about why you would shut me out. It's like we've been living in different worlds for the last two days, and I didn't even know it. While I was in the clouds, thinking of you moving into our home, you were…" Luke hid his face in his hands.

Seeing Luke so hurt and knowing that her lack of trust was the cause of it made Ashley's heart collapse. It felt as if all the air had left the room, and she couldn't find enough for a breath. What had she done? How had she not thought this through better?

"I shut you out." Ashley repeated the words as if they were a revelation. "You surprised me with the most generous, thoughtful gift, and I shut you out."

"*Why* did you shut me out? I love you so much, and you said you love me, too, so what I can't understand, Ashley, is why you didn't trust me with something this important to you. Something this important to *us*. I don't get it." He moved farther away on the couch as if touching her right now stung him, and she immediately missed his warmth, his nearness. It was an instantaneous emptiness that swamped her core and spread its dark nothingness through her limbs.

"I think I was scared."

"Scared of what?"

"Of losing you."

"And so, you thought not telling me about going to another country for four months was the answer? You didn't trust me to support you?" She could sense his anger rising, and it made her cower. She couldn't understand her actions herself.

"I'm sorry, Luke," she said in a threadbare whisper. "I handled this all wrong. All wrong. You're right. I had no courage." A small sob caught in her throat. "But it wasn't you I didn't trust. It was me."

Luke winced and leaned back and closed his eyes.

Ashley's voice was small. "Luke, I…" She gulped. "There's more to the story."

Luke didn't open his eyes. "What *else* didn't you tell me?" Betrayal sharpened his tone, though his voice was soft.

Ashley pulled in a big breath and kneaded at her neck with her fingers. "Before I married Mark, I had applied for this position in Huayllabamba. And I got it. First try. And when I told Mark, he said, *Don't go.* He said, *Stay. I want to be with you.* And he asked me to marry him. Of course, what he really needed was my small paycheck and a meal ticket," she added bitterly.

"But I thought I was staying for love. And so, I turned down my dream." She licked her lips, her throat and mouth suddenly unbearably dry. "And I, I was just so afraid that if I told you about getting the job, you would ask me not to go." She looked at her lap, afraid of the anger she saw rising in Luke's body.

"Do you hear yourself? You're comparing me to your ex-husband? Did you really believe I would not support you going?"

"Would you? Support me leaving for four months?"

"I don't know! It would be hard. I think I would. I hope I would. I think I would have hated it, but I would have helped you think of ways we could make it work. Like me coming to visit you. Like getting you tickets to come home once a month. Or, or *something*. But you didn't even give me the courtesy to *talk* about it." Though his voice was still relatively quiet, it was filled with such ferocious intensity it was even more powerful than shouting would have been.

"I would have liked the chance, Ashley, to have talked about it with you. We are in a *relationship*. At least, *I* thought we were. And *you* made a decision that changes *us*. I feel shortchanged. And betrayed. And so, so hurt. So fucking hurt. I can't believe…"

He made a fist and held it for several long seconds, then watched his own hand as his fingers slowly opened like a lily. Ashley watched him as if she were both herself and, in some strange, disembodied way, as if she were watching the whole scene from a few feet away.

Luke's voice was so quiet she had to lean forward to hear him. "Of course I would help you live your dream, Ashley. And of course it would hurt to let you leave. But that's nothing compared to how much it hurts right now knowing you would hide something from me that is so important to you—that you would keep me out of your thoughts, your struggles, your heart."

Ashley could feel him slipping further and further away, and there was nothing she could do to reach him. By not telling him right away, she had created the very scenario she most wanted to avoid. "I don't want to lose you, Luke." She swallowed. "And please understand, I just didn't want to lose this chance at my dream. The timing is just so—"

Luke shook his head and interrupted. "Don't blame the timing, Ashley. Life is always full of big choices. I just wish we could have made this choice together. I wish I could have been part of sharing your excitement. Now…" His voice trailed off as he looked at the tickets he had placed in the envelope. He looked so lost. "I think you better go home."

CHAPTER 9

ASHLEY FELT AS IF she had measured the last three days not in hours but in heartbeats, each beat like a long sharp nail being hammered into a coffin. She felt as if there was gray sludge in her veins instead of blood. She could hardly move. She could hardly eat. And she was so full of guilt and shame. If only she could bend the space-time fabric and change the way she'd made her decision.

Luke's words from that night kept returning to her. *Don't blame the timing, Ashley. Life is always full of big choices. I just wish we could have made this choice together.* If only she had given him the trust he deserved.

So many if onlys. Though she was sitting at the computer at her kitchen counter, trying to respond to emails, Ashley wasn't getting much done. The text blurred in front of her. Every few minutes, she looked at her phone to see if Luke had texted or emailed or called. He hadn't. *Of course he's not calling. Because you shattered his heart, you ass. You had the most beautiful, generous, funny man who had finally opened to love, who had just blossomed into his own amazing, loving self, and in that most vulnerable moment, you demolished him. What the hell did you expect?*

Ashley had texted him four times the day after their ill-fated conversation. She'd called him once a day since then, each time forcing herself to have just a tiny shred of hope. She'd sent him flowers, white lilies, with the words, *Please forgive me.*

Nothing.

"I screwed up so bad," she confessed to the cat, who had climbed on her. "I had it all, and now I have nothing."

If only she'd been braver. If only she'd been clearer about her own baggage. If only she'd trusted the silken cocoon of their love, trusted that it was strong enough to allow them to transform inside it. Why was it so hard for her to trust love, to trust men? Why had she lumped Luke in with the other men who had let her down? *What an idiot!* And now, as Luke had pointed out so clearly, *she* was the one who was leaving. *She* was the one who left him! *How fucked-up is that? I became the thing I most fear?*

Her stomach hurt. She'd had little to eat in three days. Everything tasted like dust. She let out a humorless laugh. She was following her dream, sure, but at what cost? She had just emotionally train-wrecked the man she loved by not letting him in.

"I am such a jerk." She pressed her fingers to her temples, then dragged them through her hair, relishing the pain when she pulled at the roots.

To make matters worse, her sister wasn't available to talk because she was off gallivanting with her new fellow every night. *I never knew love could be so great!* she'd texted, along with where they would be tonight. Ashley was happy for Jewel, of course, but Jewel's boyfriend bliss was an ironic counterweight to her own misery.

The cat jumped up and left Ashley's lap to go curl up on the couch.

"Et tu, Bamba?" she sighed and let her eyes blur on the emails in front of her. Not only had she screwed up with Luke, but she'd *really* screwed up with STEAMEA. She had sent a note to the board explaining she would be leaving for Peru for four months, and she was planning to run the organization from there. The blowback had been immediate.

"I'm very disappointed," wrote one board member. "The organization is growing exponentially now and needs your full attention."

Said another, "I was in that region recently, and the internet connection is highly undependable. Too much happening with our program now for you to not reliably be able to work online."

And: "What we need *right now* is hands-on leadership—with our donors and with our board. Though you could do much online with logistics, we need someone to represent and lead us here with enthusiasm, vision, and energy."

And so, the board members and financial investors in STEAMEA were calling for her to step down as executive director and transfer the reins, perhaps temporarily, perhaps for good. She would stay on as a board member.

She'd been overly confident, not for the first time. Ashley hated this irresponsible feeling that fit like a too-tight sweater she couldn't get out of.

Everything she treasured was upside down. She wanted to throw up.

The board members were right, of course. She had been unrealistically ambitious about leading a burgeoning nonprofit while teaching in a remote village in the Andes. The organization needed someone right now with charisma and direction. Being a director wasn't just about getting tasks done; it was about being a *leader.*

The last straw: her mentee, Emilia, really needed a strong presence right now. She was fresh out of rehab, and they had been walking in Memorial Park once a week. When Ashley had told her she was leaving for four months, Emilia's fear and sadness had wrenched Ashley's heart and stabbed at her sense of responsibility. So much was at stake right now.

She put her head in her hands and felt the dense weight of it. Over the years, she'd developed a rational, analytical, logical way of meeting the world to protect her from feeling like *this*. She had bungled *everything*.

"But I didn't screw up Peru," she said out loud, her voice surprisingly vulnerable. It was true. She hadn't bungled that. She was going to Peru. To Peru! To Tica's hometown. To honor her mentor. To pass on Tica's legacy of helping up the next generation. But sitting here, in her torn-up apartment, missing Luke and worrying about what would become of her mentee and her brainchild program, she was not finding joy in the long-held dream.

What is some good deed you can do right now?
Galvanize.

She wrote an email to her senators about crafting new legislation to protect the endangered waterways and riparian areas that provide important habitats for the millions of migratory birds that pass through the region every year.

There. One thing done right.

The phone buzzed on the counter next to her, and she jumped, eager to see if the text had come from Luke.

John: Peru? It's finally happening
         Well, at least one STEAMEA board member wasn't berating her.

Ashley: Yeah!

She so was not feeling that exclamation point, but the word looked too naked without it, almost like a four-letter dirge.

John: That's a lot of heat from the board today. You want me to back you up?

Ashley took a deep breath and shook her head with a smile. John was one of the only people she personally had invited to be on the board, and it was so thoughtful of him now to offer to be her champion. Even after she'd turned down his invitation to date, he was a friend through and through.

Ashley: Thank you, John. Idk. Idk. So much Idk

John: It would be great if you would meet me for coffee in a half hour. At our usual?

Ashley rubbed her temples with one hand.

Ashley: That would be great

―――――

"So, you haven't talked to him for three days," John reflected as he sipped his coffee sitting across from Ashley in the coffee shop window.

It felt so weird talking to John about Luke. Ashley knew he was not completely impartial, and yet she felt desperate to talk to someone, and John had made a point of asking about how things with Luke were going. She wanted to believe she and John had slipped back into their roles as good friends.

"I should have let him in on my plans sooner."

"Maybe you didn't want to? Maybe you were looking for a way to get out of the relationship."

Ashley sat with John's words for a while before answering. Had she unconsciously but deliberately sabotaged her relationship with Luke?

"No."

"Hmm. I'm not surprised you're going, but it does seem weird you didn't tell Luke about it until *after* you made your decision."

Ashley sighed. Her stomach ached. "Yeah." *Is his smile a little smug?*

John shrugged. "So, tell me more about the program."

Ashley told him about the town and the school and the place she would stay and how much she was looking forward to working again with kids. "I didn't realize until I said yes to this program just how much I miss being in the classroom. I love planning STEAMEA, and I like the tutoring I'm doing, but it's nothing like the energy of the classroom."

"You're a natural teacher, Ashley. It's like you were made for it." John had always been one of her biggest fans. She tried to let his compliment in instead of shrugging it away.

"Hey, speaking of classrooms, I have a big favor, John."

"Anything."

"It's Emilia. Lift will get her another official mentor while I am gone, but she needs someone in school on her side, John— unofficial, of course—but someone who—"

"I'll do it."

Ashley heaved a sigh of relief. "Thank you. She knows you, she trusts you, and I can't imagine anyone I would trust more to help her stay on the up-and-up for the start of her senior year."

They talked more about Peru, but the whole time, Ashley was nagged by John's suggestion that she had subconsciously intended to damage her relationship with Luke. Of course, he might have had an agenda with that comment, but she pushed herself to see if there weren't some truth in it. By the time they'd gotten to the bottom of their cups, she was in a full-blown tizzy.

"So, Ashley." John ruffled his hand through his blond hair, and as always, it fell back perfectly into place. He was such a handsome man—his features were Viking-like, very masculine, but his brown eyes were exceedingly gentle. "Do you want me to speak out to the rest of the board and defend you staying director while you're gone?"

"John, thank you. No."

He nodded and leaned forward. "I'll always be your champion, Ashley. I believe in you." He took one of her hands and held it in his, looking at how they joined, and then he looked up at her.

Ashley opened her mouth, but no words came out.

"You don't have to say anything now. But if you wanted me to come visit you in Peru, I would. I'd skip school and be there on the next flight."

They were exactly the words she wanted to hear. From the wrong man.

———

Ashley raced across the room to the phone, praying the person on the other end of the call was Luke. She'd been sitting on the couch reading *Meditations* by Marcus Aurelius, the book Luke had given her a few months ago. In the last few days, she'd started to flip through the pages and let her eyes land anywhere, reading the book like an omen. It was the closest to fortune-telling she'd ever done. Today's reading: "Not to assume it's impossible because you find it hard."

She reached the phone just in time to see she'd missed the call. From Luke. *Damn. Please leave a message, please leave a message.* She watched the phone, waiting for an alert that a message had been left. *Yes!*

Her heart beat an erratic tempo inside her chest as she listened to the message:

> *Ashley. I have these two tickets we bought for Grease at Theater Under the Stars for tomorrow night. I know you were excited about it. I can't go. I'll have them at will call under your name.*

It wasn't the call she'd hoped for. But it was a start.

Don't assume it's impossible because you find it hard. She took a steadying breath. *Okay, girl. This is your chance.*

Ashley: Let's go to Grease together

Luke: No

Ashley: Please

Luke: Not up for it

Ashley: I'll be there at 6:02 to pick you up

She waited.

Ashley: We were born to work together like feet, hands, and eyes.

That had been yesterday's quote from *Meditations* on how to think about people who make you angry. She hoped Luke would know the reference. Again, she waited. Nothing.

Ashley: Not taking no for an answer. See you tomorrow at 6:02.
            I will wait for you

And that was it. No response to her suggestion that she pick him up. But that wasn't a no.

———

Pulling up to Luke's high-rise, Ashley was literally sweating it. It was Houston summer hot. It was 6:08. She was late, even though she'd left early. *Damn traffic.* With her heart aflame and eyes agog, she searched the folks clustered in front of the building for Luke's tall, athletic silhouette.

And Luke wasn't there.

All day, she'd been praying he would come with her to the show. All day, as she'd tutored and packed and prepared for Peru, she'd been counting the minutes until she would see him, could talk to him, could acknowledge all the ways she'd messed up and beg him to let her back into his life. And now, she was six minutes late. And she'd screwed up. Again.

Ashley parked her car in the reception circle, stared at the space on the sidewalk where he wasn't, put her head down on the steering wheel, and felt all the air leak out of her lungs. She felt deflated. Frustrated. Lost. A small whimper formed inside her and escaped in an inelegant sound somewhere between a snivel and a hiccup. She felt as if she were a glass sculpture with a thousand thin fractures and the slightest touch would make her shatter.

Now what?

Now that Luke wasn't here, she realized just how much she had planned that he *would* be here, standing outside his building, open to seeing her, waiting for her to drive up and apologize and take him away for a wonderful evening. A horrible thought unfolded in her. *What if he came down and I wasn't here at 6:02? He knows I'm always on time. I abandoned him. Again.*

What kind of stupid fantasy was that? Why would he just get over her not including him in her decision? Maybe he could forgive her, given time, but not all that much time had passed, and she had broken his heart *real good*, as Jewel would say. Even if he did show up, chances were he'd still be pissed.

But I'd rather be with pissed Luke than not with him at all. And that was true. *Dante had it right.* Nothing could be worse than this eighth circle of hell being without him.

It hurts so much because I need him. Not just for the evening, for life. The thought flattened her.

All the tears she hadn't been letting herself cry for the last three days now broke the floodgates she'd placed on her emotions. She was overwhelmed with disappointment. Self-loathing. Loss. Fear. A whole cauldron of roiling negative emotions all competed to bubble up first. Hot tears spilled out of her eyes, and she let them. As if she could stop them. As if she had any control of any part of her life.

Of course he hadn't come. He'd said he wouldn't. She'd just hoped...

Sobs racked her back, and every breath seemed an effort, as if all she could do was achieve the next inhale. How had she screwed everything up so badly? All she'd wanted was to do the right thing. But in the process, she'd hurt Luke. Herself. Nothing made sense anymore. Nothing. And the tears fell into her lap, splatting against her legs. *Drowning in my own tears.* She might have laughed if she had the energy.

"You okay?"

Ashley startled at the sound of a masculine voice. Someone was rapping against her window. She shot back in her seat with a quick swipe of a hand over her eyes, as if she could hide the fact that she'd been weeping. Was it—?

She rolled down the window with a self-conscious sigh as she stared into the worried brown eyes of the familiar valet. "Sorry. I'm—I'm fine. Just waiting for someone. Well, I was waiting for someone."

He looked at her with compassion. "I see." He nodded. "Perhaps you are referring to Mr. Dalton?"

"Yeah." She sniffed and rolled her eyes. Of course he would know who she had been here visiting the last four months. "I'm sorry, I'll move the car. I know there's rules for—"

"He's standing right there, ma'am."

"He's—" Ashley looked up, slightly crazed. Hope leapt up in her chest and tried to flutter its white wings, but there was such thick gloom in her still. If hope was a bird, then doubt was an oil slick that covered its white feathers in crude until that hope bird was barely able to move.

Luke is here? Did he come just to give me the tickets? To say goodbye? Is he ready to talk to me?

From this angle, she could see only his waist and thighs, but then he bent down so she could see his face through the window. He looked like shit. His eyes were ringed with dark circles. A slight coolness controlled his expression. Once he saw her, though, the features of his face tightened with concern.

God, she must look a mess. With a sudden shock, she realized how she must appear—eyes red and puffy, cheeks tearstained, face etched with shame and wretchedness, like a woman who was ready to beg for her life. And that was exactly who she was.

"Luke."

Luke continued to stare at her through the window. She stared back, their gaze a lifeline. Though he was reserved—she could feel it from here—and though she understood *why* he was reserved, she also understood with deep clarity *now* was the time for her to be unerringly honest and open about her feelings, her thoughts, her hopes for them. Her pounding heart whispered a little pep talk to her brain. *You must let him know how much you love him. You must let him know that you know you screwed up and promise to do better. And you must be, right now and in the future, the woman who is worthy of this man.*

She took a deep breath as the valet opened the passenger door and helped Luke enter the car.

She turned her whole body in her seat to face him as he folded his long limbs into the small confines of her car and turned his body to face hers. Their eyes met and locked again. "Luke." She tried to breathe, but it was an effort that taxed her body, her lungs like brittle balloons. She wanted to reach for him, but her hands sat heavy and useless in her lap.

"Hi, Ashley." Luke's voice was gentle, but it was wearing protective gear. One side of his lips just barely slid up in a wan almost-smile that seemed to say *My heart is broken, and yet, here I am.*

"I am so sorry. I'm so sorry, Luke. I'm so sorry I didn't let you in." Tears were streaming down her face again. "I am so ashamed. I messed up. I took your trust too lightly and got caught up in my own fear. I let my past completely derail us, and I am so, so sorry." She pressed a trembling hand against her heart and felt it leaping erratically into her palm. *Go on*, it seemed to say. She bowed her head slightly. It was too much to look at him right now. "And knowing that I hurt you, it's killing me. It hurts so bad. I *hate* that I hurt you. Please, Luke, please will you try to forgive me? I want to be a better person with you, and I promise—"

"Hey," he whispered, lightly touching her knee. "Hey. Ashley. Look at me." She lifted her head. "It's taken me a while, but I understand why you did what you did. As much as I don't like being lumped with your ex and your deadbeat dad, I get why you went there."

She took a deep shuddering breath and nodded, embarrassed.

"And look." He held his open palm out to her, and she slipped her hand in, relishing the feel of his skin, the security of his touch. That simple touch felt like the most precious gift anyone had ever given her. She felt his life rushing into hers. "I don't know where we'll go from here. I know how I wanted it to go. I know four months is not a long time, but people change—especially when they go on a new path following their life's dream. I also know we have no chance at all if I don't try now. So, I'm going to try."

No words came to her, but she felt some of the oil drip off the feathers of that white-winged hope bird as she stared at Luke in amazement. He was offering her a second chance. She felt the heat of his palm rising into hers.

"Thanks for the flowers, Ashley. I've missed you." He raised his other hand as if he were going to touch her cheek, but he didn't. "I hate that you excluded me. I hate feeling locked out of your life. But I totally support you. And I want us to work on being better at telling each other what is going on, especially if we are going to be trusting each other from 3,356 miles away."

A small laugh made its way through her tears. "You didn't—"

"Of course I looked up exactly how many miles I'm going to be away from the woman I love."

The woman I love. She repeated that phrase again and again in her mind, turning it over like a beautiful stone, looking at it from every side and finding every side the most beautiful.

A thin, warm trickle of possibility filtered through her inner sludge. *Another chance.*

"I love you, Ashley," he whispered.

"I love you, Luke." And in her chest, she felt the full extension of that graceful white bird as it rose, and she trembled as at last she felt the powerful, unobstructed wing beat of hope.

This time, she showed up early.

Ashley made her way through the crowded restaurant to the bar where she'd said she'd meet Luke. The loud chatter and laughter of the after-work crowd filled the air and somehow felt like the appropriate soundtrack for her clamoring nerves.

She and Luke were back together, yes, but things were different. Very different. Last night, they had treated each other carefully, as if the other was made of fine porcelain. The truth was, of course, they both *were* very fragile. It was so different from the giddy, playful openness that they'd shared just a week ago, when everything felt so easy and happily ever after seemed so possible.

Second chances are strange. You're not really at square one; in some ways, you've taken a step back behind the starting line. And now there's an obstacle in the path.

It had helped that they went to a frivolous show last night. The troubles of Danny and Sandy in *Grease* seemed so laughable, so juvenile, really, but then again, when love was what was at stake, even the smallest obstacles mattered. She thought about how both characters had needed to change to make it work, even though Sandy's major changes were wearing tight pants and red lipstick. *If only it were that easy.*

On the way home, they'd sung "You're the One That I Want" in the car, Luke with his rich and velvety baritone and her giving it her best attempt to stay in tune. Corny as it was, it had turned her on and made her long to feel his hard body beneath her, inside her, but when she pulled her car up to Luke's building, he had not invited her up. In fact, as she'd ruminated on her way home, he hadn't even kissed her.

Of course you don't get to pick up where you left off. But that logic didn't make it any easier to climb into her lonely bed. Would he still be able to kiss her without the scaffolding of fantasy? It had taken them four months to develop that level of trust and intimacy. What would happen with that now? At this point, she wanted any kiss from Luke, any proof that they were on track to be together.

She understood he might need to take it slow, but they now had less than two weeks before she would leave. Though she wanted to give him all the space and time he needed to heal, she also desperately wanted to spend these last days together communing with him in that mind-blowing, heart-opening sexual intimacy they shared. She understood what glue it was for them, how it was so much more than just a physical act but also a building block for devotion. And they were going to need all the building blocks they could gather after she'd taken the wrecking ball to their trust.

Apparently, the part of her hoping for immediate sexual intimacy had won out tonight when Ashley had dressed to meet him. She had chosen her simple black dress. Made of soft jersey, it was loose but slinky enough to show off her curves—just a hint of cleavage—and the ruffled half sleeve hit just above the elbow and flounced flirtatiously when she spoke with her hands. She'd pulled back her honey-brown hair in a jeweled barrette, and she had to admit, though she still looked sleep-deprived and love-starved, she looked pretty good. She was never the most beautiful woman in the room, but tonight, with her nude heels and her red satin lipstick, she looked, she hoped, desirable. And with luck, she didn't look as nervous as she felt.

"What can I get you?" the bartender asked, setting down a napkin on the bar in front of her.

"House white, please." She really wanted a cosmo, but she couldn't justify spending more than ten dollars on a drink, no matter how special the night seemed.

"My buddy and I are wondering which one of us can buy you that drink," said a man with slicked-back hair and glittering brown eyes who appeared on her left.

"And I think it's going to be me," said another man who appeared on her right, tall and rugged with short curly hair and a deep tenor drawl.

Ashley laughed. She was unused to being the object of male attention, and at the moment, it helped buoy her fragile self-esteem. At the same time, the last thing she wanted was for there to be any reason at all for Luke to feel insecure about her faithfulness or intentions, so she gave them each a polite smile and said, "Thank you, both. I got this."

"I think there's a conspiracy tonight," the slick-haired man said to his curly-haired friend, raising an eyebrow and grinning. "The women of Houston have all decided not to accept drinks from us."

Ashley smirked. "That's a pretty boring conspiracy theory." She took her glass from the bartender, pulled out a ten and two ones, and prepared to walk away when Curly asked, "If you were going to start a conspiracy, what would it be?"

"The Nine," Ashley responded immediately.

"The Nine?" echoed Slick.

"Yeah, a cohort that would do whatever it takes to get nine women on the supreme court." Ashley took a sip of wine.

"Whoa! The woman's got a vision!" Curly nodded, clearly interested in her answer.

Slick, on the other hand, looked dubious. "Don't you think nine women would be a little out of balance?"

Ashley shrugged. "As RBG once noted, no one thought twice when nine men were on the court." She moved to walk away again.

"Huh." Slick cracked a grin and kept the conversation going. "That would be a lot of estrogen, but then, guys do come with certain baggage, too. What's the difference between government bonds and men?" He paused, his head slightly cocked as he waited a mere nanosecond to deliver the punchline. "Bonds mature."

Ashley shook her head, but Curly lifted an eyebrow as if to say *game on.* "What do you call a man with half a brain?"

Ashley couldn't help it. She jumped in. "Gifted."

Both men laughed with delight. "Nice!" Slick gave Ashley a fist bump, and she half-heartedly met it. "Whaddya know? A gal who can hang with our humor. I like this one."

Her body was still slightly turned away from the duo, but she deadpanned over her shoulder, "What did God say after creating man?"

Slick and Curly grinned at each other as if they were editing their comments but somehow knew what the other was thinking.

The tattooed bartender leaned across the bar. "I could do better!"

The four of them laughed, more at themselves than at the joke. The bartender gave Ashley a fist bump across the bar and walked away. Meanwhile, the men each lifted their drinks to clink with Ashley, cheering her and welcoming her into their bad-joke club.

"My girlfriend's beautiful, isn't she?" said a familiar deep voice behind her. Ashley felt Luke's hand curl possessively around her waist. Part of her worried—did Luke think she was flirting with these men? *Oh, shit. What a bad foot to start the night on.* But leaning back into Luke's strong chest, she wasn't getting a jealous vibe. More amused. Relief flooded her, and she relaxed into his body, breathing in the subtle male smell of him. *Mmm.* It was the first time he'd touched her in almost a week. And it was heaven.

Slick and Curly both regarded Luke as if they were wolves standing tall with their tails high, showing dominance. But Luke straightened even taller, and he tightened his hold on her slightly, bunching the soft fabric of her dress in his hand as he flexed his fingers into her hip. Though she couldn't see his face, she imagined the confident ferocity in his eyes. She saw the evidence of it in the other two men. In that moment, if Slick and Curly had been canine, they would have rolled over in submission and shown Luke their bellies. As it was, they raised their glasses to him as if congratulating him on getting the girl. *My alpha wolf.* Something about the whole primitive exchange warmed her.

"Hey, *boyfriend*," she cooed. He was so not a boy, but the moment he uttered the words *My girlfriend's beautiful, isn't she,* Ashley was instantly aware they were playing out the same scene they had in Telluride when Luke had walked into a bar when she was getting hit on. Only then he *wasn't* her boyfriend. At that point, she had only been fantasizing about him in her bed. And now...*I have a chance with him again, this glorious, wonderful man.*

She reached up and caressed his face, loving the prickle of the shadowy stubble. *Please be my boyfriend.* Instantly, she was fantasizing about all the places she was hoping to be chafed by that stubble. *Tonight, Luke, you are mine.*

She tilted her head up to look at him, aware that Slick and Curly were still their audience. "What took you so long? Get caught up practicing with the band?" Her head bounced slightly against his chest as he chuckled in pleasure that she, too, recognized the scenario from Telluride, and she felt wrapped up in the intimacy of their inside joke.

"Joe was having an issue with his bagpipes." He looked at his watch, stifling his smile. "But it's going to be a great show tonight." Luke released Ashley's hip to take her hand. "We gotta get going. Bye, guys."

"Bye, guys," Ashley echoed, tossing a smile to the men at the bar, and then she gave all her attention to the man who had won her heart long ago. "Bagpipes?" she whispered as they walked away.

"Aaooogah," he toned in his best bagpipe imitation, sending her into a riot of giggles. This was the playfulness she'd missed last night, the sweet ease they had with each other, and god, it felt so good right now to laugh with him, to fall back on their history and feel it support them.

She thrilled in the feeling of her small hand clasped possessively by Luke's big one. She so loved being with this man, this powerful, sexy man who could intimidate every other man even when he was being playful. *Perhaps* especially *because he's playful?*

Luke was wearing a blue-and-white-striped button-down shirt, fitted and crisply pressed. And his jeans hugged his legs just right when he moved—but she was somehow viscerally aware it wasn't just how he looked in his clothes; it was how he *moved* in them—powerful, virile, confident. It was so far from how hurt he had looked on his couch. *Ouch.* It still killed her she'd wounded him so. How much of this confidence was an act? Some, anyway, she was sure. *Fake it till you make it,* she thought, as she realized her own dressed-up appearance was also intended to convey a confidence she didn't completely own.

We'll get through this. We will.

Luke led her to the maître d', who took one look at Luke and nodded, then led the couple off to a secluded table in the busy restaurant. *We're together. We're doing this.* She was still so full of relief, her feathered hope still so new. Though she was walking, she felt as if she were flying, flitting like a sparrow, her heart dizzy and giddy.

Luke pulled out her chair for her, and once she had seated herself, he leaned in to smell her hair and trail a tender hand down her neck and shoulder.

"Hi, boyfriend," she whispered, leaning across the table toward him as he sat.

"Hi, girlfriend," he crooned. His smile melted her.

"I love you so much."

"I love you, Ashley."

"Thank you." With those two words, she was trying to convey so much. *Thank you for loving me. Thank you for letting me be here with you tonight. Thank you for trying with me again.*

Ashley watched as he rolled up his sleeves, revealing his strong forearms. She watched them flex and relax and felt oddly turned on by the small expanses of exposed skin, thinking of how easily those arms could lift her as he carried her to bed, her legs wrapped around him. God, she wanted— *Be here now.* "How was your day?"

Luke looked at her, amused, as if he could sense her interest in his flexors and extensors. "How was *your* day?" he said, flipping the question without answering it.

"Good." *All day, I thought about kissing you from top to bottom.*

"I couldn't help but notice you seemed to like having the attention of two men."

He didn't think she was leading them on, did he? Her eyes flicked up to his to ascertain his emotional tenor. But he was heavily guarded right now, and she couldn't tell the bent of his questioning.

The truth was, despite her efforts to disentangle from Slick and Curly, she kind of *had* enjoyed it, but she hadn't been inappropriately flirty, had she? Had she offended him? "They were entertaining."

He cocked his head.

"I wasn't flirting, Luke," Ashley assured him, suddenly quite serious.

Luke's low laugh was warm. "I could tell, Ashley. I was reading your body. You were having fun, but you weren't flirting. Those men, however, they would have been happy to have shared you at the hotel across the street, taking turns satisfying you until you—"

"Luke, I—"

"To be honest, I kind of enjoyed watching from a distance for a while as both of those good-looking men tried to seduce you, *especially* because you didn't seem very interested."

Ashley furrowed her brow. *He liked watching me get hit on?*

"Sweetness." Luke chuckled. "You look beautiful tonight. Really. Beautiful. *Of course* those men were attracted to you. What man wouldn't be? And I am so glad you are here with me."

"Thank you." She blushed, relief flooding her again. Seemed to be the theme for tonight. She was really on edge, so desperate for things to go well between them.

"Do you think you'd like that?"

"What?" She sipped her wine.

"Having two men please you."

Ashley choked on her chardonnay. Spluttering, she angled her chin and wrinkled her forehead. "What are you talking about, Luke? You know you're the only man I want." She could tell by the look on Luke's face that he was starting to really enjoy this. It reminded her, in a way, of how he had been earlier in their relationship—teasing, charming, warm but distant.

"But have you ever fantasized about it? Having two lovers at the same time? Two men to touch you completely differently? Two men who both delight in your body and take turns pleasing you?" His eyes darkened and locked on hers with erotic intensity, and she felt her arousal stipple across her skin, like invisible goose bumps, as if her skin were panting. Still, she felt slightly insecure, as if there were a trap somewhere she couldn't see.

What was Luke playing at? Was he being sincere? Testing her ability right now to tell the truth? Who hadn't fantasized about a ménage à trois? But it was nothing she would ever do. In fact, the thought of anyone besides Luke touching her made her positively queasy.

But if she could extract herself from who she was and the loving relationship she was trying to repair right now, what *would* it be like to have two men pleasing her? Would one watch while she had sex with the other? Would one man tell the other what to do? Or would they all be touching and kissing and exploring ways to slip into each other's bodies at the same time? The thought of four hands and two tongues and two cocks and one her—Ashley felt a warm pink flush rise into her cheeks.

His blue eyes sparkled wickedly. "So, it *does* turn you on?"

"Yes." Her admission was soft.

Luke's breath hitched, and she could tell her confession turned *him* on. But he would never want to have another man in their bed. Would he?

He leaned forward and spoke in a conspiratorial hush, his voice hooded so no one else could hear. "Perhaps one man who touches you like you're a queen, like your body is a priceless jewel. And another man who likes it rough and savage and wants to subject you to his...*darker* desires." His lip curled up when he said the word *darker*, and he touched his tongue to his lips, as if the word itself tasted curious in his mouth.

"Can I get you started with something to drink?" said the server, standing at their table. *When did he get here?* "I see you have a glass of wine." He nodded at Ashley. She took a big gulp to hide her embarrassment.

How much had he heard of their conversation? Take it with grace. Sit tall.

"How about you, sir?"

The practiced poker-faced look on the waiter led her to believe he had not heard Luke's question. But after Luke ordered a whiskey neat, she saw the waiter break into an amused grin as he walked away. She blushed deeper and gave Luke a pointed look, warning him to drop the subject of threesomes.

But he had already moved on. "So, I noticed you'll be in Huayllabamba for the big festival in the middle of September."

Ashley startled. "You looked it up?"

"Of course I looked it up. What else do you think I did for three days while I was brokenhearted and pissed at you? I studied my competition."

Ashley laughed and shook her head. That was like Luke—to get straight to the point, yes, and to research what he didn't understand. It was something they had in common. The fact that he cared enough to research where she was going made her heart glow like a neon welcome sign.

"What else did you learn?"

"They grow a lot of corn."

"Biggest in the world!" she laughed.

"And one of the local delicacies is soup with eyeballs."

Ashley almost spit out her water. "*That* is something I did *not* know."

"It's supposed to be good luck if it ends up in your bowl."

"Is it rude to say I don't want to be lucky?"

"That, I don't know. And, I learned, the internet is unreliable."

Ashley's shoulders slumped on that one. "I know."

Luke gave her a compassionate nod. "That was a big deal for you to step down from STEAMEA. I know it wasn't an easy choice. But it does show me just how committed you are to this endeavor in Peru. Never thought I'd be president of the board without you as director."

Ashley grimaced.

Luke leaned across the table, and with one hand, he rubbed the frown lines from her forehead, then literally beamed positive energy into her, as if he believed she was the most worthwhile woman in the world. "Ashley. I'll take good care of your baby while you're gone."

And just like that, a crack appeared in the dam she'd constructed to hold the strong currents of her competing emotions. A single tear slipped down her cheek.

"Sweetness." Luke brushed the tear away with the backs of his curved fingers. "I was trying to assure you, not make you cry."

"I'm so torn up, Luke. It's like I'm two women in one body—one who desperately wants to follow through with my dream in Peru and one who desperately wants to be here making new dreams with you. I don't know how to hold it all." Her heart longed to fly toward him, but it battered around inside her instead like a butterfly with a broken wing.

"I understand." Luke nodded. "Believe me, I understand."

After the dramatic start to dinner, the meal progressed with talk of Peru and the small town Ashley would soon call home—how the religion was a fusion of Catholicism and Quechua beliefs. How it was a mecca for downhill bike racers. And how it would be a far cooler climate than she was used to.

"Speaking of climate," Luke said, "and you may already know this—the Arctic drilling plans you overheard in London have been delayed."

Ashley looked at him warily. "I'd heard rumors."

"No need to be shy about it. I think we should toast." He held up his whiskey. "Here's to the grassroots people from around the world who helped put a halt to drilling while new safety systems are put in place."

Ashley raised her glass but held it back. Luke didn't seem upset about the news. In fact, he seemed rather pleased. "But aren't you—"

"It's got the industry in a spin, but Ashley, although it's a headache at work, you know it's what I want, too—what is best for the planet. And although this whole thing caused a big rift between us for a while, I have to admit I'm proud of you for sending the rallying cry out into the world so fast, galvanizing all the other Ashleys out there who are brave enough to stand up to big oil and say *do it better.*"

"You're *proud* of me?" She moved her glass toward his.

"Don't ever doubt it." They clinked.

All through the rest of dinner, Ashley's feet trespassed to Luke's side of the table, teasing him beneath the tablecloth with her toes, letting them explore inside the hems of his pants, hooking her feet gently against the back of his calves, tracing the shape of his ankle. She hoped the slow-burn seduction was working as well on him as it was on her. Would he ask her to come over tonight? She could feel how ready she was, her whole body buzzing with anticipation. She daydreamed his hands between her legs, spreading her open for him, dreamed of him entering her, filling her, driving into her, fantasized his mouth moving against her neck…

Excusing himself to use the restroom, Luke interrupted her reverie as he pushed back his chair and stood up. On his way past her chair, he stood behind her and leaned down to whisper into her left ear. "Tonight, I will play your body like the most exquisite instrument." His voice was a silken curl, intimate and lyrical, plucking hidden strings in her thoughts. "I will find the music hiding in your lovely neck, your perfect breasts, that sensitive place inside your thigh, the tender arches of your feet—I will kiss you and taste you and please you until every inch of you quivers and trembles and you fall open for me like a night-blooming lily."

Holy shit. Ashley's lips parted as he spoke, and her head lolled back in wanton acquiescence. She let out a trembling breath. *Yes, please.* He pulled away, and she closed her eyes, fantasizing about the evening ahead, the sensuous tenor of Luke's words still resonant in her head. *I guess he answered* that *question.* A giddy, amorous excitement bubbled in her. She closed her eyes and leaned back in her chair and drifted into a vision of his room with all the candles lit, their sacred scent, and his hard, naked torso suspended above hers. She imagined the soft moan he would make as he dipped his head to take her breast in his mouth and—

"I want you on your hands and knees tonight," he gritted into her other ear in a low and gravelly command. "I'm going to slam my hard cock into your gorgeous cunt until you're gushing cream and begging me to let you come."

Ashley's eyes shot open, and her nostrils flared. *Whoa.*

He growled against her throat, and he was gone.

CHAPTER 10

EVEN THOUGH SHE'D BEEN in Luke's bedroom dozens of times before, tonight, it felt surreal. He'd lit a dozen white and cream candles all around the room, filling the space with golden light. Long shadows flickered on every wall. The room smelled like lilies—he'd placed the flowers she'd sent him on the table beside the bed. They'd all opened, and the honeyed, ripe perfume floated in the air.

Ashley trailed her fingers across the soft cream comforter. Just over a week ago, she had thought this room would be hers. This bed would be hers. And the man in it. And all the pleasure between them. And then, just days later, she'd thought she might never see or feel any of it again. Now, she experienced being in this room as if it were both familiar and oddly new. It was like tasting a tree-ripened peach—though you've had a peach before and know the taste of peach, it's nothing like eating it sun-warmed and ripe right off the tree, and in that moment, it's as if you've never experienced the taste before.

Her whole body felt rich with that aliveness right now—full of hunger and anticipation and thrill. Luke had left her alone in the room to get something, and his absence made her even more aware of how all seven trillion of her nerves were like tiny lightning rods, each of them straining to meet the charge of the moment.

"There you are." Luke's voice was a low caress. Excitement rushed through her as he stepped slowly toward her. "Beautiful. You are so beautiful." She let the words in, loving that he found her attractive. The closer he came, the more furiously her pulse beat. Finally, he stood before her, taking her in with his gaze. With one hand, he smoothed her long hair, whispering praise as he pulled his fingers through the length of it. His other hand found the slow curve of her hip, and he gently, firmly pulled her in closer.

"Luke." Ashley stared up at him, her breathing uneven, her heart drumming against her chest. His blue eyes moved across her face like radiant beacons, searching her for something.

He leaned in to whisper in her left ear. "Do you want this, Ashley?"

"Mmm." She leaned into his body to nuzzle her face into his hard chest, but he stepped back and cupped her chin gently, urging her to look up.

"I want to hear you say yes, yes you want me to please you, you want me to take care of you again and again." His fingertips flirted with her skin just below the hem of her dress. "Tell me *yes*, Ashley," he whispered into her ear as the backs of his fingers lightly brushed against her inner thigh.

Was he asking for more than just permission to kiss her? If there was any fantasy involved, she couldn't yet detect it. Part of her ached, worrying that she'd damaged the trust that had enabled them to make completely authentic, unguarded love. And part of her tingled in sweet anticipation of an evening of erotic, unpredictable play. They hadn't done that for weeks, and somewhat to Ashley's surprise, she had found she had missed it.

With a sudden clarity, she realized that whatever Luke was asking her to say yes to, she would. She trusted him. She trusted him completely. She wanted *this*, wanted *him* in any way he was able to meet her.

"Yes." She flushed, molding her fingers and palms into his hard chest, reveling in the warmth that radiated through the cotton of his shirt. She looked into his eyes, those sapphire pools. "Yes, please."

"Good answer." He smiled with devilish charm as his head descended until his lips were covering hers with soft, insistent pressure in a seductive kiss that obliterated every other thought. Her mouth opened for him, and he swept his tongue into her waiting warmth in sweet penetrating strokes. Awash with pleasure, she arched into him, her hands on his waist kneading into the strong muscles of his back, every part of her throbbing with hunger. She struggled to deepen the kiss, but Luke nibbled and tasted and playfully skimmed her lips with his as if he had all the time in the world.

"Let me," he whispered against her open mouth. "Let me go slow. I want to savor every note of you." He dragged his lips across her jaw and down the long, smooth expanse of her neck, grazing and nuzzling with his open mouth, lavishing attention on all her most sensitive places. Oh, how he knew her. She leaned back to grant him access, draping over his one-armed embrace, his strong arm supporting the cantilevering of her torso.

The whole time he explored her, he braided strands of sweet praise into the kisses, ribbons of *how beautiful you are, so perfect for me, such soft skin*, and she shivered at his gentleness, twisting and arcing as desire commandeered her motions, making her an erotic animal, a creature of instinct.

In an elegant sweep, Luke scooped her into his arms, floated her to the bed, and laid her down so her arms were arranged above her and her knees dangled over the edge. Luke kneeled between her legs and traveled his hands up and down her calves. "So beautiful," he murmured, entranced by the shades of her skin.

With one foot in each hand, he eased her legs open, purring his approval as she let him stretch her, wider, wider. Though she had shared with him her body many times before, Ashley felt a tinge of insecurity, perhaps because of their separation. *Am I sexy enough? Am I good enough? Am I beautiful enough?* She watched his shadowy stare travel across her legs to where the soft fabric of her dress pooled over her sex, watched as his gaze continued to move over the landscape of her torso and heaving breasts. The heat in his eyes melted her self-doubt and transformed it into sensual certainty. *We are so perfect together.* Her brain shut up, and her body warmed as he slipped his hands beneath her dress and slowly, slowly pulled it up. Her senses swarmed, her pulse an erratic bumblebee. *Touch me, touch me now.* He was going so deliciously slow that she wanted to pull up her own dress and—

Luke growled somewhere deep in his throat. She sighed in acquiescence and smiled an inner naughty smile. Right about now was when Luke would realize what she wasn't wearing beneath her dress.

Luke's low grunt as he found her intimate skin bare for him beneath the thin black fabric caused a sharp clenching deep inside her. He paused, and she froze, waiting for his next touch, missing the confirmation of his presence, and then, with the lightest touch, as if she were a delicate flower, he traced the seam of her outer folds with a slow, sly finger, bending and pulsing against her ever so slightly, but not exerting enough pressure to slip inside. She gasped. So slowly, so feather-soft, he was playing at parting her sex, but he did not, and it spurred her, inflamed her, and she arched in response, her hips rising off the bed.

"Shhhh," he calmed her, stilling his exploration until her body relaxed. Once she had melted back into the bed, he began again to stroke her with his finger, this time letting it dip through her lips, finding her wetness and pulling it through her slit, moistening the dark passage with each sweet curl of his fingertip.

Ashley moaned, acutely aware of how precise he was, aware of how her whole body flooded with sensation, all stemming from one single point of contact. Her whole world had been reduced to this here, this now, this man, this touch, this tantalizingly slow movement. Though her eyes were closed, she could feel his gaze on her, watching her response to his slightest caress, reading her merest quiver, attuning to her every twist and shudder and gasp.

"You are so beautiful, Ashley." And now he slid his wicked finger deep into her secret entrance, such welcome invasion, and she bucked in blind pleasure. Deeper, he slid into her, massaging unhurried circles inside her, flirting with her G-spot, the soft pad of his thumb floating lightly above her sensitized clit.

Ashley almost wailed at the breathtaking torture, the heat in her building, her body clamoring, baying for release. She could smell her own arousal spreading through the room, the musk-heavy scent of craving.

"Yes, Ashley," Luke crooned. "Everything you want, *everything* you want."

Gentle, heat-seeking kisses began at her inner knee, and Ashley whimpered as Luke's mouth drifted languidly up her leg, grazing the delicate flesh with his teeth and warm tongue. Bliss-muddled, she slurred his name on each exhale, reveling in his warm breath against her sex, his finger still gently swirling and curling inside her. He blew on the tip of her exposed clit, and she shivered and arched in desperate search of contact.

Only the tip of his tongue met the elusive bud where she most wanted to be touched, and she felt her satiny walls squeeze hungrily around his finger. *More, please more,* her body screamed inside, but the only sound that came out was a quivering breath that shimmered above her like the haze of visible heat rippling above the desert floor.

Luke lifted his head just a bit. "That's it. I want to hear you. Let me hear how much you want me."

He licked her again, and as requested, she immediately groaned in response.

"Yes." Luke was pleased. "I love the sounds you make."

Ashley obliged, unmuting the erotic sighs and moans that were forming in her, letting them rise from her throat through her lips, letting them sing through the air in resonant pleasure. Luke hummed his appreciation, clearly turned on by the crescendos and diminuendos of her desire. With his playful, agile tongue, he provoked her, fluttering the flat edge against her hard bud with wing-light strokes, exciting her with his tenderness, butterfly gentleness. In her lust-heightened state, she longed for a leonine savagery, craved something stronger, something that would release her from this tightening, coiling torment. And the softer he was, the louder she became, her body shaking and literally buzzing with longing.

"Please. Luke. *Please*," she gasped as her body craved up toward him. He sucked at her clit with his lips, then indulgently flicked the tender bud with his tongue until at last she felt the surge and swirl of ecstasy rush and crest in a glittering, churning climax. "Yes, yes," she cried, opening into rapture. She could swear a thousand suns were rising in her body with their luminous and radiant, beaconing energy, transforming her whole being into pure light.

Breathless, she panted his name, her whole body convulsing. He continued to slide his finger in and out of her, pulling more and more pleasure through her limbs, coaxing her into trembling aftershocks of heaven.

"Luke." Her voice was hoarse with lust, and she watched as he rose between her legs until he was standing over her. She pushed back on the bed to receive him. Her eyes took in all of him—the thick bulge of his cock pressing against his jeans, his glistening chin, the playful glint in his dark, hungry eyes.

He leaned down over her so she could feel the heat of him hovering above her as he whispered in her left ear, "You are so beautiful, every inch of your body, so divinely beautiful." His voice was lush and sweet, like a long and resonant note of a cello, and she was all too aware of the emptiness inside her aching for his hard length to fill her, complete her. She lifted her hands to untuck his shirt and find the tight knit of his abs beneath, but he caught her hands and pinned them beside her, and then he kissed a hot trail up to her right ear and bit it. Hard.

"You need more, don't you?" he growled, then pulled back to meet her eyes. "Say *yes*, Ashley." His grin was wicked, ruthless, even callous, and his posture became increasingly authoritative.

The change in tone was so dramatic Ashley inhaled sharply, but she stared into his eyes, so intense, so charged with control and devotion. She felt herself opening up instead of shutting down.

Ménage à trois. That's what's happening. The realization hit her as his words from earlier echoed in her thoughts: *So, it does turn you on? Two men touching you completely differently. Two men who both delight in your body and want to take turns pleasing you.* He was giving her a threesome of sorts. A shock of astonishment rippled through her core.

"Say. It. Now." His voice was thick with control.

A soft pant escaped her as her mind short-circuited. *Holy shit.* This was crazy hot. Feeling herself blush, she nodded.

"You know I need to hear you say it."

She knew she was saying yes to so much—yes to wanting him, yes to whatever he was planning, yes to a new invitation. Suddenly shy, she tried to look away but couldn't.

"Say it," he coaxed. He lifted his chin.

"Yes." She was breathless.

"Good." His eyes glinted a commanding blue in the candle-light. He leaned back on his heels, crossed his arms in front of his chest, and gazed at her with a regal confidence. Her heart beat wild, almost feral in her chest. When he spoke again, it was in a dominant purr. "Take off your dress."

Ashley sat at the edge of the bed and slipped the soft black fabric over her head. Now all she was wearing were her heeled shoes, her black lace bra, and a full-body blush. Luke looked at her nakedness as if he would not be satisfied until he had pos-sessed every inch of her body, until he owned every beat of her heart. She felt a damp heat growing between her legs. *So good.*

"Take off the bra."

She reached back to undo the clasp and noticed how Luke's eyes hooded with approval when her chest slightly jutted out and her back arched. She loved watching him get turned on, loved knowing how her actions affected him. She felt the heavy spilling of her breasts as the scrap of lace draped and then dropped to the floor, but she kept her eyes on his face, marking every change in his expression.

"Kiss me." His tone was smoldering, more forceful, more moonless than just a moment before. He slid a hand into her hair and formed a fist, pulling on her hair not so much that it hurt but enough that she knew his hand was there, a remind-er of his immense physical strength, a display of potency. He pulled her closer and kissed her with a grinding ferocity. All the sweetness of their previous kisses was gone. Instead, Luke was raw, untamed, almost savage as he crushed his lips into hers, demanding she respond with equal intensity.

Instantly, her body answered his with an untamed passion. It was like wildfire—what began as a small, heated pulse inside her soon overtook her senses, and she moaned in breathless ex-citement. He tugged on the roots of her hair, angling her head so her mouth fit his perfectly, and he took what he wanted from her lips.

And then he was gone from her, leaving her body bereft. He nodded his head toward the center of the bed. "Get on your hands and knees." Though his voice was commanding, it wasn't cold or condescending. More like a strong massage—powerful and enlivening.

She moved to do as he asked, slipping out of her heels.

"Those you leave on."

Oh-kaaay.

Ashley pressed her hands and knees into the mattress, faced the headboard, and waited for her next instruction. Her heart knocked hard in her chest. She felt Luke's eyes on her as he prowled the perimeter of the bed, appreciating every angle of her body.

"Your body likes it when I tell you what to do." His voice was low, curious, hoarse, and the words brushed across her like long strips of suede, giving her goose bumps. She was startlingly aroused.

She bit her lip, almost embarrassed by the truth. "Yes."

"I like giving you pleasure. In so many ways." She could hear a dark smile lurking in his raspy voice. "Crawl back to the edge of the bed." Ashley exaggerated the swing in her hips as her knees took turns sliding back, delighting in Luke's groan as she teased him with her swaying.

When she reached the edge, she stopped and waited, forcing herself not to turn her head to see what Luke was doing. She watched the candlelight flicker against the wall and felt a similar flickering inside her—some strange hypnotic dance between shadow and light. She heard the metallic clink as Luke undid his buckle and the swoosh as he pulled the belt from its loops, then let it drop to the floor. She heard the telltale whisper of a button coming undone, the quick buzz of the teeth of his zipper, the rustle of his pants as he stepped out of them. She had never been so turned on by waiting before, but she quivered in restless anticipation of being touched, and each second that went by flamed her arousal.

"It's hard to wait, isn't it." There was little question in his gruff voice. "Touch yourself, Ashley. Show me how you make yourself feel good. Show me what you'll be doing when you're alone in the mountains of Peru."

Ashley let out a short exhale, something between astonishment, embarrassment, and arousal. She peeked beneath her chest and between her legs, and she saw Luke standing behind her, the muscles of his strong naked legs bunching and one hand stroking his long, stiff cock. An electrified flutter rippled through her sex.

"Show me," he repeated, his voice a smoky purr.

Any embarrassment she might have felt was overcome through sheer need—the need to please Luke, the need to please herself. Balancing on her left hand, she lifted her right and slipped her middle finger through her thickened folds, already slick from Luke's lavish licks and the silky cream of her own release. Despite herself, a small moan of relief escaped her, her body writhing into her own hand, her fingers craving toward the tight wet entrance of her body.

"That's it," he crooned. "It feels so good, doesn't it? But not as good as cock. Let me see you slide that pretty little finger in."

Ashley teased her fingers through the smooth furrow to her entry, then slipped one tip slightly in. All the while, she kept her eyes focused on Luke's hand as he squeezed and slowly fisted his length.

"Deeper."

One knuckle disappeared, and then another slid deeper inside her channel until her finger was wholly in her, then pumping, curling into the soft walls, searching for her G-spot, relishing her own wet slickness as she rode her own hand, grinding her palm into the swollen bud of her clit. Touching herself in front of Luke, letting him watch her like this, turned her on more than she thought it would—and the thrill of him telling her what he wanted, the thrill of knowing she was pleasing him right now by fulfilling his fantasy, flooded her like a dizzying aphrodisiac.

"Now two fingers. I want your tight body so open for my cock that all you feel is pleasure when I take you."

Ashley did as he asked. She could feel the burn of his eyes on her fingers as they disappeared into the dark pucker of her entrance. She heard the slight catch in his breathing, and his arousal emboldened her. She gave in to a deep shudder, feeling the stretch of two fingers. Her back arched as she drove herself toward climax, unable to keep herself from accelerating the heady rhythm of thrust and release, thrust and release. *So close.* Her breath shortened, and she felt her thighs start to clamp and her inner muscles start to tauten.

"Don't come."

Ashley stopped the motion of her hand and began to pant. A small desperate whimper escaped her.

Luke rasped, "Let me."

She gasped as she felt his strong hands slide down the curve past her waist, kneading into the soft flesh above her hips before pulling her back to meet his bare cock. His knees were bent, so the hard upright jut of his arousal pressed into the opened crack of her bare ass, and he bent his knees more to slide his length up and down the warm groove, groaning at the friction.

She reached her cream-slick fingers back to cup and stroke his balls, and he grunted his pleasure. He repositioned himself so that the tip of his shaft was poised at the soft, wet folds of her beauty. He pushed in the barest inch. She felt a tension build in his hips, felt him pull back as if about to piston forward. Just in time, she returned her hand to the mattress to steady herself as he commanded, "Now," and sunk his full cock into her body in one strong plunge.

With a sharp cry of pleasure, she received him, grateful he'd prepared her so well before deep thrusting into her. She felt so wanted, so wanton, so deliciously full of his hard arousal. The fit was tight but not painful, and they both stilled for a moment as her body accommodated the deep pressure of his length.

She felt his hand slide up the back of her neck and massage her scalp before he twisted her hair into his fist and firmly tugged so that her head was forced up and her back arched more acutely, allowing him to push in more deeply.

"Open," he huffed, a one-word command that had an extraordinary effect on her. As if Luke could control her autonomic nervous system, Ashley felt her body open even more to receive him, and he moaned in response, feeling it, too.

She'd been so close to coming before, and now her body was edging some glorious abyss. Just one slight move of his cock and she thought for sure she would slip into the oblivion of pleasure. She undulated beneath him, seeking the friction she craved.

He steadied her with his hands. "Don't. Come," he gritted through clenched teeth as he slowly withdrew his cock, pulling through her snug sheath, then slamming hard again into her body as at the same time he tugged at her hair. Again and again: the delirious impact, her breasts swinging with each deep thrust. The animal of her body craved the animal of his body, relished the rushing tides of his breaths that seemed timed to his movements.

A low, wild moan that began somewhere deep inside her escaped her lips. She couldn't even recognize it as a sound she'd made before. She desperately wanted to do what Luke said, but she doubted she could hold back the roiling flood of pleasure that threatened to overtake her.

"You want to come?" he chuffed as he pumped into her hard, his flesh slapping against hers. "Is that what you want?"

Yes, yes! She tried to speak, but words eluded her, so she whimpered in affirmation.

"Ask," he commanded. "I want to hear you ask for it."

What were the words?

"Ask me to come."

"Please, Luke," she mustered. "Please." She was so close to falling into the abyss, and she struggled to keep herself at the edge.

"Please what?"

"Please, can I come?"

He pulled out.

No! Did she really say *no* out loud? Or was it just in her head? Her body crumpled with unfulfilled longing.

In the silence of the room, all that could be heard was their panting, their breathing uneven, each of them recovering from the shock of separation.

"Luke?" Sweating, shivering, hungering, desperate, Ashley turned to face her lover, his cock in full salute.

He leaned forward to whisper in her left ear, "I'm going to take such good care of you."

Registering the change in him, Ashley almost laughed despite her near desperate need to come as she realized he was playing with her as only Luke could. She wanted to sob, to scream, to plead with him to fill her again with his cock. And at the same time, she melted into bewildered pleasure, realizing he'd returned to the role of sweet and gentle lover, making real her fantasy to make love at the same time to two very different men. Every part of her hummed, as if there were an entire sky full of starlings all looping and swirling and diving through her body.

He laughed, too, clearly enjoying the way the scene was unfolding. He ran his tongue across his upper lip, sending a message straight to her clit. "Yes, beautiful." His voice fell on her nakedness, feather soft. "I'm going to give your beauty exactly what you need." He knelt at the edge of the bed and gently lifted his lips to her throbbing clit. And with a single, perfect lick angled at the tip of her layered flesh, he sent her into spasms of brilliant release, and she soared, her body a bright, lustrous, lyrical vessel filled with light and song, overspilling with warmth. Her hips bucked as he continued to lick and bite and nip, and she rode wave after wave of climax, pleasure filling her like an ovation until she collapsed, spent on the bed.

She felt Luke stretch his long, limber body alongside her on the bed, moving his hand so lightly over her skin that Ashley almost wondered if he were actually touching her or if she just felt the energetic charge of his hand as it moved.

She opened her eyes to the honeyed radiance of the candlelit room and gazed intently into the twin cut gems of Luke's eyes.

"May I touch you?" she asked with a sly grin, her hands already reaching for him. He smiled and acquiesced, rolling onto his back, and she admired his well-muscled chest, his taut abs, the flagpole of his cock. "I want to touch you."

"I want that, too."

Ashley let her hands roam across his biceps, tracing his shoulders, tracking his collarbone. "You're so perfect," she murmured, running her hands across his taut chest, delighting in the feel of his tiny nipples pressing up into her palms.

She straddled him, his cock rising like a temple between the triangle of her legs, and she continued to massage her fingers into the hardened muscles of his chest and shoulders, pressing him down into the mattress.

She leaned over him and whispered in one ear, "I like the way you make me come." She shifted slightly to whisper in his other ear, "And I like the way you drive my body crazy."

She lifted her hips to fit the head of Luke's cock right at the damp seam of her opening, eager to slide down his thick circumference, to feel him hot and hard inside her, to give him pleasure the way he had pleasured her.

"Go slow," Luke rasped as he reached his hands up to cup both breasts as they strained into his skin, craving his touch. "I want tonight to last forever." He ran both thumbs ever so lightly over her nipples, and they stiffened to meet him.

Slowly, so slowly, she shifted her weight to rub her wetness over the slick head of his cock, teasing him with her wet folds. She watched his face as his lips opened and closed and opened again, and his head fell back. As she slipped his shaft inside her, just past her entrance, she felt his body tense, heard the quick intake of breath, as if it were taking all his energy not to come. *Payback.*

She teased her legs slightly more open, making more room for him to enter her, and then she repeatedly squeezed and released her slick warmth around his cock, milking him as she lowered herself with deliberate leisure onto his rigid length, inhaling the musk-heavy scent of their sex. It took all her self-control to go slow, *but damn,* judging from the blissed-out look on Luke's face, the effort to delay gratification was worth it. He hissed in appreciation, his breath whistling through his teeth, his blue eyes, pleasure-lit, fluttered closed, and a groan of appreciation slipped through his lips as if he'd just been given something sweet and rich to eat. But even while lost in his own paradise, his hands continued to torment her breasts until her erect nipples felt so exquisitely sensitive she couldn't tell if she wanted to beg him to stop or squeeze harder.

At last, she felt herself fully seated on him, and she squirmed slightly to accommodate the full feeling inside her. She lifted, dragging her body up his thick erection—

"Don't move, beautiful," he slurred, his hands arresting her, holding her gently in place. "Don't want to come yet."

How long did they remain that way in the silence of his room—her body suspended and still above his? It felt an eternity as she watched his face while his eyes were closed in concentration, marveling at how much she loved this man beneath her.

And then with a savage growl that shocked and surprised her, Luke's grip on her tightened, and he wrestled her to her back. She found herself trapped beneath his muscled weight, their bodies still connected. Though fuzzy with lust, she realized by the change in his energy, he'd transformed roles again.

With a strong rock of his hips, he pinned her to the bed, her body gladly receiving his almost brutal ownership as he buried himself so deep she felt roughly ripped apart. Behind her eyelids, stars exploded. Luke's hands caged her on either side of her shoulders, his muscled arms rippling with tension. With a brutish lunge, he buried his face in her neck, nuzzling and biting at the tender skin.

"You. Are. Mine," he grunted into her ear, his gruff voice bestial and charged with possession. He punctuated each word with strokes so forceful Ashley's whole body shuddered with the deep penetration. He stared into her eyes, his gaze unrelenting. Ramming his cock into her again, he rasped, "Who takes care of this pussy?"

"You do." The words came out in a huff as he drove into her.

"Damn right I do. Bend your knees. I want you to feel every inch of me."

Ashley obediently bent her legs into the air and dug her high heels into the mattress, marveling at how the change of angle intensified the sensation. She lifted her hips to meet him as he pounded deep into her again and again, touching places inside her she couldn't remember ever feeling before. Then he grabbed her legs and lifted them to wrap around his shoulders, leaning forward in a way that allowed his cock to enter her even deeper. Lost in sensation, she closed her eyes.

"Look at me," he commanded. "Never stop looking at me." Though her head wanted to fall back, though her eyes wanted to close, she did as he asked. She watched how pleasure played across his features as he leaned farther forward, changing the angle of his cock in her, positioning her just as he wanted her. She felt her legs, her whole body, relax in a delicious surrender to his power, his passion. She let herself be taken by him.

Luke's voice was a steady stream of filthy talk. How he loved slamming his aching cock into her slick heat, how he wanted her to beg for him, how he owned her and wanted to mark her bare skin with his cum. The dirty words and his expert thrusting took her again to the edge of oblivion, and she felt the effervescent sparkle of orgasm starting in her toes.

His eyes intent on hers, he noticed the way her mouth began to open, the way her body began to tremble. "Oh, you like that dirty talk. Does it make you want to come again, honey?" She moaned in response. "Oh, I'll make you come again." He sank to his elbows so that his body hovered right above hers as he continued his delicious onslaught. Smoky and gruff, his voice urged her on. "I'll make you forget every cock you ever had but mine. I'll make you come and come and come. We're so goddamn good, so fucking good together, and still you're going to leave me. You're fucking going to leave me."

Just as Luke spoke the last words, Ashley soared into orgasm, stars exploding in her head, wild sparkling waves of pleasure crashing in and through her, nerves firing through the core of her into her stomach, her chest, her thighs. And at the same time, those words, *you're fucking going to leave me,* crashed through her heart and ripped at it, tore through it like ragged ruthless teeth—not just the words themselves but the desperate, desolate tone that he'd said them in.

"Oh, Luke." Ashley gasped through her haze, her throbbing heart trying to push the orgasm away. She wanted to soothe him. "Oh, love."

But he was chasing his own orgasm now, driven by instinct and hunger and hurt. With each thrust, he guttered, "You're leaving me, you're leaving me, you're leaving me." His face was torn with anguish—not the beautiful, joyful look of an orgasm, but more as if he were being destroyed from the inside, stroke by stroke. His movements slowed as he started to come in her, his cheeks a hot mess of sweat and tears. He closed his eyes, and in a voice she barely recognized, he panted, "Red. Red. Red."

"I WON'T BE LONG." Luke gave Ashley a lingering glance and a mischievous smile as he walked toward the elevator to go buy pancake mix.

"Oatmeal will be just fine—" Ashley spluttered.

"My gal wants pancakes, she'll have pancakes. I'll be back before you know I'm gone."

Ashley leaned back into the warmth of the sofa and cradled the coffee Luke had made for her. She smiled as she sipped the black and bitter brew laced with the barest taste of sweetness. He always got it just right.

She stared out the window at the Houston skyline, the morning light glinting on the windows of the high-rises. She admired, as always, how beautiful the city was from up high. *He asked me to live here. I almost lived here. With this view, this sofa, this mug, this man. I could have woken up with Luke every morning. Could have stayed with him forever.*

Was it still possible? Could she go to Peru and come back to this home? Not only, but also?

Ashley flashed back to the unresolved angst of the night before. Luke had safe-worded himself, apparently so caught up in their fantasy he spoke to powerful feelings that had scared him. Scared both of them. Or, Ashley wondered, had he been safe-wording their *situation*—in which she was leaving him, and that's what he was trying to stop?

She shivered, remembering his face, how raw it had been, how wounded. Almost as if the sex itself had allowed him to step into his deepest fear. After he came, he'd collapsed on her, and they had held each other tight, as if trying to pull the other's being inside their own, to be even more connected than sex would allow. She'd felt the wet of his tears in her hair. They'd fallen asleep that way. This morning, they hadn't talked about it. Ashley didn't know how to bring it up or even if she should.

Maybe it's time to pull out that wooden elephant...

Although she knew Luke was doing his best to reconcile her leaving, it was clear from last night that there were a lot of feelings he was covering up, perhaps from himself as well.

What did she want? To go away from this man who loved her? Who she loved? And for what? For a promise she'd made to a woman who died? For some sense of responsibility and pride? Was she a fool to throw away all her new dreams in favor of an old one? What kind of hurt was she still causing in Luke? Nothing seemed clear. A growing despair grew in the pit of her stomach, like a black hole that threatened to pull everything in—her happiness, her sense of who she was, any certainty she had about what she wanted.

"I'm sorry, Luke," she whispered. "I'm so sorry."

She was jolted by the sound of the intercom. She walked to the door and saw on the security screen an image of Savannah on the other side.

"Are you kidding me?" Ashley said to the screen, watching as Savannah smoothed her hair and rolled her shoulders back to thrust out her chest, no doubt preparing to see Luke. Surely, she knew that whoever was on the other side of the door could see her. *Shit.* Knowing Luke would let her in, Ashley felt obligated to let in Luke's jealous ex. She blew out a breath, steeled herself, and opened the door.

The door to hell.

"Hi, Savannah." She forced her voice to be cheerful, even though Savannah made every effort to be rude to her in their every interaction.

"Oh, aren't you *cute*?" Savannah cooed, noting Ashley was wearing Luke's robe. "I wore that robe a thousand times." She pushed past Ashley into the room.

Okay, so it's war. "Looks like you *tried* to be cute," Ashley quipped back, her words soaked in saccharine. Truth was, Savannah didn't look cute. She looked like sex in slippers.

Slippers?

Savannah was wearing designer sweats and slippers, and her face looked as if she'd just spent an hour doing her makeup to make it seem as if she'd only just awoken with smeary sex-kitten eyes and messy bedhead.

"Where's our Luke?"

Mine, not ours. "He'll be back in a while. Can I help you, Savannah?

"Oh, sure." She turned to face Ashley with a sultry stance, one hip cocked back. She thrust a large mug forward. "I just need to borrow some sugar. And some measuring cups. I'm making a chocolate cake, and silly me, I must have forgotten to pack my measuring cups when I moved."

Ashley's jaw slackened.

"Oh, you didn't know? So funny Luke didn't tell you. I moved in just two floors below this week, thanks to Lukey. It's not easy to get a place here. So exclusive. Good thing I have an *in* with the building owner."

Luke owns the building? Ashley didn't know that and suddenly felt wildly out of her game. She understood why he might not have told her he owned the building; he was quiet and humble about money. But why hadn't he mentioned Savannah was moving in? *Because you two weren't talking, dummy. Because you're leaving him.*

Seeing Ashley was momentarily dumbstruck, Savannah took the chance to plunge the knife in deeper. And twist it. "Oh, and I hear you'll be moving to Ecuador." She gave a wide-eyed innocent look and batted her lashes.

Seriously, who bats their lashes?

"Peru," Ashley corrected her.

"Right. Well, all the same, I'll take care of our Luke. It's a good thing we're such close friends. He counts on me for a lot— and we are, of course, involved in many prestigious city activities together." Savannah narrowed her gaze, a predator moving in for the kill. "And I'm glad I know where I can get some *sugar.*" She flipped her hair and walked toward the kitchen. "In fact, I know *exactly* where it is. I helped him move in. Just like he helped me."

Did Luke really help her move in? Jealousy choked her.

"And here are the measuring cups, right in the drawer where I put them a few years ago." Savannah bumped the drawer closed with her hip. "Don't worry, honey. I'll make sure Luke is very, very comfortable. And that he has plenty of cake to eat."

Did she really say—

"Oh yeah. I mean it that way. Luke always spoiled me in the kitchen. Playing chef, if you know what I mean—"

"Goodbye, Savannah." Ashley managed to keep her voice level and calm. "I'll let Luke know you came by."

"Oh, you do that, Ashley. Life in Ecuador will be splendid, and you can build a wonderful life there."

Ashley couldn't help herself. "Peru." Her voice sounded weak, even to her, as if she knew she was losing the catfight.

Savannah smirked.

"And it's only four months."

"Right. I'll have things covered here. *Bon voyage.*"

Long after Savannah left, Ashley couldn't stop thinking of what she'd said about playing chef. Over and over, she imagined Luke's head buried in Savannah's legs, eating her out, speaking French, finding creative, playful, sensual ways of making her come.

She sat in the corner of the couch again but no longer felt enveloped by it, her coffee now bitter and cold.

———

Ashley could tell her mother didn't believe her.

"Is that so?" Ashley's mom offered Ashley her favorite blue mug. The familiar scent of licorice and mint swirled into Ashley's nose and calmed her. Slightly.

"Yeah, that's so." Ashley had just told her mom she had no second thoughts about going to Peru in two days. In fact, she had *only* second thoughts. And third thoughts. And fourth thoughts. *Why am I leaving? I'm risking too much. If this is my dream, why am I so miserable?*

"You look delighted." Her mom sipped her tea from a mug with a giant yellow sunshine, an innocent look on her face.

Since when is Mom such a devil?

"It's the most important thing, Mom."

That's not true.

That is true!

Ashley took a sip of tea in an attempt to turn off the constant war in her thoughts. She was careful to meet her mother's gaze because her impulse was to avoid it. She had never been so at odds with herself. Never. And the *last* thing she needed now, two days before getting on the plane to Peru, was for her mother to change her mind.

"I admire your clarity, Ashling. And you will be a blessing there—a gift to everyone you meet. You honor Tica. You honor yourself and your promises. And, my dear, I am sure that Huayllabamba will be a blessing to you, too. You will come home changed."

Yeah. Changed. That's what Luke had said, too. That Peru would change her. And he was right, of course. Of course she would change. But did that mean that she and Luke couldn't still be together? That wasn't what he'd said, of course. But that was what he'd implied.

"Speaking of change, what have you heard from Emilia?" Ashley's mom had always had a soft spot for Emilia.

"She's doing so much better, Mom. She's out of rehab, though I haven't given Emilia her job back with STEAMEA yet. Her new Lift mentor is going to help her work toward it. And John's looking out for her at school."

"And how is she with you leaving?"

"She says she's all right."

"Hmm. I hope so. Sometimes people tell you what they think you want to hear." She smiled sweetly, but Ashley got the hint. Her mom was onto her.

"I hope so, too. She's such a great kid."

"You really put your heart into helping her. And sweetheart, sometimes you just must let things go. But sometimes, sometimes you need to hold on." Her mom leaned forward to push a heavy lock of hair away from Ashley's face. "Ashling, you look miserable. I know you must be worried about leaving Luke. He is a lovely man. Our dinner together here the other night was wonderful. He loves you so."

Ashley gave her mom a querying look.

Her mom shrugged. "Based on the way he looks at you, my darling, that man is really struggling—both wanting to support you and devastated by you leaving."

Ashley opened her mouth to interrupt, but her mother raised her hand to stop her.

"The fact you are trying to tell me *everything is fine* lets me know just how torn up you are. It is not like you to sugarcoat things."

"But I *am* fi—"

"Oh, my darling. Of *course* you are fine. And of course you are *not* fine. This has been such a difficult choice for you. And sometimes those difficult choices are the ones that help us grow the most." She rested her hand on Ashley's. "I may not be an example of how to make a romantic relationship work. But I do know one thing that is true in all parts of life: Sometimes you can try and try to make something happen, yet it doesn't. But if something is meant to be, then it will ripen and rise up, and there won't be a damn thing you can do to stop it."

Ashley nodded.

"Trust, sweetheart. Trust yourself. Trust that when you follow your heart, the doors of the world will open for you."

———

"Take a moment to look around and find your closest exit. Keep in mind this may be behind you."

Ashley craned her head to see that there was, in fact, an exit behind her.

"If only real life had exit doors, right?" said the woman sitting next to her.

Ashley laughed. "Yeah." In fact, that was basically what she was doing right now. Exiting her life. She clicked her seat belt on.

Ashley was grateful for a window seat and stared out, her eyes blurring. The airplane engines whirred beneath her. *I'm doing it. I'm really doing it. I'm going to Peru.*

She missed Luke. She missed the shapes his mouth made as he formed words. She missed waking with the weight of his hand on her hip. The missing was less a thought and more a full-body ache. He had left four days ago for a meeting in Tel-luride. It was hard enough that she had spent her last few days in Houston without him. But it was even harder thinking of him in Telluride, of all places, where they had fallen in love. Where he'd taught her to ski, and they'd snuggled in the gondo-la. Where they'd gazed at stars on the balcony and talked about their dreams.

What are you doing now, Luke?

And *who* was he with? Her thoughts curdled, thinking of Savannah in Telluride with him now as she had been before. She sighed, trying to push the jealousy away.

I'm going to Peru.

She tried to be excited. But the truth was, she was heartbro-ken. She reached into her backpack down by her feet to take out the small, tightly wrapped box that held Tica's ashes. She set it in her lap and closed her hands over it.

"Is Houston home?" said the friendly woman beside her.

Ashley gave the woman a weak smile. "Yeah." *And I'm leaving the man I love, the man who loves me, and it feels like a thousand knives are stabbing me.*

The flight attendant's voice interrupted them. "If you still own a watch that needs to be set, relax. The local time in Peru is the same as in Houston."

"Actually," the experienced flyer said, "when you arrive in Peru, it's more like you should set your watch to a hundred years ago. The villages in the Andes are still using *oxen* to plow their fields."

"Huh." Ashley gave a lukewarm smile and put in her ear-buds. There was no way she could chitchat right now.

Leaning back in her seat, she started the playlist that Luke had made for her. "For the plane," he'd said. "No cheating and listening or peeking first." And so, she'd waited for this moment to listen and noted the first song was by a band named Purple

Moon. She exhaled long. Would she ever be able to see or hear the word *purple* again without a sharp twinge of simultaneous thrill and loss?

She closed her eyes as the soft solo guitar began playing a haunting melody. The music swirled through her, opening her, honoring heartbreak and love and loss and beauty. And then a man's voice began singing. Luke? She opened her eyes. That was *Luke*.

> *Even as you leave, I love you*
> *There is nowhere my love can't reach.*
> *It walks wherever you walk,*
> *It cradles your heart in sleep.*

Oh my god. His voice. Velvety soft and earthy as vetiver. Was it Luke on guitar, too? She'd seen the guitar in his living room but had never seen him pick it up, never heard him play.

> *Even as you leave, I love you*
> *I feel you here with me.*
> *Your absence is present in every room*
> *Your love is present in me.*

The words steeped in her like strong tea, infusing every part of her with their love, their longing, their devotion.

> *Don't you hear*
> *there's a question in the air*
> *and it waits for dawn,*
> *a dawn that's yet to come.*

Tears prickled her eyes, then streamed down her cheeks. The lump in her throat threatened to choke her.

Can't you hear
a lover singing in the night
and I wait for dawn,
a dawn that's yet to come.

She stared out the window as the plane left the ground. *I hear you, Luke, I hear you.* And as she hurtled toward a new country, oh, how she ached for that dawn.

CHAPTER 12

"PERHAPS YOU'VE HEARD WHAT they call Huayllabamba." The woman walking beside Ashley was just under five feet tall, but she had an enormous presence. Her somewhat formal deportment felt incongruous with the lively and friendly villagers around them, and Ashley couldn't help but feel that the townsfolk were intimidated by the woman—or perhaps it was her own intimidation she was projecting on others?

Chaska, a woman about the same age as Ashley, was Ashley's landlord and one of the most influential people in Huayllabamba. Her Spanish was fluent, but her Quechua accent was strong. Ashley recognized it as the same accent Tica had. It sounded so familiar to her ears that despite Chaska's cool demeanor, Ashley felt a rush of warmth for the stiff woman.

Chaska was giving Ashley a tour of the village—no more than ten square streets surrounded by terraced fields, all of it nestled between a wide brown river and the steep brown rise of the Andes cliffs. There was a central square with a church, a huge tree filled with singing birds, and a handful of small shops with brightly painted doors. The buildings were made of adobe or concrete with a gypsum stucco. The tops of the buildings were clean, but the bottom halves were splattered with dried mud from the rainy season.

In response to Chaska's question about the origins of Huayl-labamba's name, she asked, "The name means *prairie* in Quechua, yes?"

Chaska nodded, but she gave Ashley a cool glance. "And they call us *los layq'as*."

Ashley puzzled for a moment. "What does it mean?"

"Sorcerers. Or witch doctors." Chaska seemed to be watching Ashley for her response, even though her eyes were on the cobblestone road in front of them.

"Please, tell me more."

Chaska didn't smile, but she seemed pleased by Ashley's response, and Ashley felt as if she'd passed some kind of test. "They used to say the heads of the witches would separate from their bodies so only the heads would follow you. But no one believes that anymore."

"I see." Ashley nodded, but her logical, scientific brain was being scrambled, not only by the talk of witches but also the combination of lack of sleep, excitement, exhaustion, and being surrounded by the Spanish and Quechua languages. Everything combined was having a strange effect on her—as if the harder edges of her were being softened and eroded, like a sandstone canyon. Perhaps it was being in this valley, too, infused as it was with a joyous and shadowy beauty. Perhaps it was the people themselves who met her with open curiosity. Though she didn't believe in witches, she couldn't help but believe that something mysterious and wonderful could happen to her here—was, in fact, already happening.

"*Allillanchu!*" A group of kids playing in a courtyard shouted a greeting at her. Most of the homes had courtyards with outdoor kitchens filled with chickens pecking around and guinea pigs running around. Some even had cows and sheep. The kids were waving at Ashley, pushing each other aside trying to get a peek at her, tripping over each other and giggling.

"*Allillanmi*," Ashley shouted back and gave a friendly wave. Surely these would be some of her students. She was so excited for school to begin in a week.

"You speak some Quechua." Chaska's tone bordered on approval, and Ashley was grateful she'd learned at least a few phrases during her teacher training in Cusco the last few days. Though she'd be teaching in English and Spanish, most of the students spoke Quechua as a primary language and had only studied Spanish in school.

"Why do the houses have a pair of bulls on top of the roof?" She pointed to a pair of brightly painted clay bulls that had been affixed to the top of one house.

Chaska replied matter-of-factly, "*Cusco toros* keep the house safe with a blessing to the Apus, the mountain gods, and they ensure health, wealth, and unity for the occupants of the house."

"And why the ladder and cross between them?"

"To allow easy passage to heaven when the final call comes."

Ashley took in the information and wondered at the strange marriage of Quechua and Christian beliefs, just as she'd read. As they walked closer to the school, Ashley noticed the signs in many shop windows for Donofrio and Lamborghini. "Perhaps on our way back, we can stop for ice cream?"

Chaska frowned. "Can't buy ice cream here."

Ashley gestured to the store window signs, and Chaska gave a closed-mouth smirk. "Perhaps once the freezers were full here, but not anymore. Not enough money to spend on ice cream. Plus, most of the young people have gone to cities with better schools. Look around."

Ashley saw a handful of gray-haired women wearing bright woven blankets sitting on a park bench, gossiping in Quechua. An old man was leading his cow down the street, taking it to pasture. It *was* mostly older people. Would any of them have known Tica? Just then, two young girls ran past them down the street, squealing, their plastic flip-flops thwacking against the stones. Two young boys were right on their heels, laughing.

"It's good you are here," Chaska said. "The kids who are still here need you."

What a curious place she had arrived in. A town filled with witch doctors whose heads might detach and follow her? Advertisements for ice cream everywhere with no ice cream available? Fields all around them tended by oxen pulling farm implements and irrigated by canals. The clucking of chickens and the squealing of guinea pigs and the shouts of children. Huayllabamba felt both endangered and vital at the same time—as if not much had changed in six hundred years, but it was about to.

Ashley longed to share everything she was experiencing with Luke, though she couldn't quite imagine him here. He'd be over a foot taller than everyone. He would barely fit in her small room she was renting from Chaska with its tiny bed and brightly woven bedspread. Could he even stand up in it?

She had to admit she was happier now that she was out of the room. When she'd first arrived a few hours ago and Chaska had given her some time to rest, she'd felt empty and full of doubt. Her phone didn't work well enough to make a call, and there was no Wi-Fi in her room; the service was blocked by the thick adobe walls. In fact, service was spotty all throughout the town, though Chaska said she could get Wi-Fi and make calls if she went to the corner of their courtyard.

Now, out in the street, the large multistory concrete school ahead of her, the majestic mountains above her, and the windswept air of the Sacred Valley tugging at her hair, the empty feeling was giving way to a growing sense of purpose. *This.* This was Tica's world. This was the dream she couldn't imagine in Houston. The real faces on the kids. The scent of roasting corn and potatoes and chiles. She felt wildly in touch with the earth, with her life.

I wish I could share this with you, Luke.

When the surge of longing threatened to crash over her and a thick lump formed in her throat, she made her imaginary black box in her mind, put her longing for Luke in it, shut the lid, and gave all her focus to the world around her.

Was it her imagination, or did Chaska give her a knowing look as she turned the box's imaginary key?

———

"So, tell me more about Tica," Chaska said as she continued to tend the earthen oven, or *huatia*, she'd made with clods of dirt. The delicious scent of charred wood and earth and baking potato wafted through the air, and Ashley realized she was salivating. Her pension included one midday meal that Chaska provided, and in the evenings, like the locals, she ate bread and jam with coffee. At first, she'd been dubious about having someone cook for her, but now she was grateful to have someone serve her local delicacies. There was something so wonderful, so natural, about cooking *in* the earth and sitting beside the smoldering pile of dirt that was the *huatia*, Ashley continued to marvel at her new circumstances.

"Tica dreamed of coming back from Cusco to be a teacher here," Ashley said. "But then she and Cusi moved to Texas for his work. And then they had four boys—"

Chaska interrupted. "And you became her daughter."

Ashley didn't hesitate. "Yes. She was a second mother to me."

"She was a blessed woman, then. I, too, have prayed for a daughter to whom I can pass on my knowledge, but—" She stopped speaking, as if realizing she'd shared more than she wanted to. She gestured to her home. "Well. No matter. It is just me."

Ashley was surprised, actually, that Chaska had shared about wishing she had a daughter. It was the first personal information she'd volunteered, even though they'd spent meals together the last few days. Ashley had gathered that Chaska's relatively well-to-do father had died, and because he had no sons, he had somewhat reluctantly left his fields and herds to his daughter. Chaska took her responsibility very seriously, and for the most part, she was all business. While most of the locals Ashley had met had been gregarious, Chaska seldom had conversations that went beyond hello—even with other locals. In fact, Ashley's first assessment that other people were somewhat afraid of Chaska seemed true. But as Chaska and Ashley shared meals, Ashley had warmed to the woman, and, to her surprise, Chaska seemed not only receptive but eager for companionship in her awkward, stilted way.

"Tica used to tell me about the corn here—how it is the largest corn in all of Peru."

"In all the *world*." Chaska didn't say it with pride, merely stated it as a fact. "Surely Tica spoke about her family here."

Ashley shook her head. "She never spoke of them except to say they told her when she left, she should never come back."

"But you brought her here, didn't you."

"Well, yes, in a way I..." At first, Ashley thought Chaska meant she was bringing Tica's memory here. Then she realized that Chaska somehow knew she had Tica's ashes. Goose bumps rose on her arms. "Yes. In fact, I did."

"Good. Did she have a request of you?"

Chaska's intuition was uncanny. "Yes. She asked me to take the ashes to the chapel on the hill." In addition to the Catholic church in the heart of Huayllabamba, the small chapel on the hill had been built after the Virgin Mary had appeared on the mountain, and it was the place the locals considered most sacred, a place connected not only to the Virgin Mary but also to the spirits of the mountain.

Chaska considered this. "It is good you are here. She will finally be able to rest."

Hot tears prickled against Ashley's eyes. "Thank you," she whispered. "Thank you for this message."

When the potatoes were done, Chaska used a *pico*, a pick, to look for the potatoes and pull them out. She cleaned the potatoes off on her pants, put one on a plate, added a dollop of dark green *uchukuta* sauce, and handed the plate to Ashley. Though her lips didn't smile, her eyes did.

"Tell me, is there someone else you wish were here? Someone with whom you wish you could share this meal?"

"Yes."

"Before you take a bite, think of that person, blow on the potato, and send the blessing to the person far away."

Ashley closed her eyes and pictured Luke. He had been in the Middle East on business since she'd gotten here, and they'd had almost no contact. But she could feel him—sometimes she missed him so much she swore she could smell him, could feel his hand on the back of her neck, could hear his voice in her ear saying her name.

She lifted the potato to her face, and the delicious scent curled into her nose. She blew on the steam. Though she didn't know what she was supposed to say, words formed easily in her mind.

Luke, I share all this goodness with you. How I miss you, Luke.

Ashley took a bite of the hot gold flesh of the potato and the creamy, spicy cilantro sauce and almost moaned.

"It is good," Chaska said, reading Ashley's face, and then she raised her own potato to the sky and spoke clearly in prayer. "Thank you, God, for this wonderful potato, so delicious even the farmers don't have potatoes this delicious. Thank you for this generous gift. We are blessed."

Ashley marveled as the other woman held the potato with such immense reverence and gratitude. *All for a potato.* Some of Chaska's devotion spilled into her—she could taste the respect for the earth, for God.

She blew across the food again, sending joy all the way to the Middle East, imagining that Luke, wherever he was, whatever he was doing, could connect with her in this moment. *Join me,* she thought. *Please, Luke, join me.*

The path up to the small chapel was not long, but it was steep and had many switchbacks. Chaska had said if Ashley wanted to go into the chapel, Chaska could ask her cousin to open it, but Ashley declined. She felt strongly that Tica cared more about the sacred site of the chapel than the building itself.

Chaska had offered to come with her to release Tica's ashes, and Ashley appreciated the offer, but she wanted to do this alone. Well, not alone—she was with Tica. She carried the small box with the ashes in her hands now as she climbed the mountain. And tied around her back was a Peruvian *manta*—a colorful striped cloth made from alpaca wool—in which she carried numerous things that Chaska had helped her procure for a small ritual. "Your heart will tell you what to do with them," Chaska had said.

Ashley had watched Chaska the day before as she performed a rite she called *Pago de la Tierra*, payment to the land. Chaska explained that every August, her people paid tribute to Pachamama, essentially Mother Earth, giving offerings in gratitude for life, plants, and animals that the earth provides for the people. Ashley had quietly observed, and she could tell Chaska was pleased that she gave it her attention. Such a curious friendship was developing between them. Though the two women were so different on the surface—one of them cool and profoundly spiritual, the other warm and profoundly scientific—they both shared a deep love for the earth, though they expressed it differently.

As Chaska had lit her altar on fire and they watched it burn, she'd explained that the ritual was done for the home but also for the fields before planting, for new businesses, for new building projects, even for luck in love. Ashley couldn't help but wonder how different the world would be if all businesses—including mining companies such as Luke's—had ceremonies thanking the earth before they dug a new mine or new landfill or new foundation for a high-rise. *That's what's missing in the world right now—a fundamental respect for the earth, for life, a sense of reciprocity, of giving back.*

"Tica, thank you for bringing me here," Ashley said aloud as she continued her climb. "I am learning so much in just these few days. And soon I will go and work in the school where you thought you would teach. Remember how we used to sit at your table? And you would serve me hot cocoa and tell me to take my studies seriously? I didn't know then what a difference you were making in my life. I just knew I was grateful you were there."

The wind picked up and whipped her loose hair around her face, and Ashley inhaled the scent of dust and earth.

"Is that you, Tica? Is that you?"

As she climbed through the shrubbery, she looked out to the fields where locals were planting corn together in a system of reciprocity where the members of different households helped each other. The locals called it *ayni,* mutual aid and trust that grow out of the belief that everything and everyone are connected.

"This is where you learned to help others, isn't it?" She spoke aloud as if Tica were there, which she truly seemed to be—some vital presence, though Ashley couldn't help but wonder if she were making it up. "This is why you stepped in to help me—you trusted our connection. And now it is my turn to help you and to give back to your birth community the way you gave to mine." Though she felt flooded with purpose, she stopped often to catch her breath, still unaccustomed to the altitude. It reminded her of when she and Luke had been in Telluride and how thin the air had been there, too.

"Remember the time when I found my dad's old recipes in the back of the cookbook, and you helped me make them so I could taste something my dad loved? Thanks for that. Who would ever think to put za'atar in a blueberry tart? And remember how you'd grown thyme in your yard and let me use it for another recipe?"

Ashley paused a moment and looked down the mountain toward the small town below. She felt so small in this great valley and yet somehow so a part of it.

"And remember that time when I was so afraid for my mom's health and you had me write my fears on paper, and we burned them together in your sink? And the smoke detector went off?"

The wind pushed her up the hill, and she laughed. "All right, all right. I'll go faster. After waiting all these years, you sure are eager."

Am I really talking to Tica? Do I really think she's the wind?

Ashley laughed at her mind trying to make sense of things. All she knew was that she was high on emotion—filled with purpose and near elation.

"Remember how you called me *urpicha*, little dove? I've always cherished that nickname. It suits me. I heard someone call a little girl *urpicha* in the marketplace yesterday. It almost made me cry."

At last, Ashley reached the grassy terrace beneath the chapel. "We're here, Tica, we're here."

Ashley took off the *manta* and set it on the ground, then raised her hands to the sky, feeling herself a bridge between the two. She caught the wind in her hands and gulped it into her lungs. "Tica. We made it."

She knelt on the ground and untied the knot in the *manta*, then spread it across the earth to make an altar.

"I don't really know what I'm doing, Tica, but I want you to know I'm doing it with love. And with gratitude. I know how much you wanted to return home, the home that shaped you into the wonderful woman you were." She was struck by the idea that Tica had left Huayllabamba to move to Houston to be with the man she loved.

And I left the man I love in Houston to come to Huayllabamba.

The thought did strange things to her heart.

She placed the box of ashes in the center, then attended to some of the things Chaska had sent her with: a small bottle of *pisco*—a clear brandy that Tica had enjoyed in the States that was very popular here. She poured that into the earth, whispering, "Thank you." There was a bouquet of red flowers wrapped in newspaper, which Ashley de-petalled. She strewed the petals in a circle around her and the *manta*. The wind died down, and the petals stayed in place. She placed cookies and garbanzo beans in a pattern around the box. And then she opened a small paper bag of coca leaves and placed the leaves dark green side up on the cloth as Chaska had done. With each leaf she placed, she whispered, "Thank you, thank you."

For a long time, Ashley knelt there, staring out into the Sacred Valley, feeling present with Tica, flooded with gratitude for the woman who had helped raise her, who had inspired her to become a teacher.

Ashley opened the box and stared into it.

"Welcome home, Tica," she said as she sprinkled the ashes into the flowers. "Welcome home."

As the box emptied, Ashley felt a simultaneous surge of overwhelming joy and a mounting sense of agonizing loss, and the two mingled in her the way two rivers become one—churning and swirling and spreading. "Oh!" she cried as the wind picked up again and blew the last of the ashes into her clothes and mouth and eyes and hair. "Oh!" And she wept with the certainty that Tica was with her, was somehow part of her, and she wept with the finality of the loss. Tica was gone. Ashley didn't even have her ashes anymore. She was returned to the earth, to the Pachamama that she had spoken of so often. And Ashley felt a rush of completion. And the sense that she was now profoundly, terribly alone.

CHAPTER 13

"*S*EÑORITA!*"

Ashley was aware of someone knocking hard on her door, each rap causing spasms of pain in her head.

"*Señorita*! Are you there?" The door creaked as it opened.

Ashley groaned. She could vaguely remember the night before she'd seen the telltale flashes of light in her vision, felt the tingling in her arm, and she'd known a debilitating headache was coming. She'd gone straight to bed and shut the blinds in her room, but now a severe ache pulsed in the right side of her head. She was in the throes of a full-blown attack. Shuddering as the light streamed into her room through the door, she gingerly pulled the covers over her face and felt a wave of nausea rise from the slight movement. A billion bells rang in her head.

Chaska came to her bedside and spoke in quiet Spanish through the bedsheet. "Ashley. Tell me. What is happening?"

"*Migraña*," Ashley managed.

"I see. Do you have medicine?"

"On the dresser. White bottle. Painkillers."

Ashley heard Chaska walk toward the sink, and then she said very quietly, "Please trust me," and disappeared.

When she returned, she had brought a mug with a strong green scent. "Here. It's tea made with healing herbs. Please sit and drink."

Ashley whimpered, knowing that sitting was not possible for her.

"I will spoon this into your mouth."

Ashley felt like a little bird as she sipped the bitter tea from the teaspoon Chaska slid into her mouth. Then she fell into oblivion.

When Ashley opened her eyes again, it was dark outside. How long had she slept?

The first thing she noticed was that her head was clear. Usually, after one of these headaches, she felt drained and confused, but instead, she had a feeling of clarity, almost elation. *It's gone?* She had heard rumors from some of the other teachers at the school that Chaska was a shaman, a healer. Ashley sensed that her coworkers had more fear than admiration for her landlord, but in this moment, Ashley had never respected anyone more.

The pain is gone!

And then the most terrible thought grabbed her, shook her out like a rag. *No. No!* Panic filled her chest like a thousand crickets had landed in there and a patch of thistles with their pricklesome leaves grew in her gut. *Please, no!* She stared at the blue dress she'd carefully laid out still draped over the chair, ready for her to slip into it.

It had been the first day of school. And she'd missed it.

"Ah, *La Professora*! Welcome!" The handsome Peruvian man behind the counter at the bakery spoke in clear Spanish, but his voice was musical, like a Spanish guitar, resonant and light, and it was almost as if he had sung to her instead of speaking.

Ashley was a little taken aback that he knew who she was. Then again, her fair coloring did stand out in Huayllabamba.

"Of course, I know who you are. This town is so small we know if someone sneezes across it."

Ashley laughed, immediately feeling at ease with the friend-ly baker. In a town where it seemed most of the population was older, he was quite young, perhaps in his early thirties like she was.

"Plus," he added, "my daughter Mayu is one of your students. And I am Mayua. It is nice to meet you, sister."

Ashley loved the way people here referred to each other as brother and sister—though there were different words for the terms based on the gender of who was speaking to them and to whom they were speaking, and she was still nervous to get the terms wrong. Still, she responded in her stilted Quechua, "I am glad to meet you, brother. I am Ashley."

Mayua rewarded her with a bright smile. "You told me that your mother-in-law is a donkey."

Ashley cringed, then realized the beaming man was a trick-ster. "Forgive me." He chuckled with a shake of his head. As he smiled, she noted that unlike many people in the town, he had very straight and white teeth. He wore his dark and shiny hair long to his shoulders. His features were chiseled, regal, and his almost obsidian eyes glittered with amusement as they held her curious gaze.

"I can't help myself. You are very brave to learn Quechua, and you spoke perfectly. And I add, you are very brave to come and get a pastry at this bakery. I've seen you walk by many times without coming in. You are, perhaps, afraid of pastries."

Ashley laughed. She had walked past the bright blue door of the small bakery several times without entering, but today, she couldn't help herself. It smelled so good as she passed by, and she had so much to celebrate—her first day of actually teaching at the school had gone better than she'd ever hoped. Chaska had given her a small puma trinket to carry in her pocket. "Pow-er and strength," she had said as she pressed the silver charm into Ashley's hands that morning. And the students had been so respectful, so enthusiastic to learn, despite their very humble classroom. Their shining, eager faces, so unlike many of her students in Texas, reminded her why she was here.

But what had her heart soaring was the giant bouquet of flowers that had arrived at the school yesterday from the florist in Urubamba—arriving for what was supposed to be her first day. Not only was Luke thinking of her, but he was also cheering for her. The card read, "*Every time you are tempted to react in the same old way, ask if you want to be a prisoner of the past or a pioneer of the future. I'm so proud of you, Ms. Pioneer.*"

Her heart melted again just thinking of it. Those were the words she had read to him from Deepak Chopra's *The Path to Love* the first day they had met in the bookstore.

"What would you like? Perhaps one of these?" Mayua pushed up the sleeves of the blue linen shirt he wore beneath the full-length white apron, and Ashley caught herself admiring his strong arms as he pointed at the *pan huaro*, a roll similar to ones that Tica used to bake, but Ashley had already spotted a sweet-looking cake confection. The man followed her eyes. "Oh yes, a very good choice. Much to celebrate, yes? And you are feeling better?"

Ashley tilted her head slightly. How did he know she hadn't been feeling good? *Oh yeah, if someone sneezes across town.* She was used to the anonymity of Houston. She couldn't tell if she was put off by the small-town dynamic or thrilled by it.

"Yes, thank you. I'm feeling better." She took the sugary confection that he passed over the counter, her mouth already watering. "How much does it cost?"

"No, *Professora*, it is my treat."

"But—"

"I insist. You honor our town by teaching our children. A pastry is the least I can offer you in gratitude."

"Thank you."

"Plus, I am about to ask you to do something for me. Or rather, something *with* me." His eyes sparkled mischievously.

Ashley felt her guard go up. "I see."

"I would like you to dance with me." Ashley gave him a strange look.

Here? Now? Is he flirting?

"Well, with my group. As part of the *Festividad Virgen de Natividad.*"

Ashley had seen videos of the ecstatic dancing and feasting that took place during the annual Festival for the Virgin, a weeklong celebration that drew thousands of people and happened to be synched with the anniversary of the town.

"What is it you Americans say? Anyone *worth their salt* will be in someone's dance. And you, *Professora*, you are worth salt." He scratched his head with some drama. "But that is a very strange phrase."

Slightly overwhelmed by Mayua's exuberance, Ashley hesitated.

"Or have you already been asked by someone else to join their group?" He looked disappointed. Ashley shook her head and smiled at him shyly. She knew already she would need to march with the rest of the teachers in the civic parade—she'd had to buy a gray suit for the occasion. But to be a dancer meant she would dance in colorful regalia with the locals, and she desperately missed dancing. A sudden surge of delight made her do a happy wiggle.

"I would *love* to be part of your dance."

Mayua's whole face lit up. "Ah, now we will have the best dance at the festival! It will take much training. And we will drink much *pisco*. And the Virgin will be very pleased with our offerings."

"It's a competition?"

Mayua raised an eyebrow. "There's a rivalry to be sure. But let's just say we all want to do our best. When we come together and do our best, well…we have a Quechua saying. *Llaqtakunaq atipayninwan tiqsimuyuta kuyuchisunchis.*"

"What does it mean?"

"When the villages work together, we will turn this world around."

Ashley turned the words over in her mind, thinking of just how much that related to so many parts of her life—her work with STEAMEA, environmental activism, and teaching. "That's what I believe, too, I just never knew how to say it so well."

"Ah, *Professora.*" Mayua's voice thickened with layered meanings. "Perhaps you come to Peru not just to teach but to learn."

―――

When Luke answered the phone, Ashley was completely unprepared for what his voice would do to her equilibrium. She knew he'd just come back from his work trip to the Middle East, and she'd thought he might be asleep.

"Ashley," he said, and just those two syllables in his lush baritone voice made every cell of her come to life—as if she were a desert landscape and his voice was the rain that made everything come into instantaneous bloom.

"Luke, oh thank god you answered."

In the silence between them before he spoke again, she felt a strong, almost violent desire twist through her body—as if it had claws and it ripped a spiral through her. She inhaled, taking in the strange blend of lust and relief and longing and satisfaction, such wonderful torture, before she managed to say, "I've missed you."

I've missed you was an understatement. She hadn't heard his voice in over a week, except for his voice singing on her playlist, which she had played *over and over and over.*

"I've missed you, too."

Her nervous heart leaned into the words, but she didn't find the comfort there she was longing for. There was something distant about his tone. Ashley supposed she wanted him to gush about how *much* he missed her, how his body craved her, how his days were empty without her. She wanted to hear in his voice something that matched the ferocity she was feeling.

Don't read anything into his quietness, she placated herself. *Surely, Luke is tired from his transatlantic flight.*

"Thank you for the flowers, Luke. They were beautiful. I can't imagine how you got them here."

And I wish you were here so badly. I miss your mouth, I miss your hands on my cheeks, I miss the way you gently push my hair out of my face.

"I'm glad they arrived. How was your first day?" His tone was polite.

She told him about the headache, the bright eyes of the students, the humble but clean school rooms, the friendly teachers who had welcomed her so warmly. "But Luke, it's crazy how strict the government here is with teachers. Many of them live in the city and travel here. We all have to clock in and out, and if any of the teachers are late, their salaries are docked."

"That's not that unreasonable."

She felt defensive on the teachers' behalf. "Considering the trip they have to make to get here? And another thing—if the students write in their books or rip them or whatever, the *teachers* are charged. So even though we have a lot of resources from the government, everything's locked in cabinets—books, calculators. No one wants to use them because the teachers are held responsible for loss and damage. They all think I'm brave to have the kids use computers—and believe me, the word *computer* is generous for what we are using—but I really need to use them to teach."

"Is that different from what you would have expected there?"

"Oh, I don't know—I'm just thinking of my classroom back in Houston, and even though our school had a super-low budget, I wasn't worried for myself each time a kid dropped a beaker—I wasn't penalized for it."

"Eat any eyeballs yet?"

Ashley laughed. "No, but I did eat something called *soltero*—which is basically a mix of cold beans, onions, carrots, and algae."

"Um, delicious?"

"Um, no? But after we started eating it, the woman who served it to me said she made it because I am single, and it would help me to find a husband." As soon as the words left her mouth, she regretted it. It had made her laugh at the time, but now, saying it aloud to Luke with him a continent away, it made her feel uncomfortable—and she could tell it made him uncomfortable, too.

"I see. So, is it working, the soup?" There was no humor in his voice.

"No, Luke." *You're the only one I am interested in.* Though on that note, the thought of marriage to anyone did not appeal to her. She was permanently soured on that institution.

A long, stroppy pause extended between them. Ashley looked around the courtyard where she was standing—the only place at Chaska's where the signal was strong enough to sustain a call. She became aware of the birds singing nearby, the squeal of the pigs in the nearby yard. Suddenly, she felt more than a continent away from Luke; she felt a whole *galaxy* away.

"Well—" They both began at the time. Then both stopped.

"You go first," Luke said.

"No, you go first."

"Actually, I should go." Her heart did an uncomfortable lurch. He had to go already? "I'm on my way to Alexander's Bistro for dinner, and I need to get dressed."

"Oh, how nice." *Oh, that hurts.* Alexander's Bistro was where she had met Luke on their first night together in Houston, where they'd sipped champagne and made silly puns and she realized just how completely she was falling for him. It was where they'd gone for dinner the night he'd procured two new donors for STEAMEA. It was *their* place.

She wanted to ask who he was going with. She wanted to ask if he, too, felt part of him had been cut away. She wanted to tell him she had pictured him in every part of this small town—walking through the colorful marketplace. Climbing the trail to the chapel. Leaning against the centuries-old Pisonay tree in the main square where lovers were supposed to kiss. Slipping with her into her narrow bed where he would cover her body with his hard, lean weight, pressing his hips into—

"Thanks for calling, Ashley." His voice was wearing its most reserved robes.

"Good to hear your voice." She felt a big dull gray lump form in her throat and stick there. "Luke." *I love you.* But the words lodged tight beneath the lump.

She heard the click. Then empty air.

⁓

Ashley was eating *soltero.* Again.

It wasn't that she hated it, though the cold beans and algae were not her favorite. It was more that she resisted the implication that the people in Huayllabamba felt it was their job to help her find a husband. Though she had told them she had a boyfriend, she was starting to wonder about that herself—she and Luke had barely contacted each other in the last two weeks since their brief and awkward phone call when he had returned from the Middle East. They texted most days, but it felt thin compared to the luxuriant love they'd had.

Though she was consumed with meeting new people and trying new things and going to new places and throwing herself into her work, the lack of connection was painful. Excruciating, actually. Unfortunately, it felt like an extension of the last few awkward days they'd been together after he'd safe-worded. Really, ever since she'd unilaterally made her decision to come to Huayllabamba, though he'd tried to give her a second chance, they hadn't really had enough time to get their relationship back in good standing before she left. It wasn't that anything heartbreaking had been said—it was more a feeling of drifting apart, and it was eating her alive.

In fact, Ashley had taken to lurking on Facebook, checking Savannah's page to see if she would post anything about Luke. To Ashley's dismay, she often did. There had been a couple of photos where Luke had been included in group shots—one at a happy hour, one at Alexander's Bistro with others from his office whom she'd met. She stared at the picture, zooming in on Luke's handsome face, as if it could answer her questions. Where else were he and Savannah meeting? And how often? Ashley all too frequently played back Savannah's words: *Luke and I are close.*

It made her stomach queasy. Or maybe that was the *soltero.*

"*Eh, ñanay!** Perhaps you would like the recipe for the *soltero*?" her hostess asked, interrupting Ashley's thoughts. Though her hostess addressed her in Quechua, she spoke with Ashley in Spanish. Ashley was eating with about a dozen other people of all ages who had shown up for an impromptu gathering. That was one thing that took some getting used to—no one really invited anyone anywhere; you just showed up. It was expected.

---

* Sister

She noted that Chaska was never at these gatherings. And Mayua always was.

"Oh, thank you, I have it. Thank you for the soup." She stopped short of lying and saying she liked it.

The hostess leaned in to whisper in Ashley's ear, "I think perhaps the *soltero* is working." She gave an ever so slight nod with her head in the direction of Mayua, who was looking at Ashley from across the courtyard, smiling as if to say he knew they were speaking of him, and it made him very happy.

To her horror, Ashley blushed. They had been spending a lot of time together preparing for the *Festividad Virgen de Natividad*, though always with a group. And he was very funny and made her laugh. Mayua was droll and warm, but he didn't feel romantically toward her. Did he?

Ashley's blush caught the attention of several other young women at the party who were also single, and they were not at all amused by what they saw happening. Their eyes sharpened, and Ashley felt their jealousy like talons in her chest.

Stand tall.

Ashley started to move toward them, as if to diffuse the tension she felt, but her hostess intervened, stepping between them. "Do not mind them. The girls of Huayllabamba are renowned throughout the Sacred Valley for their beauty and for being flirts. They think Mayua is a catch—and he comes with such a lovely child—but there are many other good men for them to catch."

"But—" Ashley hastened to put any speculation about her and Mayua to rest.

"They are perhaps jealous, too, because the whole town is so enamored with you. The kids in the school love you. And the old married men are happy because you dance the *huala* with them. And the old women are happy because you help us in our kitchens—it isn't always that the white people are willing to make food with us and serve it."

Ashley smiled at that. Though she had come with the intention to connect with the kids here the way Tica had connected with her, she was really loving her interaction with Huayllabamba's older citizens. They reminded her so much of Tica and her husband, Cusi. Having come now to several parties, she had learned that the younger people would eventually leave, and the older people would sit around drinking and dancing and singing. Ashley always stayed. She loved being with the older generation and listening in, even when they spoke in their native tongue and their conversation became like birdsong—something beautiful she could appreciate even if she couldn't understand it.

Tonight, as usual, the younger folks left early. One of the women her age asked if she'd like to join them at the *discoteca*—the dance club—in Urubamba. Ashley had asked for a rain check.

Mayua also stayed—he never went to the *discoteca*. Of course, he had to wake early to make bread, but the truth was he seemed content to spend his evenings with his daughter, who even now sat beside him, giggling as he animatedly spoke about something that had happened that day at the bakery. Ashley loved watching Mayua and Mayu, the way his eyes sparkled when she came into a room, the way he listened to her with his whole body, the way they shared many inside jokes and laughed often with each other. It emphasized the empty space in her where there were no happy memories of her dad, really no memories at all, just a blank where the love should be. Would she carry this abandoned feeling forever?

And what of Mayu's mother? Had she left? Did she die? She realized she was staring at Mayua when he looked up and

caught her eye. A warm smile spread across his face as he acknowledged her, then returned his attention to his daughter.

The host was quite drunk, not uncommon for most of the
men at these parties, and Ashley knew they would soon begin
singing songs from their youth.

"And tonight," said the host, "let us sing for our new friend.
For Ashley!" And he launched into a sloppy but enthusiastic
rendition of "*La Professorita*."

"That is the song that we met with," the hostess said to Ashley, smiling wide. "It is his favorite song." She shrugged. "Perhaps mine, too." And she walked to her husband, humming
along. Soon, everyone was singing along, raising their voices
in celebration of Ashley, but mostly, she could tell they just enjoyed singing together.

"What a gift you are to our community," Mayua said softly,
appearing at her side when the song was over. "Now the old
men have more reasons to sing." Actually, now they had put on
YouTube to find music for dancing. What a crazy contradiction
this place was.

Ashley chuckled. "What a gift Huayllabamba is to me."

"See how it goes both ways?" he said. "When the villages
work together—"

"—we will turn this world around," she finished for him.

Mayua took her by the hand, and with a confident flair, he
turned her in his arms and led her in the *huala*. Ashley hadn't
totally mastered it yet, so she was slightly clumsy, but Mayua
guided her gently, smiling all the time until she stepped on his
foot, and he winced.

"I'm so sorry!" She stopped dancing and stared at him,
embarrassed.

"I see a man must be very brave to dance with you, sister," he
teased, his smile big again.

They laughed together, and Ashley shook her head as if disapproving of his teasing, but it was clear she loved it. It was so easy to be with Mayua. She appreciated his easygoing nature, his willingness to joke. It was nothing like being with Luke. Luke made her feel in full technicolor—both vulnerable and safe, both desired and desirous. With Luke, she felt 150 percent alive. Mayua felt like a brother, though Ashley couldn't help but wonder if her heart weren't already so completely given to another man if she wouldn't be interested in the handsome baker in the same way the other young women in the village all were.

"Your daughter is so lucky to have such a good father."

"She does not think so when I start singing."

"Mayua, I don't want to pry, but what happened to Mayu's mother?"

"Ah, sister." His face went from ebullient to sober. "I will tell you something very sad. She was perfect in every way. The most beautiful woman in the mountains. One day, she was with me in the garden with the peppers, singing as she picked them. Three days later, we were burying her."

He took a deep breath and gave her a sad smile. "Life is fragile. And love, love is everything."

Ashley opened her mouth, on the verge of saying she was sorry for his loss, but Mayua anticipated her words and stopped her.

"No. Do not feel sorry for me. I have known great love. I *still* know it. I would do anything for the chance to spend just one more day with her. Just one more hour. But because this is not possible, I live my life knowing that I loved her the best I could. I carry our love with me, and it continues to grow. I shine her light everywhere I go. Every day we were together, I told her I loved her, I showed her I loved her. And she told me, too. Every night, before we went to bed, I made sure things were clear between us. When she died, even though it was so unexpected,

I knew that she loved me and that she was sure of my love, and that was a small comfort."

Ashley nodded. Was Luke sure of her love? If she died tomorrow, would he know she loved him? They had been so distant since she'd come to Peru.

Because it is scary to love someone knowing they might leave you.

What had she been doing? Why had she let their communication slip? While they were distant, it was more important than ever for her to assure him she loved him, but instead, driven by fear, she'd pulled back.

"Thank you, brother, for sharing that with me. You teach me so much," Ashley said quietly. Mayua was called away by his daughter, and he gave Ashley's hand a warm squeeze before going to his girl. Ashley stood there alone for a moment, surrounded by singing and laughter and the *tuk-tuk-tuk* of chickens and the squeal of the guinea pigs, and she felt her heart stretch toward a high-rise penthouse in Houston, hoping that the man there could feel the Morse code of her heartbeats like some enchanted telegram: *I love you. I love you. I love you.*

CHAPTER 14

"O H, LUKE, I'M so glad you answered the phone," Ashley gushed. She was standing in the corner of the courtyard of Chaska's house. She had waited to call until she knew Chaska would be gone. Sometimes her landlord seemed to be listening in on her conversations, and she intuited this one would be too private to be overheard.

"Is everything okay?" Luke's voice was laced with worry.

"Better now that I hear your voice. It's hard to not be with you, Luke."

"Well," he purred. "I don't want to sound like a jerk, but I'm glad?"

She took a deep breath, and then the words spilled out in frothy desperation. "I've been the jerk, Luke. Not because I left for Peru—I know that was the right thing for me to do. But now that I'm here, I feel myself shutting down emotionally—trying to protect myself in case you decide it's too hard to have a long-distance relationship. Since we haven't been talking much, I make up stories, and I—"

Shit. Just keep telling him how you feel.

"I don't want to mess up again. You're too important. *We* are too important."

She'd rehearsed what to say in her mind after the party last night, had fallen asleep thinking of what she might say to Luke.

But now that she was speaking with him, there was nothing elegant about it—her words were raw, and each one felt as if it had a small chunk of her heart attached to it. She felt dizzy with vulnerability, but now was not the time to stop.

"I love you, Luke. I love you so much. I need you to know that. And even though things feel strained right now between us, even though I left to follow my dream, I love you. And I can see now that I have been building up a wall around my heart, but I didn't do it on purpose. And I'm tearing it down, even right now talking to you. I just, I can't think of life without you. Being here alone, half of my heart is missing, and I am so afraid that me being here is undoing all the beauty we created, undermining our future—"

"Whoa, whoa, whoa. Hey. Ashley. It's okay. It's okay."

"I hope I'm not too late." She waited a moment, noticing that she wanted him to rush in and say she wasn't too late. When he didn't, she leaned into the uncomfortableness of that and forced her heart to stay open. "I miss you, Luke."

The silence on the other end of the phone lasted too many heartbeats. Ashley felt herself bracing against the worst.

Luke took a deep breath, then whispered, "I miss you more."

Ashley almost laughed, though it sounded more like a gurgle than a giggle. Her relief at those four words had her on the edge of tears.

"I even miss the way you slurp your coffee," he said.

"I do *not* slurp coffee."

Luke made slurping sounds into the phone that actually did sound vaguely familiar.

"I do *not* sound like that." She paused. "Do I?"

Luke just laughed. "I miss the smell of your shampoo on my pillow."

A high, giddy sigh escaped her.

"I miss how you steal the covers, so I have to snuggle up to your soft body to get warm again."

"I don't st—" she began. "Actually, I do, huh."

"Yeah. You do. And I miss your little snores."

"I snore?"

"Just little, um, snarls of air, really."

"What?"

"And I miss your hands." His voice was shaded with layered meanings. "I miss what you do with your hands."

Ashley felt the sharp pang of arousal tug in her core. Luke's voice played her desire like fingers pulling on harp strings. Her longing to connect with him blossomed into a full-body ache, as if fiery petals were unfurling in her bloodstream. She closed her eyes and easily imagined his large frame solid against her, his full lips crushing hers, the erotic melding of flesh and breath.

No one is here, she thought. *We could—* "Luke," she rasped, her voice notched with need. "Let me tell you what I want to do to you with my hands. I want to—"

"Ashley," he interrupted, the teasing and warmth gone, his voice like cold water on her passion.

"Yes?"

"I...I can't do that right now."

"You can't—" she echoed, twin currents of excitement and disappointment eddied through her. "Oh. Okay."

You can't do that right now? Why not?

And all the courage she'd had when she began the call fell away like dry petals, one petal after another, until all that was left of her was a bare stem.

"I think I should go."

"Oh. Okay?" *What is happening? How did we go from laughing to lost in three seconds?* "Luke, is something wrong?"

Duh. Something *is wrong.*

"I just—I'm sorry, Ashley. Can we talk tomorrow?"

"Sure?"

"Great. Let's talk tomorrow."

"Bye?" She felt the question in her farewell slur through her, a gray, damp fog that extinguished all the joy and desire she'd felt just moments ago.

He'd never said I love you back.

She wilted. And just like that, her bare stem was gone, too.

———

Ashley's feet and legs throbbed with exhaustion. She, like the other dancers in the *Festividad Virgen de Natividad*, had been dancing for hours. Thank heavens they'd been training for a month, or she wouldn't still be stepping and sashaying. This was nothing like doing salsa for a night—this was hours and hours of small, lilting, repetitive steps. Her full skirt lifted and swirled around her thighs each time she twisted her hips, she was sweating inside the bright red top, and her arms strained as she held and twisted the colorful garland above her head.

"Give your pain to the Virgin," Mayua had said to all the dancers each time they had trained. "It is your offering." And though she felt in some ways an outsider to the religion, she felt very much a part of the community as they danced together. In the last five weeks, she'd come to love the people of this mountain town. And tired as she was, the smile on her face was real.

A young boy, maybe four years old, was running through the dancers, laughing and twirling, and Ashley marveled at how at home she felt here in this community, her feet moving to the pounding of the drums, her thoughts weaving like the notes of the flute.

But ironically, it was almost as if noticing how grounded she felt in this moment led her to remembering how uneasy she'd been the last two weeks. She'd had almost no interaction with Luke, in fact, none in the last three days. He'd gone from intermittent texting to no response at all. Somehow, her radical vulnerability had backfired, and now those protective walls around her heart were higher than ever.

So much for absence makes the heart grow fonder.

Of course, she was worried something had happened to him. She'd looked on Savannah's Facebook page for any hints of what might be happening. Nothing.

She stumbled, her ankle twisting slightly—not enough to stop dancing, just enough to make her wince. From across the circle of dancers, Mayua caught her eye. The smile on his face was so artless, so real—infused with joy and gratitude, an ecstasy that comes with complete surrender to the moment. Had she ever felt such a sense of belonging as he seemed to feel right now? Had she ever felt such certainty that she was in the right place at the right time with the right people and that all was right with the world? The ache for Luke that had begun as a seed she'd tried to shut away in a box now sprouted and grew in her like an enchanted vine spurred on by the music—it wrapped itself around her with terrible speed, shocking her with its spiraling strength.

And suddenly, it was as if she were watching herself from outside of herself, dancing in the Sacred Valley ringed by the rugged Andes, surrounded by thousands of people in colorful outfits dancing and feasting and laughing and making music and celebrating their town, their people, their religion, and their life. She could see how her own honey-brown hair and fair skin marked her as a stranger here. A strangled gasp escaped her.

In seconds, she'd gone from profound happiness to feeling completely estranged from her own life. Did she belong here? Did she belong with Luke? Where was he? Why was he so distant? What was the right thing to do?

And with her heart breaking, her sense of self shattered, she danced, and she danced, and she danced.

———

"What?" Ashley said into the phone, straining to hear her sister's voice above the sounds of revelry and music still ringing through Huayllabamba after the dancing had ended. Feeling sideways, she'd come home, but the rest of the town was electric with celebration.

"I said, *I'm sorry*," Jewel shouted, sounding annoyed that Ashley couldn't hear her well.

"For what?"

"You don't know?" Disbelief laced Jewel's voice.

"Is Mom okay? Are you okay?"

"Mom's fine. I'm fine." A loud cheer from next door ripped through the silence as Jewel hesitated. "Has Luke called you?"

Ashley felt her heart become stone in her chest and drop into her gut.

"He hasn't. Not in days."

And he got off the phone so abruptly. And now he hasn't even returned texts. And why do you *know what's happening with Luke?*

"I know you're going to be angry, and I didn't want to tell you—"

"Tell me *what*, Jewel?" Ashley could hear in the ensuing silence that her sister was trying to choose her words carefully, not something Jewel often did.

"I didn't mean to fall in love with him. I mean—"

"What?"

"He isn't my usual type, and I—"

Luke! What? Luke! With Jewel? With her sister? No *wonder* Luke hadn't called her. "So, this is why you were so secretive every time I asked you if I could meet your new man." Bitterness clawed through her voice.

"It is a little delicate, right, but we belong to each other."

"I. Can't. Believe. You."

"Well, you're always telling me to find someone more responsible, and I'd say an oilman is—"

"Jewel!" Ashley felt such anger coursing through her she couldn't even form a word on her lips.

How dare you? How dare *you?*

"And I know it's wrong that he's married, but—"

"Married?"

"Aaaactually, he's going to leave his wife. We're in *love*, Ashley, and I know that this must be hard for you, but I hope you will find a way to be happy for me and—"

Luke is married?

"—Jimmy. We're in love, and there is only beauty in love. Our love."

"Jimmy? You mean *James*? Luke's *dad*? The person you've been calling J.J.?" Ashley's brain felt as if its neurons had turned to oatmeal.

"Yeah, who did you think I was—oh, oh, that's rich. You thought I was talking about *Luke*?" Jewel laughed. She had the audacity to *laugh*.

"It's not funny." She was trying to remember everything Jewel had told her about her new boyfriend. He was responsible. Generous. Older. *Fuck.* She'd never called the number Jewel had given her.

"It's pretty funny! Luke is sooooo not my type," Jewel hooted.

"And James is?"

Jewel's voice instantly softened. "He is. He *is*, Ashley. We're going to get married."

"You're *what*?" Ashley tried to imagine how her sister would have met the elder Dalton. "How did you even—" She paused as it dawned on her.

"At the party you invited me to, the one at Jimmy's house."

"Jewel! It was his fortieth-*anniversary* party."

Where he groped me in his study and said the most disgusting, lewd things.

"Yeah, some anniversary. Margaret was drunk, as usual, and she went to bed, and you and Luke *left*, and Jimmy and I, well, we—"

"Don't tell me. Don't tell me. I don't want to know what you—"

"We talked. We sat in his study and talked after everyone else had left. And we have such a good connection, Ashley, and, well, he needs me."

"For sex?" Ashley's voice came out strident.

"He sure as hell hasn't had sex with his *wife* for twenty-six years. Twenty-six *years*. Ever since the accident—yeah, he told me about that—ever since then, she's blamed him for what happened and treated him like shit. Their marriage is dead."

"But Jewel—"

"What, did you think he and his wife were *happy*? That's what Luke told you, right? They've been putting on a show for Luke and Elaine and Corinna for *years*. I am *not* the first affair Jimmy's had. There've been many. But I'll be the last. He loves me enough to leave that drunk. He's ready to be happy."

That man is a slime bag. "Are you crazy?"

"Crazy in love. Why are you defending Margaret? Can't you be happy for me?"

"Jewel! Are you thinking about anyone besides yourself? This isn't just about Margaret. This is about your integrity. This is about Luke and Elaine and their family. Did you think about how this might affect my relationship with Luke?"

"You're kidding. You think *I* might hurt your relationship with Luke? I think you did that all by yourself."

"What do you—"

"You're the one who left him. Jimmy told me Luke has been angry and argumentative, and then when Jimmy pressed him,

Luke said it was nothing, but Jimmy knows his son, and Ashley, the way I see it, you *abandoned* him. He loved you, and you *left. You're* the crazy one."

"I don't..." Ashley desperately wanted to make an excuse for herself, but she knew that the truth was that the way she'd left for Peru had really hurt him. And as much as he said he wanted to forgive her and make it work, well, it was hard to resuscitate a relationship long distance.

Especially if your sister and your lover's dad are screwing.

Ashley's stomach hurt. "It's not like I was leaving him forever."

"I think your timing sucked. He was in a pretty fragile state. Anyway, I thought you would want to know, and I am sorry to tell you this. Jimmy says Luke's spending time with Savannah again."

"Oh." Ashley's voice was small. She remembered seeing the pictures of the two of them on Facebook and inwardly crumpled.

Jewel's voice softened. "Look. I don't know what that means, Ash. Maybe he's just turning to her for friendship?"

Ashley said nothing. She couldn't. She felt her stomach cramp and bile rise in her throat.

"Look, I knew this was going to be hard. But mostly, I just wanted to let you know. Jimmy and I are hoping you'll be happy for us."

Ashley tried hard to steer herself away from her own heartache to speak to her sister's situation. Her big sister instincts kicked in hard. "Jewel."

Do I tell her about the incident at the party? What else could she say?

"He's got to be at least, what, thirty years older than you?"

"So?"

"So don't you think it's just a little too father figure-ish?" A sharp edge returned to Jewel's voice. "Don't you lecture me about acting out because of our dad. Age is irrelevant. This is *love*."

"But—"

"If anything, *you* are the one who's acting out, leaving the man you supposedly love to go have your own experience—"

"Jewel!" Ashley felt as if she'd been punched in the gut.

There was a long pause on the other side. "Truth hurts, huh?"

Ashley was quiet for a moment. "So why are you telling me about you and James now? Why didn't you tell me before?"

"Well, we had planned to tell everyone after he put a ring on my finger—"

"That man is *never* putting a ring on your finger."

"You are so wrong."

No, you *are so wrong.* "Does Margaret know?"

"Yeah. Luke told her. Surprise, surprise, she went and got drunk."

"So, Luke knows?"

"Yeaaah. He walked right in on us while we were in the middle of—"

Ashley interrupted, "I don't want to know."

"Anyway, Lukey didn't take it very well."

"Don't call him that."

"Oh-kay."

"Does Mom know?"

"She knows I'm really happy. Jimmy's buying a condo for us and—"

"Does. Mom. Know."

"She doesn't know who it is."

"Doesn't the fact that you're embarrassed about telling people who he is set off any alarms for you?"

"*That's* why I'm telling you now. So that it *isn't* a secret anymore. Anyway, I'm a little surprised Luke didn't call to tell you. I know he went to his cabin in Austin, but he still has cell service."

"Luke has a cabin in Austin?"

"I think, sis, there's maybe a lot you don't know about Luke."

~

Fifteen. Sixteen. Seventeen. Ashley was counting the cracks in the adobe wall of her bedroom. *Eighteen. Nineteen.*

What am I doing here? Why is everything such a mess? How do I fix this?

The sound of a drum drove its resonant rhythm through this never-ending night festival, and Ashley switched to counting drumbeats.

One. Two. Three. Four. Laughter erupted on the street as drunken revelers stumbled, their shoes scuffing the cobblestones.

I've got to reach Luke. I've got to figure out how to make things right.

She had tried, of course, to call him right away. The call had gone straight to voicemail: *Hi, you've reached Luke Dalton. Please leave a message.* Pathetic as she was, she almost called it again just to hear his voice on the recording. In the end, she'd hung up without leaving a message, but she'd texted him.

Ashley: Need to talk. Please. I know about Jewel and your dad

There was so much more she had wanted to say. Like, *I hate how I messed things up between us.* Like, *Please tell me you'll give me another second chance.* Like, *Is it true you're back with Savannah?* Like, *I love you.*

Ashley groaned. She had too much anxiety to continue lying on the bed. *How can I calm myself down?* She turned on the lamp beside her bed and picked up the metal singing bowl Luke had given her that she kept on her bedside table. It was sitting beside the silver puma that Chaska had given her. She held the trinket in her hand for a moment. "Power and strength," she whispered, then set the puma back on the table.

Ashley sat on the floor in the middle of her room and tried to rim the bowl with the wooden baton the way Luke had taught her, but all she could produce was a scratchy sound. After almost twenty circlings, she kept waiting for the melodic tone. It never came.

Well, this isn't helping. She set the baton down in frustration. *Are you really going to give up so quickly?*

Yes.

She huffed. *No.*

She tried rimming the bowl with the baton again. *One. Two. Three.* After counting to twenty, she realized she'd tightened all her muscles and stopped breathing because she was so intent on making the bowl sing. But it didn't sing. She lifted her arm to hurl the baton against the wall. And set the baton down.

Okay. Something else.

She tried crossing her legs, closing her eyes, and focusing on the sound of her breath. Instead, she heard a cruel inner voice: *You are the one who is always talking about how you were abandoned, but then you went and did the same thing to Luke.*

"I did *not* abandon him," she said out loud, her fists clenching in her lap.

The silence around her said nothing.

She slumped. "Okay. I kinda did. I chose to leave him without talking to him about it first."

And sitting there with her eyes closed, she felt rage kindle in her—a hot fury for her father.

It is your *fault I have such a terrible time knowing how to have a healthy relationship with men. It is* your *fault I'm so afraid of being vulnerable. It is* your *fault that I am not with Luke and Jewel is with Jimmy. It is* your *fault, your* fault, *your* fault.

She opened her eyes and uncrossed her legs. Some meditation. Her exhale was heavy with frustration. "*This* is not working." She let out a huge, rattled breath and fairly stomped back to her bed, even more agitated than she'd been before.

"Hello, Mr. Aurelius," she said, pulling the *Meditations* book out from underneath her pillow. Since she was a little girl, that was her favorite place for keeping whatever book she was reading. "I guess it's up to you now, Marcus. Because everything else has failed."

She flopped onto the bed, picked up the book, and broke it open to a random page. She scanned it until she focused on a few lines from the old Roman general. "It's silly to try to escape other people's faults. They are inescapable. Just try to escape your own."

"Escape my own faults, huh?" She rolled her eyes.

She heard something Tica used to say to her when she was angry. *Can you meet the anger?* When she was a girl, she'd imagined what that meeting with "the anger" might look like in a very literal way. Anger was a pacing tiger. *Can you meet it?* And she would picture herself walking toward it. And slowly, the tiger, as if all it needed was for her to face it, would disappear.

She tried it now, tried to move toward the anger instead of holding it at bay. In her mind, she imagined going toe to toe with the powerful feline, her heart pounding, jaw clenched. *I am so angry,* she thought, conjuring her father's desertion, her sister's behavior, her uncle who'd tried to take advantage of her when there was no father in the house to protect her, her mother working her hands till they cracked because she was the sole source of income. She bristled with rage, her skin hot, her throat tight, her chest heaving.

And what's under that feeling of anger?

Ashley didn't know whose voice was asking that question. Her own?

She stood in that anger for a long time before she recognized what was beneath it. Sadness. A big ocean of sadness met her.

Decades of sadness. Wave after wave of sadness. Ashley floated for a time on the rollers of sorrow, felt herself drifting through memories of fatherless Father's Days, picturing the empty chair where her father hadn't sat at the kitchen table, the empty bleacher where he hadn't attended her college graduation, the letters she'd written to him in her diary, the picture on the wall in her apartment in Houston of some strange man holding the hand of some strange little girl.

And what's under that sadness? Ashley imagined her mother telling stories at that same kitchen table where her father hadn't been. Her mother at the graduation, proud tears gathering in her eyes. Her mother tucking her into bed. Her mother on Christmas morning, smiling at the picture Ashley had drawn of her and Jewel and their mother as if it were a treasure. Gratitude flooded her like spring perfume, like sunshine, like radiant heat.

And what's under that gratitude? Ashley felt herself breathing, felt an ease in her body, a pleasant exhaustion, as if she had climbed a peak and was now looking out at the world below. Clarity.

It's silly to try to escape other people's faults. Just try to escape your own.

She may not be able to do anything in this moment about her and Luke. But there was one man she could do something about.

———

Several days had gone by, and still no word from Luke. She had texted him every day. Short texts. No response.

Ashley was walking away from the school after teaching. She felt like a walking wound. Surely everyone could tell. Sure, she still opened every class with a joke—a ritual she'd started when she did her student teaching over ten years ago. But her heart was a raw and throbbing pulp in her chest, and she could tell she was, well, dull with the students. Not shiny. Not bright. It didn't help that the bread rolls the government had sent to give the kids were moldy today. Many of the kids in this region were poor and depended on the food subsidy. It had broken her heart when she'd handed the rolls out and the kids had unwrapped the plastic only to find green-spotted bread. Some of them had eaten it anyway.

She would pay Mayua to make extra rolls she could bring for the kids tomorrow. She didn't care how much it cost.

A wan smile found her face as she remembered the way Mayua's daughter had come up to hug her after Ashley had dismissed class today. *Thank you, Mayu,* she'd said as she stood rather awkwardly in the embrace. The girl had held on to her for a long time, held her until Ashley felt herself soften. Then Mayu had looked up shyly, as if there was something she'd wanted to say, but she left without a word. Poor Mayu. No mother. Ashley had some idea of how hard that loss might be.

Instead of walking straight toward her room at Chaska's, Ashley turned right to walk to the river. There were lots of flies and mosquitoes there, and she usually avoided it. Not today.

When she arrived at the banks, Ashley stared at the wide muddy river below and followed a bottle with her eyes as it bobbed its way downstream.

She'd felt into her sadness around her father, and over the last few days, she had written him a letter about her anger, her sense of betrayal, her enduring sadness. She'd been shaken when these words arrived on their own: *I forgive you.* Those three words had shocked her. They'd arrived so naturally, the way the sun arrives in the morning, first just as a suggestion of light and then startlingly bright, pushing away the darkness. Ashley now felt that glow of forgiveness inside her body, an inexplicable lightness. All these years, she hadn't been able to force forgiveness to happen, but then, when it did come, almost of its own accord, there was no stopping it. It was mysterious and utterly inexplicable. And yet so real.

She laughed to herself now, reminding herself again of her favorite analogy for framing time: *Even uranium has a half-life—albeit four and a half billion years.*

With that as comparison, how much sooner forgiveness had come. She'd been holding on to anger about her disappeared father long enough, to the point where it was hurting her relationships now. For this moment, she had such clarity about it. Could it last?

She had folded the letter into a small paper boat, her scrawlings like blue decorations on the boat's sides. She pulled it from her bag and stared at the tiny vessel in her hand. It looked so small. The river looked so vast.

"I forgive you, Dad." And she threw the paper boat into the waves.

CHAPTER 15

"DID YOU KNOW?" LUKE asked, his voice dry, almost formal, but his speech was slightly slurred. Ashley was pretty sure he had been drinking.

"No."

"Bullshit." An acid tone came through the phone, a more bitter version of Luke than Ashley had ever heard before. This was *not* how she'd imagined this conversation would go. A full week had gone by since Jewel had called her, and Ashley had somehow managed to convince herself that once she and Luke talked, their love would find a way forward. At the moment, bitterness presented an impassable wall.

"Luke," Ashley blurted. "How could you think I would know something like your father and my sister were having an affair and not tell you?"

"You didn't exactly tell me about Peru right away, did you?"

The words stung. Because she hadn't.

"You have to believe me."

"No. I don't. I don't have to believe you. In fact, I don't believe much right now. I found out, Ashley, that most of my life has been a lie. Everything I thought I knew about my family—"

"*We're* not a lie."

A tortured laugh. "And you're still lying to me. You had to know. You and Jewel are so close. Of course she'd tell you. Your sister broke up my family. And you did nothing to stop it."

"No—"

"I have done *everything* I could, Ashley, *everything* to make my parents happy, the way they were before Jimmy died. I went into oil instead of exploring *my* interests. I squashed my own *dreams*. I'd go to football games with my father. I *hate* football. I'd drink root beer floats with my mother. I *hate* root beer floats. But I have tried to be like two sons for them. I tried to make things whole again."

"Luke—"

"Don't you see, even *I* was a lie. My whole life has been a lie, but I did it so my parents could be happy. And after all these years, your sister destroyed our family. She took that away from me."

Ashley was torn between compassion for Luke and a need to defend her sister. "This is not just Jewel's fault."

Your dad is an immoral sleazebag who tried to put his hand up my dress that night we went to your parents' anniversary party, and I didn't have the heart to tell you. He'll try to fuck anything in a dress.

"You're right. It's your fault, too. You did nothing to stop your sister. You didn't tell me about it so I could stop it. And on top of it all, *you* were the one who helped me let my guard down, Ashley. Helped me get stronger. Made me believe I deserve love in a way I never felt before. With my parents, I always thought I needed to be more than myself to deserve their love. But with you, with you I thought maybe I was enough, that I could be my authentic self. That I didn't need to fake it."

"You *are* enough."

"But I wasn't, was I?" Self-loathing curled into his voice. "You left. I understand why. You needed what you needed. I get it. I do. But—"

"You deserve love, Luke," she whispered, but Luke continued, perhaps not hearing her.

"I've been so afraid since the accident that I might inadvertently hurt the people I love. I've done everything to keep that from happening. And now I'm the one who's broken because the people I love most are hurting *me*."

"Let me help."

"You are exactly the person who cannot help me right now. I can't do it anymore, Ashley. I tried, I wanted to believe in us, but the truth is I was too broken when you left to know how to stay in our relationship. It's been hard, Ashley. And now this."

No. Ashley thought the word, but nothing came to her lips.

"Tell your sister to find some other man to fuck. That would help. The damage is done, but I don't want to see her with my father." His volume lowered to a whisper. "And I don't want any reminders of you."

And he was gone.

———

"Ah, *La Professorita*, it would seem you are in desperate need of a pastry." Mayua's Spanish was warm and tender.

"*Allillanchu, turay*."*

"Ah, you hear that?" Mayua held up a pastry and spoke directly to it. "She says the right words, but they do not meet her eyes. Her eyes have lost their sparkle. Come, pastry, you have much work to do." He held it to her and smiled. "You are lucky, sister. Today I have made special pastries that bring sparkle again to the eyes of those who are mourning."

---

* Hello, brother.

Ashley raised an eyebrow.

"Do you think I do not notice everything? That is a baker's job—not to make bread and pastries, no, but to make the food the people *need*. And this, sister, is what you need."

Ashley took the plate. Truly, since her talk with Luke, she had hardly had an appetite. But this fresh-baked confection smelled of cinnamon and nuts and had a fan of thinly sliced apples atop it. For the first time in a week and a half, she felt her mouth salivate.

"*Professorita*, looking at the pastry is not enough. It can only do its work if you *eat* it."

Ashley fought a smirk. She bit in, tasted the soft, delicious flakiness, and her eyes closed in pleasure. A small moan of appreciation escaped her lips. "Oh, it's good."

When she opened her eyes, Mayua was staring intently at her face from behind the counter. He gave a small nod. "Ah, already, it's working. Just a small sparkle, but I see it begins."

"*Sulpayki*,"* she said, smiling her first real smile in weeks, it seemed. She set the pastry down.

Mayua gave a small, humble shrug and said in a faraway voice, "*Llakita mallispaqa, manañam mikuytaqa munanichu.*"

"What does it mean?"

"After tasting sadness, I am no longer hungry."

Ashley nodded.

"You do not need to tell me why you are so sad, *bonita*, but I understand sorrow. Perhaps what you need is a picnic, to go sit on the earth beneath the Apus and feel the sun on your face. This weekend, please join me and Mayu, and we will go to my brother's land. I will close the bakery for a few hours that day. Please say yes."

---

* Thank you

Ashley hadn't wanted to do anything but work at the school and sit in her small room at Chaska's. She'd declined invitations from people to feed her and had been taking the meals Chaska prepared for her in her room. She'd barely been keeping up with the emails about STEAMEA meetings. Hadn't reached out to any of her friends back in Houston. She was living a husk of a life. Mayua's invitation sounded like a chance to be alive again.

He raised an eyebrow. "You must rescue me, sister. I must get out of this bakery. Otherwise, I start talking to pastries."

Ashley laughed. "Yes. I'll go. It sounds lovely."

As it was, Mayu did not join them for the picnic. "She said she did not want to be a *third wheel*," Mayua said in Spanish, scrunching his face. "This *tercera rueda* is some phrase you have taught her to say? Something you say in English?"

Ashley laughed. In Mayu's English class, Ashley had been doing a unit on idioms.

"Perhaps this unlucky wheel is what we call here the *violinista*, the one who is playing the violin while the other two are…" His voice trailed off.

Are what? What are we doing?

In actuality, they were walking on a well-worn trail through the brush, and Ashley was glad Mayua was in front of her so he couldn't see the confusion that was surely written on her face. She stared at his strong back and shoulders as they flexed beneath the blue linen of his shirt. He carried their picnic in a colorful Peruvian *manta* he'd tied around his neck and shoulder.

Is this a date?

Mayua pointed to the hacienda ahead. "We are almost there, *Professora*."

When they reached his brother's house, Ashley noted the shift in Mayua. He was almost formal in the way he introduced her to the family. Mayua's niece and nephew were too young to go to school, but he told them that Ashley was a teacher and that they would be very lucky someday if they had a teacher as good as she was. "You must give her great respect," he said, and he showed them how to shake her hand.

They left the small family in their yard, and Mayua led her to a place on the land where llamas with bright yellow and blue tassels affixed to their ears were grazing. The wind pulled through her hair like fingers, but it was a warm breeze, and she didn't mind it.

Mayua pulled a small flask from the manta and spilled *pisco* on the ground. "When we honor Pachamama, the land rewards us abundantly." He pulled out three coca leaves, fanned them, blessed them, blew on them, and offered them to the mountain spirits. Then he spread the *manta* on the ground and gestured for Ashley to sit. He sat beside her, then produced two of her favorite rolls, *pan huaro*, a small bit of butter, and a knife. He let her serve herself, and then he did the same and took a big bite of bread. While chewing, he looked across the valley with great satisfaction before turning his face toward her. He seemed almost serious. His gaze was unreadable.

"It is beautiful here, yes, Ashley?"

It was the first time he had ever said her name—even to his brother and sister-in-law, he'd introduced her as *La Professora*. Her name sounded like music in his mouth.

"It *is* beautiful," she agreed.

"And so are—" He halted. Ashley felt a shadow cross her, but when she turned to see what it was, she realized the woman casting it was too far away for her really to feel the shadow.

"Ah, *La Layq'a*, do you care to join us?" Though Mayua's voice was friendly, his body stiffened.

It was Chaska, wearing a black Peruvian hat and holding a tall wooden staff. She was glaring at Ashley and Mayua as if her eyes were blades and she was searing them, spearing them, damning them.

"*Allianchu*, Chaska," Ashley called out, but the woman said nothing and continued to stare at her with an expression so malicious Ashley felt a shiver run through her whole body, and the hairs on her arms stood at attention. Ashley wanted to turn away from her gaze but found it impossible, as if she were a butterfly being pinned on a wall. At last, Chaska turned and walked away.

"That is her land she is walking on," Mayua said, as if explaining to himself why Chaska had appeared. He looked at Ashley, his obsidian eyes squinting with concern. "There might be news around town tomorrow, sister. People do love to talk. I am sorry if it will negatively affect you. Me, I will get slapped on the back. But you—"

"—will be fine. I will be fine. But Chaska seemed very unhappy."

"That was the evil eye. If it were *only* the evil eye, I could handle it." He pointed to the band on his hat woven in black and white diamonds. "This design reflects the bad energy away. But with Chaska, there is so much more."

Ashley's scientific brain rejected the threat, but her body shuddered anyway. "That can't be real."

"Sometimes, adults joke about it when a child has a crying jag or a fever or can't stop yawning. They say some stranger must have given their child the evil eye. But this, this is no joke." He shook his head.

"What was it you called her? *La Layq'a*. What does that mean?" It had sounded strangely familiar, but she couldn't place it.

"The witch, sister. *La Bruja*." His voice was grave. "Chaska is a powerful witch."

———

"I cannot believe I am doing this," Ashley muttered.

Ashley had returned to Chaska's home, and upon discovering that her hostess was not here, she had set out to do what Mayua had told her to do.

"You must select one of her guinea pigs in her yard," he'd instructed as they walked back to town. "Choose the whitest one. And you must blow on it three times and then rub it all over your body."

At first, she had laughed, thinking this was one of Mayua's jokes, but his face was terribly serious.

"No, sister. Do not laugh. I would not joke about this. If it were not Chaska herself who had given us the evil eye, then I would ask you to go to *her* and have her perform the cleansing ritual on you. She knows the old spells, the old ways that most people in our town have forgotten. And she would sacrifice the guinea pig once she had finished rubbing it on you and study its entrails for hints of how your soul has been separated from your body."

Study its entrails?

"Mayua, please. I'll be fine."

Mayua had then held her arm to make her stop walking and forced her to look him in the eye. "I know you are not from here. I know you believe in science. I am not saying you are wrong to do so. But we are a very old culture. There is much I do not understand but I know is true. And I know you are in danger. Please. Promise me. Promise me you will rub the guinea pig on all parts of your body. Your head. Your chest. Your front. Your back."

"But I am not going to kill it."

"I assumed you would not. And we will have to hope that the cleansing will be enough without the sacrifice."

The whole walk back, he had cut small bits of cactus off with his knife and then flung them behind them into the air. When she'd asked what he was doing, he explained that his father had told him that witches' heads sometimes separated from their bodies to follow those they might hex and that you could stop them by throwing cactus spines behind you to catch in their hair.

And so here she was, more than a little discombobulated, clutching a small, mostly white guinea pig in her hand, and it was squealing and squeaking as she rubbed it in her hair, on her face, on her arms.

"I'm sorry, little guy," she apologized, looking him in the face, remembering she was supposed to blow on him. "This is awkward for me, too."

What was becoming of Ashley the scientist? How was it she had let herself promise to rub a coarse-haired feisty rodent all over her? "Touch as much skin as possible," Mayua had insisted. Certainly, she didn't believe this was helping. She was just doing this because she had promised.

She finished the cleansing and let the traumatized *cuy* run loose around the outdoor kitchen again, looking over her shoulder to make sure no one had seen her and that Chaska hadn't returned.

"This is nuts."

She went up to her room and lost herself for hours reading a romance book she had loaded onto her phone before leaving Houston. Somehow, vampire romance seemed normal and comforting compared to the weirdness of the day. As the sun was going down, she rolled over to turn on the light and noticed the silver puma was missing from her bedside table.

She looked on the floor in case she had inadvertently knocked it off, but she knew she wouldn't find it. She knew Chaska had entered her room and taken the very trinket she'd given Ashley.

And what is she doing with it now?

Visions of voodoo movies she had watched as a teenager slipped into her thoughts unbidden, and Ashley felt her skin prickle.

"Stop it," she said aloud to herself. "Pull yourself together. You are fine, Ashley. Everything is fine."

If she had been home in Houston, she would have walked to her drawer and pulled out her gun so she could feel safe, but this present insecurity was very different from being threatened by an intruder. She could barely understand the nature of this threat. She remembered again Chaska's eyes, how they had stared so intently, how her whole face had contorted. She'd felt shriveled inside somehow.

Outside her window, the wind was blowing hard through the town as if it were as unsettled as she was. Ashley tried to hear if Chaska had entered the house and was even now below her, but she found herself listening more to her fear than to reality.

Why was Chaska so angry? Ashley felt certain it had to do with her and Mayua spending time together. Was she jealous? It seemed obvious. But Chaska had nothing to be jealous of. Ashley felt nothing but friendship for the baker.

"So, you *talk* to her about it," Ashley said out loud. "You talk to her like a *rational* human being."

A rational human being who rubbed a guinea pig all over her body and is talking to herself in a windstorm, wishing she had a gun to fight the curse of the evil eye.

Ashley groaned and flopped back on her bed.

You talk about it.

That's what she had *not* done with Luke, and that's why she was in this mess now. She thought of Luke and the small wooden elephant and how from the beginning, he'd tried to convince her to talk with him openly about things that bothered her, things that challenged her, things that were obstacles in their relationship.

Will I learn? Will I ever figure out how to talk instead of shutting down?

That was when she realized that all the drama of the day had for some hours pushed Luke out of her mind. Before today, the terrible ache she felt from the loss of him had not subsided for more than ten minutes at a time. And now that she remembered again how much it hurt to be out of his life for good, it hit her doubly hard. She would leave this small Peruvian town eventually, and all this drama would go away. But what did she have to return to? Not her sister. Not Luke. Only her mother. And Emilia. The pain of loss overtook her like a massive mudslide.

It was hours before she found her way into broken dreams.

———

"It's so good to hear your voice, Ashling," said her mom. "Tell me everything."

Her mother was such a good listener. Ashley marveled again at the gratitude she felt for this powerful woman who had raised her. She had never once doubted that she was completely valued and loved.

Ashley had climbed up to Chaska's roof for cell service and was delighted to find it worked better up here than in the corner of the courtyard. Up here, she felt less worried about being overheard. As for that, she'd barely seen Chaska since the evil eye incident. And though Ashley had been determined to speak with Chaska, it seemed her landlord was equally determined *not* to speak with her. For the last few days, Chaska had been leaving Ashley's food out, then disappearing.

Some part of Ashley worried that Chaska had poisoned or put a spell on the food.

She wouldn't do that, right?

But hunger and reason won out, and she'd simply taken the meals up to her room to eat them.

"Well, living in Huayllabamba is certainly not what I was expecting."

Her mother laughed. "And thank heavens for that. The world is so much grander than we can imagine. Even at the diner where I worked, I never knew what to expect."

Ashley told her all about the school and the kids and how much they loved the *realia* she had brought—menus, museum brochures, maps, and all kinds of texts from her life in Houston. How strange these paper bits seemed here—so foreign. When she'd passed out the ticket stubs she'd collected when she and Luke had gone to *Grease*, she'd almost wept.

Realizing a couple of weeks had gone by since they'd talked, she updated her mom about her experience visiting Machu Picchu and how humbling it was to see the great terraced citadel. She talked about making friends with the other teachers and the spicy green sauce she now craved and the geraniums that bloomed all around town. As she spoke, she realized although some things had been quite difficult here, her time in Huayllabamba had also been quite wonderful. She felt deeply connected with the people in this town and loved the way their customs and beliefs continually surprised and pushed her to reconsider what she thought she knew about the world. It was as if she were being recalibrated.

In fact, over the past seven weeks, she had transformed in surprising ways—she was less rule-driven, less cut-and-dried, more open to spontaneity and wonder. And though she was still intent on saving the environment through activism, that commitment was now fueled by a more intimate, authentic relationship with the land itself. All the talk of Pachamama and mountain spirits and trees that connected heaven, earth, and the underworld had gotten past her gates of logic and seeded a different kind of love and respect for the planet—a love and respect that flowed both ways. It was a real relationship with the earth, a sacred bond.

"How are things going with Luke?"

"I don't think we're together anymore."

"But *maybe* you are?"

Ashley wasn't about to open the whole door on the Jewel and James thing. That was not her story to tell. "I went to Peru, Mom. It's hard to have a relationship when he's there and I'm here."

"People do that all the time, darling."

"Apparently, *we* can't. You see, I…I didn't do a very good job including him in the decision. Just before I left, I broke us."

"Are you sure?"

"There's more to it than that, Mom, and I just don't want to talk about it."

"Ashling. That man loves you. And I have seen how he brings out the very best in you. Every man wants to believe he is the most important thing in his lover's life."

Ashley let her mom's words slip in. It was almost exactly what Luke had said. It wasn't so much her leaving that hurt him but that she didn't let him help her think through it, and that made him feel unimportant, unessential.

"You know he sent your mom flowers last week."

Ashley sat straight up. "He did what?"

"He sent me white lilies."

Really? "With a note?"

"It said he knew I must miss you very much."

Ashley was stunned.

"It's true, of course, I do. But I think it was a projection. I think *he* misses you very much."

"Huh." What on earth could Luke have been thinking? Was it just him feeling generous? Was he giving too others to make himself feel better? That was his pattern. But he'd said he didn't want anything that would remind him of her. Had he changed his mind? A thunderbolt of hope jolted through her. "I can't believe you didn't tell me last week that he sent you flowers."

"I guess, my love," her mother teased, "you should call your mother more often."

———

It had been a wonderful day at school. Was it because Ashley was charged with hope about Luke after her call with her mom that everything seemed more fun, more engaged, more alive? *We carry our hope with us until it becomes us.* That's what Rena had said. And Ashley could feel the truth of it in her body.

Now that the students were gone, she sat with her laptop to look at emails and found one from the new STEAMEA director. Seeing the other woman's name as executive director was still painful for her. *Speaking of hope…*Ashley still held out hope that when she returned to Houston, she'd be able to resume the directorship again. But even she had to admit the new woman was bringing professionalism and good energy to the program, and if she were honest, Ashley was grateful the online education program was thriving in her absence.

How did I ever think I could run it from a tiny town in Peru?

Getting STEAMEA launched was a full-time job. In fact, she realized that as painful as it had been to let her position go, she was grateful not to have that pressure back home so she could be more present with her work and the people here.

When she opened the email, she was surprised to see a photo of a note in Luke's handwriting. Reading it, she saw it was something he had left on the director's desk, saying he'd gotten a new donor. The dollar amount made her jaw drop. Below the image, the director had written a note praising Luke for his dedication to the program.

Amazing. He was still dedicated to the success of STEAMEA, even though she wasn't there. Of course, he was president of the board. His commitment to the nonprofit made her heart flutter. He really believed in the program. He hadn't just been doing it for her. And, she realized, it would seem he had pulled himself out of the drunken funk and was finding ways to move forward.

But he hasn't called you.

She took a deep breath and stared out the classroom window.

Something her mother said the night before came back to her. *Every man wants to believe he is the most important thing in his lover's life.* Maybe he needed her to reach out first. To show him he was important in her life. After their phone call, she'd stopped all communication. That's what he'd wanted, right? But maybe—

In a sadistic fit of self-doubt, she found herself going to Savannah's Facebook page to see if there were any clues about her and Luke's relationship being intimate again, as Jewel had suggested.

Birthday cake! said today's post with a photo of a three-layer chocolate cake.

What day is it? October seventh. *Luke's birthday.* How could she have forgotten? She prided herself on remembering dates. But since she'd arrived in Peru, she'd never been less in touch with the calendar. She'd never been *more* in touch with the rhythms of daily life and the season.

She scrolled down to see if Savannah's page had any other pictures of Savannah and Luke and found several of them in groups of people together, maybe all work related? Often, they were smiling side by side. There were no pictures of the two of them alone, but still, jealousy squeezed Ashley's gut until she tasted bile in the back of her throat.

Why are there so many pictures of them together?

Though Savannah was a compulsive poster, Ashley couldn't help but wonder if she posted pictures of her and Luke, knowing that Ashley would be stalking him through her.

And she'd be right.

Just send him a text.

She picked up her phone.

But what if he's with Savannah right now?

She set the phone down.

Then you should really send a text and ruin their little party.

She picked the phone up.

Don't be a jerk.

She set the phone down.

Wish him a happy birthday. Let him know you are thinking of him.

She picked the phone up.

Ashley: Happy birthday, Luke

She put the phone down. What else could she say?

Ashley: I hope each day is better than the next

She pressed Send.

There. That wasn't so hard, was it?

Exhaling deeply, she closed the laptop, stood up, and gathered her things. Her phone buzzed in her hand.

Luke: Talk tonight?

What? Electricity pulsed through her.

Ashley: Yes. Please

Luke: Call me when it works for you

Ashley: K

She squealed. Screamed, actually.

Another teacher came rushing in. " You Okay?"

"Yes!" Ashley cheered, lifting both arms in a gesture of victory, leaving a puzzled but happy look on her colleague's face.

Ashley continued to gather her things, this time with a little wiggle in her step as if dancing to music only she could hear. *Call me when it works for you?* That meant he didn't have other plans tonight for his birthday. At least not plans *he* had made.

Yes!

Every atom in her entered an excited state.

As if.

She laughed, imagining her electrons returning to their ground state and emitting photons so that, in her excitement, she would actually be emitting light.

You're going nuts, Ashley.

With her questionable pitch, she started to sing a favorite song from some years back by the Black Eyed Peas. "I Gotta Feeling—" And darned if she didn't almost skip out of the school, glowing.

———

Ashley brought a glass of *pisco* with her to the rooftop and poured a bit of it out onto the courtyard dirt three stories below. *You are hilarious*, she thought. Then she blew across the top of the cup in Luke's direction, took a sip, grimaced as the strong alcohol burned down her throat, and dialed Luke. He answered on the first ring.

"Hello," he said. She drank in his voice, so rich, so familiar, so Luke. *Like velvet and vetiver.* She could hear the smile inside his one-word greeting, and it did crazy things to her very neglected lady bits, causing an almost painful tingling.

"Hello," she said. Tiny butterflies fluttered through her bloodstream. "Happy birthday, Luke."

"Thank you. I've missed you, Ashley." The words melted her. She had no idea until he said them just how desperately she needed to hear them.

"I've missed you, Luke."

There was an awkward silence, and then at the same time, they both said, "I'm sorry."

And laughed. And lapsed into another awkward silence.

"I didn't know," Ashley said. "About your dad and Jewel. I'm just as horrified about it as you are."

Though maybe not for the same reasons.

"I believe you. I was just so angry, and I wanted someone else to blame. I didn't want to blame my father, though in the last few weeks, I've really had my eyes opened about who he is. I just never wanted to see it before. Now it's so obvious. And it was easy to blame you because I was hurting so much from missing you already, and maybe subconsciously, I thought blaming you might make everything easier to handle. But it didn't. It made everything worse. I'm sorry I didn't believe you."

"I'm sorry I ever gave you any reason to believe I would withhold the truth from you." The apology was so heartfelt that she felt an immediate opening in her chest when she said it.

"Thank you," he acknowledged.

"You've taught me a lot, Luke, about the importance of talking about difficult things. I'm grateful. In fact, I think I should get an elephant tattoo on my wrist." She exhaled deeply. "How's your mom?"

"Oh, she's devastated."

"I'm sorry."

"No, it's good. She's devastated enough to check into a rehab clinic and get the help she needs. It's a giant silver lining."

"Wow. And how are you?"

"Ashley, I'm—I'm doing okay. My birthday present to myself is to take better care of myself and fight an old demon."

"What do you mean?"

"This whole thing with my parents' divorce is helping me see how I have been a pleaser. And all that pleasing didn't help anything or anyone else. It didn't fix anything, even though I gave and gave and gave."

Wow. He'd really been doing some deep reflection. "You're an incredibly generous giver, Luke. It's true."

"I love giving. I don't think that's a problem per se. I think the part I need to work on is when I change who I am to be with other people. When I try too hard to be what I think they want me to be."

"That's a pretty big epiphany."

"I think the pleasing came up because I didn't feel worthy of love in and of myself. Ever since Jimmy died. I understand why I developed this way. And I also see now why it's so important that I break that pattern."

The breeze stiffened, and Ashley turned slightly to minimize the sound in the phone.

"It sounds windy there."

"It's often windy here."

"I thought it was just because it is *Wind*sday."

"Ohhhhh." She winced and laughed. Somehow, the pun fanned an ache in her—it reminded her of all the fun they'd had playing with words and making each other giggle.

"I do know it's Tuesday, by the way," he said.

"Of course you do, *week*-ling. Hey, I saw what you did for STEAMEA. Thank you."

"It is my great joy to support that program, Ashley. You came up with something the world needs, and it's thriving as we get ready to launch."

"Thanks to you, Mr. President."

"And thanks to you, Ms. Founder. The new director is great, but I want you to know that the board members are all hoping you will return to your old job in January if you want it."

A wild cocktail of relief, nervousness, and excitement intoxicated her.

"Ashley. I owe you a giant apology. I know I laid an enormous guilt trip on you about leaving to go follow your dream in Peru. And that was the pleaser in me who expected that same dysfunctional pleasing behavior from everyone else, too. Like you were supposed to make choices in your life just to please me. But I am very clear right now that you are going to Peru and following your dream was *absolutely* the most important thing for you to do, not just for you, but for us. If we had talked about it first, I am sure I would have eventually known to trust that."

He took a deep breath. "It wasn't that you were choosing Peru over me; you were just making a choice that ensured you wouldn't resent me later for not being able to go experience this thing you'd been looking forward to for your entire adult life. I'm so sorry I made it about me. Before you left, I convinced myself I could handle it, but once you were gone, I went crazy. I guess it took stepping away to get more perspective. It's so easy now to see how important it was for you to go there so that we don't end up like my parents—lying to each other about who we are and what we need."

Ashley struggled to find the right response.

We, she thought. *He said* we.

"Ashley? Are you still there?"

"I'm right here, Luke."

"I love you, Ashley. When you come home, I want to try again. I'm learning how to be a better partner for you by taking better care of myself. I was going to call it a third chance, but I hope that both you and I can give up on counting chances. I hope we can agree to give each other infinite chances."

Ashley didn't say anything. She couldn't. She was so overcome with relief and joy and possibility, such an onslaught of feelings that they all got stuck in her throat. Her whole body was humming with elation, about to explode.

Luke seemed uncertain about how to treat her silence. "I hope I'm not too late," he rasped. "I hope you haven't been swept off your feet by some handsome Peruvian man."

Her voice trembled as she forced out a love-laden whisper. "It's not too late, Luke." Her heart opened as big as the Sacred Valley she now sat in, even bigger than that. "No, it is not too late."

—⁓—

Ashley loved walking into the local Huayllabamba market. It wasn't large—only a dozen or so stalls in a courtyard with high concrete walls and an open roof. People were squatting or sitting on their bright-colored blankets with their wares spread out. There were spring vegetables such as onions and broccoli and lettuce, flowers in every color, plus baskets and hats and trinkets and textiles. She seldom bought anything, mostly she liked just to come here and look and listen to the older folks speaking in Quechua. She wished she could understand it. Mayua had told her that the language was so rich, so sweet, that to speak and listen to poetry in Quechua was like listening to the song of honey.

Today, Ashley was drawn to one of the booths that had trinkets of all kinds—clay figurines and wooden spoons and brightly painted bulls and cloth dolls and, something she hadn't seen before, a row of small brightly painted monkeys, each with a big wide mouth tilting up.

"New," said the vendor with a grin. "You like it?"

"How much?"

The price was more than she hoped, but Ashley knew the vendor had children in her class and knew their family had meager resources, so she didn't haggle. He gave her a grateful smile when she handed over the *sols*.

"That was too much," Mayua whispered in her ear, and she startled, not having noticed him before. "You are too kind."

She stepped back and beamed at him, delighted with her purchase, delighted to see him, delighted to be alive.

"*Professora*! Look at you. Your sparkle is back."

"I've been eating so many of your pastries," she teased.

Mayua beamed with pride. "If this is the effect, I should like to see you get very, very fat."

———

Ashley had to admit she was looking forward to the weekend for the first time in a long time. On the days without school, she'd felt a little lost here. But this week had been such an emotional roller coaster with her witch doctor landlord and the phone call with Luke she couldn't wait to go for a long walk on the hillsides around the town. Who cared if she got lost—a fear that had kept her from hiking alone before this. She'd find her way. Eventually.

Excited as she was for time to herself, she loved this last class of the day when the students had returned from their lunches at home to learn English. She loved teaching science here, too, of course, but there was something so playful about this particular class. Today, they were going to start off with food puns. The knock-knock joke format had turned out to be one of the students' favorite class openers. Obviously, her enthusiasm for the genre had influenced them. First, they'd do a few together, and then she'd give them each a knock-knock joke on a strip of paper. They'd circulate, tell the jokes, help each other figure them out, and talk about their favorites. Then on to grammar.

Ashley drew a serviceable picture of a turnip on a piece of paper and showed it to the class. "A turnip is a root vegetable, similar to *maca*. Got it?" They nodded, so she began. "Knock knock."

"Who's there," the class answered.

"Turnip."

"Turnip who?"

"*Turnip* the volume, it's my favorite song."

A few of the students groaned when they got it, and Ashley beamed, then rubbed her hands together with zealous enthusiasm.

"Let's try another. Knock knock."

"Who's there?"

"Figs."

"Figs who?"

"*Figs* the doorbell, it's not working."

Half of the students stared at her blankly, and Ashley explained what a doorbell was. Again, the room rumbled with low reluctant laughter.

"You love these, right? Okay, last one before I hand you your own '*tear*-able' puns." She laughed to herself, knowing none of her students understood she was making a joke about the ripped strips of paper she'd written the puns on. She loved cracking herself up. Dang, she was in a good mood. "Knock knock."

"Who's there?"

"Lettuce," she said.

"Lettuce who?" they chorused.

"*Lettuce* in because we came a long way to see you," said a voice from the doorway.

For a moment, time turned to amber. A delicious, dangerous shiver spread through her, as if she found herself standing at the edge of a beautiful precipice she hadn't known was there. Her heart beat wildly, and her palms tingled. *That voice.* It pierced her, an arrow through the chest that took away her breath. *Could it be?* Struggling to keep herself from squealing, trying desperately to tame the thrill now rising in her, Ashley turned to the doorway to see who had spoken, but her body knew. It knew instantly, though her eyes sought proof.

"Luke?" If she could move, she would have run to his arms, but her knees had nearly buckled, and her body was pinned to where she stood, stunned into stillness. She focused on staying upright. A bloom of heat flushed through her blood, and her brain grappled to take in the truth.

He is here! Luke is here!

The gates to joy swung open in her, and her whole body was shaking with surprise and delight. The moment stretched, and the classroom blurred until all she could see was Luke.

He stood in the open doorway, filling the space with his powerful frame, though a little leaner than she remembered him. His hair fell in dark curls around his square jaw, his cheekbones were pronounced, a feature that always fascinated her and caused flutters in her belly. His blue eyes, the color of Peruvian sky, now focused on her, and light danced in them as they drank her in. He was loving this moment, too, she could tell by the curve sliding up his lips and the confidence that exuded throughout the room, as if he knew he belonged wherever she was. Could he hear her heart pounding from across the room?

He took a half step in. "Knock knock," he said.

She raised an eyebrow and cocked her head in silent challenge. "Who's there?"

"Peas."

The whole class, well trained in knock-knocks, joined in. "Peas who?"

"*Peas* let me take you away for the weekend?" Ashley shook her head in disbelief as the whole class erupted in cheers and groans and chaos. Luke took another step into the room and pulled a big bouquet of red and white flowers from behind his back, holding them out toward her.

The world was swirling, and Ashley barely heard the whispers of the students about her in both Spanish and English. "So handsome." "Who is that?" "Is he a movie star?" "I think she likes him." Then they were all staring at her, waiting for her answer.

"Yes," she said breathily. "Yes, I'll go with you."

Luke set the flowers down on an empty wooden desk, flashed her a wolfish grin, and gave her a glance so hot it could melt the glaciers not far from where they stood. Then he quickly recomposed his expression, gave a small bow to the students, and said, "Sorry to interrupt your lesson." Then to Ashley, he purred innocently, "I'll just be waiting outside until you're done."

Ashley had no idea how she made it through the rest of class. She was floating, soaring, barely tethered to the earth.

Luke is here. He's really here.

And impossibly sexier than she'd remembered. Blood pulsed in her veins just thinking of him, and her body was in full riot, every part of her wanting to touch him first. While the students told knock-knock jokes, Ashley followed them around, but several times, she'd closed her eyes for a moment to remember him, and the air in her lungs would become strangely dense: so tall and strong and masculine. Sensual. Virile. *And playful.* He'd walked in during her pun lesson? He couldn't have planned that, and yet how perfect. How right. How utterly Luke.

As much as she tried to suppress her physical response to seeing him as she taught present perfect, past perfect, and past perfect progressive, she failed. All class long, she was thinking of his full, kissable lips, his strong hands moving on her waist, her hips, and her heart rate never came down.

The kids had a good time teasing her about the handsome Americano. There were catcalls and saucy coos and fist bumps from all the students—all the students except one. Mayu looked heartbroken, as if she'd lost something special. With a tug in her gut, Ashley intuited the larger story the girl must have woven around Ashley and her father. Mayu never met Ashley's eyes for the rest of the period, and when class was dismissed, when Ashley moved to talk with her, the young girl ran.

CHAPTER 16

"I'T'S PARADISE," ASHLEY WHISPERED as they walked hand in hand through an artistic garden gate into extensive, verdant gardens. Though they had only driven half an hour, Ashley felt as if she were in another part of the world entirely—a world of calm and serenity. It was a lush, mysterious beauty so different from the bustling, working village of Huayllabamba. It had just rained, and the air smelled of petrichor and the leaves and flowers sparkled in the early evening sun. She felt like Dorothy just landing in Oz, stepping from a world of black and white into an enchanted kingdom of lambent technicolor magnificence.

Luke had booked them two nights here. The buildings were simple, humble, but the gardens were a feast for every sense. They were surrounded by white trumpet flowers, abundant hanging fuchsia, and purple passion flower vines, pink geraniums, red garden roses, and vast drapes of pink bougainvillea. The exotic perfume intoxicated her nose. All around them, the air thrummed with the hum of bees gathering pollen, and birds filled the garden with bright evening song.

"I can't believe we're here. I can't believe *you're* here." She pulled him closer, and they stood for a moment, holding each other. She met his gaze and held it, marveling at the many shades of blue in his irises, from tropical sea to stormy afternoon. She could look into his eyes all day, trying to read them like a book she wished would never end.

They hadn't really had a moment to just hold each other—there'd been too many curious eyes in Huayllabamba. And she hadn't dared take Luke into her room at Chaska's—that would have been frowned upon even if she and her landlord were on better terms.

But here in these flourishing gardens with high hedges that blocked them from inquisitive eyes, here she felt free to express and act on all the wanton energies that had awakened in her since he'd walked into her room two hours ago. She pressed her hips suggestively against him now, shameless, and was rewarded with a low growl.

Luke turned and pulled her hard against him. "You are so right for me, Ashley." The words fluttered against her skin.

He brushed his knuckles along her cheek, a gesture impossibly tender for the ferocity she read in his expression, and she knew he still was reining in his yearning. She was always astonished by the ways he'd learned to control and channel his sexual longing, and as much as she wanted to make love to him right here in this garden, she was also determined to let him lead her now in whatever way he chose, in whatever way he felt safe enough, but oh, it was so hard to wait.

He ran his hands up her arms, leaving a trail of exquisite heat where he'd touched, and she felt him shudder with sexual hunger. "Come, Ashley." His voice was low and tremulous with urgency and lust. "Let's find our hut. Now."

The "hut" was a circular adobe building, far enough away from any other structures that it felt quite private. They entered, and Ashley took in the high ceiling, the exposed wooden beams, and the dark hardwood floors. The windows looked out toward tall trees and flowering bushes that kept the room feeling both private and open. The king-sized bed was covered with a creamy white comforter and bright Peruvian throws and pillows. A small vase of red garden roses was on the bedside table, and a huge gray rock the size of a large table was somehow inside the room, as if the hut had been built around it. *Of course the geologist would want the room with the giant rock.* She chuckled to herself.

Ashley dropped her bag and clapped her hands in excitement. "Oh!" she exclaimed, and she was about to turn and gush to Luke about how much she loved the room, but then she heard the door click shut behind her, the snick of the lock, and a dark rumble from Luke. "I believe you owe me something."

Shivers ran down her spine. There was such dominance, such shadowy need in his voice, and she felt the intensity go straight to her core. She turned slowly to meet his gaze, wondering where his imagination might take them, licking her lips in anticipation, her chest barely containing her faltering breath.

"Oh, yes?" she asked, her voice silken with arousal. "What do I owe you?"

"I believe I paid for ten hours of Spanish lessons some months ago, and yet only two were delivered."

"*Claro.*"* A wicked smile slid up one side of her face. "I believe I owe you eight hours."

"I want eight *consecutive* hours," he clarified, stepping forward from the door with a brutal grace, fixing her with his hot gaze. "Do you think you can make good on my lessons?"

"Depends on what you want to learn."

"Teach me how to say *I want you very much.*"

"*Te deseo mucho.*" Just saying the words caused a spontaneous clenching in her sex.

"*Te deseo mucho, Ashley.*" Luke took another step closer.

"Quick study," she praised him.

---

* I see.

"Teach me how to say *I have dreamed about you every night and wake up hard and starved for you.*"

Ashley blushed. "*He soñado contigo todas las noches y me despierto excitado y me muero de hambre.*"

"Teach me to say that there is nothing in the world that will keep me from loving you, nothing."

Need burned in her body like five thousand candles, their radiance spreading through her. "*No hay nada en el mundo que me impida amarte, nada.*"

"*Nada,*" he growled as he closed the gap between them. He shook his head, his dark locks swinging, and she felt the fervency in his promise. "*Nada.*"

Luke lifted her from her waist, walking her to the high edge of the bed. He set her down gently, legs spread, and he stood between them. Only their legs touched. He braced his hands on either side of her body, enveloping her without touch. He moved his lips over her slowly, fanning her with the light stroke of his breath and deliberately inhaling the salt scent of her skin.

"Now tell me," he whispered, his lips almost touching her ear. "Tell me you agree to this *instruction.*" He nuzzled his nose against her cheek. "Tell me yes. I want to hear you say *yes.*"

She knew how important her consent was to this moment, to him. Her body was so on edge, like a glass poured too full with only surface tension keeping the excess from spilling over the edge. She would have promised him anything, anything to release that tension. "Oh, Luke," she whispered. "Yes."

The moment the word escaped her lips, Luke covered her lips with his own in a deeply possessive, almost punishing kiss, and she felt herself spilling, spilling into the beauty of the moment. She felt the heat of the kiss all the way down to her pinky toes, and she sensed in that moment every shred of restraint Luke had clung to was stripped away, releasing pure animal need.

Her mouth moved feverishly against his, their teeth gnashing, lips bruising, his low stubble grazing her skin, her tongue desperate for a taste of him—*cool mint and hot kisses.* Nothing else mattered but this connection, this communion, this closeness, and she felt herself drowning in the sweet pull of desire. *More, more, more* her body clamored, all of her craving his fire. She was frantic for him even as he flicked and swirled his tongue in a heated exploration of her mouth. She was almost overwhelmed by the intensity of her craving. Their noses bumped and slid, their breathing twined, their chests heaved, her hands twisted in the sheets to keep from pulling the full weight of his body down onto her. *Let him lead, let him lead.*

But her blouse felt too tight, her skin too hot, and she wanted so badly to be naked against him. As if reading her want, Luke lifted his lips and gave her a naughty, teasing glance, then drifted his attention to the long smooth landscape of her neck, licking her, nibbling her, tasting her skin. She gasped as he found the soft place where her neck met her shoulder. Nudging aside the thin fabric, he sank his teeth into her flesh and bit her sharply.

"Oh!" she panted, surprised that the endorphin rush of the pain made for a potent aphrodisiac, and she felt a warm slickening between her legs.

He pushed up on his arms and looked down at her with raw gratitude, an uninhibited devotion that took her breath away. She had never seen any expression so sexy.

He gave her a sinful grin. "Teach me to say *I want to rip your clothes off with my teeth.*"

A husky laugh escaped her, as if she were daring him to do what she taught him to say. "*Quiero arrancarte la ropa con mis dientes.*"

"*Quiero arrancarte—*" he began, then rip he did with his impatient teeth and his eager hands, pulling apart the front panels of her blouse so the small mother-of-pearl buttons went pinging around the room.

He pushed aside the cloth and stared reverently at her body, her breasts hidden by her very functional sports bra. In half a second, he'd pushed it up to expose the dark tips he sought, and he was instantly on her, taking strong, sweet pulls with his mouth, sucking and biting and worshiping her body. She whimpered in ecstasy, and instinctively, she arched her back, lifting her breasts in a silent entreaty for more.

At last, she could no longer lie there and submit to being pleasured without taking the lead herself. She was the teacher here, after all. She wrapped her legs around him and pulled him in until his hips were pressing into hers, and he groaned as she rhythmically rocked herself against his hard ridge and made a vise of her legs, pulling him in closer. Longing gnawed at her as she neared orgasm from just rubbing herself against him through their clothes.

More. More. More, came the chant in her blood. Her need distilled into a steady beat that pulsed like a one-note song in her clit, demanding satisfaction. She was ready, so ready, so longing to be penetrated by his tongue, his fingers, his thick proud cock. She wanted this, wanted *him*, wanted to own him, to be owned by him, to find euphoria together. She'd waited for months and didn't want to wait anymore.

With some astonishing semblance of clarity, Ashley considered how Ashley-the-woman-Luke-met-in-a-bookstore would never order a man to please her, to please her *now* when she was wild for it. No. That version of Ashley would wait until the man decided he was ready to make her come. Or she might beg. But *this* version of Ashley, this sensual and adventurous Ashley that Luke had released through his sexual play, this Ashley would have no problem breaking any rules or preferences if she thought it might bring her more pleasure. And at the moment, she knew exactly what would be incredibly erotic for them both.

"*Déjame enseñarte.* Let me teach you," she rasped. "Let me teach you how else you might use that clever tongue."

Luke lifted his head from her swollen breast and stared down at her in wanton delight, realizing Ashley had just turned the tables on their game. A prurient smile spread wide across his face. "Whatever the teacher wants."

———

Ashley woke to the feeling of someone lightly touching her back. There was something intentional about the single finger, the way it moved across the long expanse of skin.

"What are you doing?" she asked drowsily without moving an inch.

"Writing a secret message."

"Mmm. Start over."

Luke complied, beginning his cursive scrawling again just below her waist, and Ashley called out the letters as he drew them. "T. O. B. E. C. O. N. T." She knew where this was going. "I. N. U. E. D." A soft laugh escaped her. "Oh. And an exclamation point!"

She felt his finger circle the scar where a hook on a wall had sliced into her back while they'd been having sex. "It's healed well," he said. "I'm sorry."

She rolled over to look at her lover. "Oh, Luke. I know you would never hurt me on purpose."

"You're right, love."

"Nor would I hurt you on purpose. And yet we both do. And look. Look how we heal, too. Look how we're healing ourselves and each other."

For a long while, they simply stared at each other, a dreamy peace between them. Morning light played across his strong features, and Ashley loved the unguarded aspect of his face, his disheveled hair. She stared at him, wholly mesmerized, and gave him a sleepy smile.

"I'd say we're even," Luke said. His tone was flirty and layered with innuendo.

"We're even?"

"Well, I think you gave me *more* than my eight hours, but not all the instruction was for Spanish."

Ashley blushed, remembering the things she'd "instructed" him to do, all the wicked and hedonistic ways they had pleased each other, letting their fantasies become increasingly wild, playing them out until they were deliriously spent. And then, like devotees of desire, they'd roused from drowsy slumber and started again. And again. As if losing themselves in each other's bodies was as necessary to their survival as drinking water. As if with merging their flesh, they could rewrite all the frustration and separation and hurt of the past few months. As if through touch and sigh, they could say all they had been unable or unwilling to say. She remembered the sounds of their bodies slapping and smacking and suctioning and sliding. Remembered the moaning and grunting and panting and the roughened bellowing of breath.

"Whatever you're thinking about, I love what it does to your face."

Ashley laughed. *Busted.* One would think after ten hours of sex, she would be more interested in breakfast than fantasizing about more sex.

"I'm just considering, in light of last night's, um, progress, you deserve a bonus lesson."

"Ah, sweetness. To be continued ... now."

And the instruction began again.

Ashley was so sore as they wandered the gardens, a delicious reminder of all the pleasures they had shared since arriving here. Clearly, her body needed a break from lovemaking. But she didn't *want* to stop.

It was also clear that although Luke had done a lot of self-reflection and healing in the last few weeks since he'd walked in on his father and Jewel, there were still parts of him that were masked and too vulnerable to share. Ashley flashed back in her mind to the first time they'd had sex without fantasy, the first time Luke had told her he loved her. He'd been able to kiss her and make love to her as himself—something he'd never been able to do before, and she had loved it. Loved the headlong closeness, the lack of anything between them. No pretense, no game, no walls. Just pure, intimate love. It had been wildly vulnerable, even intimidating, to love that openly—and now that she knew it was possible, she wanted it. She understood it would take time before Luke was ready for such intimacy again. Still, it was something to aspire to—resolidifying that delicate trust and re-entering into that highwire act of vulnerable, deeply unreserved love.

Just this morning after breakfast, she'd made a spontaneous move to pull him into her arms and passionately kiss him, and he'd gently deflected and had given her hand a squeeze as if to say, "Please give me time." And she was surprised she didn't feel rebuffed. For now, she was grateful for what he was able to give her, though part of her longed for the time when they would again be able to be completely vulnerable with each other. And she knew that being able to kiss passionately without first entering some kind of role would be a litmus test.

"I've been thinking…" Luke said as he led her to a large rock to sit on in the shade. A canopy of giant white trumpet flowers hung down above them.

"What have you been thinking?"

Luke laughed. "See this rock we're sitting on? It's granite. Two-hundred-forty-six-million-year-old granite. It was magma once, and it slowly cooled, and that's why it has such well-developed crystals. And that's what makes it so good for carving, hammering, and making monumental Incan cities—its structure helps the stone fit together perfectly with no cement, no binding agent. After they've been shaped, that is."

Ashley listened, wondering if he had any idea what a turn-on it was for him to talk science with her. There were so many reasons she loved this man. His brain was certainly one of the biggest.

"You and I, we have the magma part down. We know how to be hot with each other, fluid, fiery. But we have also had times when we were able to cool slowly. And in those times, we've learned so much about who we are as people and who we are together."

Ashley cocked her head, wondering where this metaphor was going.

"We fit. We fit *together*, Ashley. Our lives have shaped us in a way that allows us to really build something—something monumental and lasting. And I know things have been tenuous with us for the past few months. So much of that is my fault."

She moved to interrupt him, but he held up his hand.

"And so, I thought I should make it clear, what I want more than anything when you come back to Houston, is for you to move in with me."

Again, she tried to speak, but he put a gentle finger to her lips.

"I made a top ten list of why you need me and should move in."

Ashley started to laugh. "Really?" Though every part of her was already a hundred percent yes, she was so curious to hear what he'd say.

"*Really.* For my gal who loves to count. Number one. I am… *Metaphor Man.*" He puffed up his chest like a superhero and flashed her a debonair and dashing look, then flexed his arms on both sides like a muscleman. "I can make meaningful metaphors out of granite"—he patted the rock they were sitting on— "out of lithium-ion batteries"—he waggled his eyebrows—"and out of any other object you give me—*voilà!* Meaningful and useful comparisons can always appear thanks to…*Metaphor Man.*" He said the last two words in a cartoon announcer's voice and had Ashley doubled over giggling.

"What?" he challenged. "You think you don't need metaphors? Just try living without them." He puffed up his chest. "I bring meaning to the mundane!"

"And you're alliterative, too." She smirked. "Okay, Metaphor Man. Number two?"

"Number two! You need me to help you spell."

"Ouch! Way to hit a girl below the belt!"

"Just sayin', I can be a real help."

"Okay…and number three?"

"Number three! You need me to *turnip* the music when it's your favorite song."

"Oh my god. You were standing in the doorway already when I said that?"

Luke nodded. "And I couldn't believe that the world handed me such a great grand entrance—you were telling knock-knock jokes? I mean, really. I knew you started classes with jokes, but that was like a giant blessing from the pun gods, who must be watching over us even now."

"It was a *pun*derful coincidence. Number four?"

"Number four!" he said in an announcer's voice again. "You need me because I can introduce you to Goofy and Loopy, the new dogs at the shelter. And believe me, these dogs will make you laugh."

"How is the shelter?"

"As you can imagine, I have been spending a *lot* of time there the last month. Again and again, those dogs have saved me."

"Luke, I'm sorry," she blurted.

"What?"

"I'm sorry I didn't handle how I left better."

"You were following your dream, Ashley."

"I know, but I've had a lot of time to think about how I handled it all, and I can see why you would feel as if I wasn't including you in my choices. And why that would hurt. And most of all, I am sorry for the way I didn't let you in on the decision, and I see how that caused a big schism in our trust. And I'm sorry."

All that without an elephant tattoo.

"I hear you, Ashley. Thank you. Like I said, we've both had a chance to grow slowly when we've been apart, and I think it will make us stronger when we are together. In Houston. In *our* home."

Ashley laughed again at his sudden determination to make sure that she would move in with him. She was already a hundred percent certain that was what she wanted, too, but she was having so much fun with his list that she urged him to go on. "Number five?"

"Number five! You need me because your hair always falls in your face while you are reading, and I am the one who will pull it back for you." He pushed a few strands behind her ear as if to prove his worthiness on that score.

"Compelling."

"Number six. You need me because I always preset the music in my car so every time you get in, I am sending you a secret message about how I feel about you."

"I thought so!" Ashley held up both hands as if claiming a discovery. "I *thought* you were doing that!"

"Not much gets past you, hmm?"

"I just didn't want to assume—"

"That I meant it all those nights about the Moondance?"

"Well, a gal can hope—"

"Number seven! I can be your trusty assistant when you need help putting your necklaces on and taking them off."

"Again, very practical."

"Just trying to set the deal in, um, stone," he said, patting the rock they sat on again.

Ashley gave him the obligatory moan.

"Number eight is you need me because I will always honor your puns by groaning, no matter how bad they are."

"Thanks for having my back, Luke. You've *groan* on me."

Ashley waited, but there was no response from Luke.

"Hello? I said you've *groan* on me." She added a groan just to be clear he got it.

"Forgive me!" And he proceeded to groan loudly—loud enough that another guest walking through the gardens looked over to be sure he was okay, which sent the two into fits of giggles.

Luke gave her a sheepish smile. "Number nine. You need me because I make an incredible peach pie. And, ladies and gentlemen, number ten! You, Ashley Barris, need me because I just happen to be the worldwide leader of the fan club for divorced women who get bad headaches, want to travel to Peru, love reading memoirs about other people's messed-up lives, and can somehow manage to be fantastically seductive while reading lines from Deepak Chopra."

Ashley stared at him in genuine astonishment as she went back to that first day she'd met him in the bookstore in Houston and had fretted about what her choice of books said about her.

"You remember what books I had?"

"Oh, I think I remember just about everything about you. Not trying to be creepy—it's just that you are my very favorite subject in the world. Will you please, Ashley, move in with me when you come back to Houston?"

Ashley beamed at this man, this man who brought her joy beyond what she'd imagined was possible, and she knew all she wanted was more of him. "Purple."

CHAPTER 17

WRAPPED IN HER TOWEL, with another towel wrapped turban-style around her hair, Ashley stood alone in the bathroom after her shower, the scent of lavender soap still clinging to her skin. Her body felt surprisingly re-energized by the warm water.

She had one thing in mind; she just didn't know how she might get there. Luke was leaving tomorrow, and no matter how sore she was today, she desperately wanted him inside her, joined to her, for as many hours as possible in the time they had left.

But how? She knew Luke was "giving her a break" because he knew how sore she was, and she doubted he would initiate sex with her out of respect for her discomfort. But if he wasn't going to initiate, and she wanted sex, then what did she do? Ask him to come up with something? Or could *she* initiate?

Most of the time, except once, really, Luke initiated their sex because she still wasn't quite comfortable instigating lovemaking in the way he needed. It wasn't as if she could just walk up and kiss him or tell him she wanted him and lead him to bed. That wouldn't feel safe to him. The truth was, coming up with fantasies came easily to him—they arose organically for him out of any situation. So basically, it was his role in their relationship to start the seduction.

But Ashley kept thinking of something Luke had said earlier that morning. *We're even.* He'd been talking, of course, about the so-called "debt" of the Spanish lessons. But she'd felt his words on a deeper level. *We're even.* She wanted them to be equals in bed. And that meant she had to figure out how to enter into spontaneous fantasy on her own.

The one time she had initiated sexual fantasy with Luke, she'd come prepared with props and a "sexy photographer" costume. She'd planned that seduction for a whole day. But right now, she didn't have a day to plan. She had minutes. *I'm just not as creative as he is*, she protested to herself. She was a *scientist*, for god's sake.

Think, think.

Nothing came. It was as if the more she reached for an idea, the more she shut down the whole creative process. And then it came to her.

Don't think. Just play.

Pretend play had never come easily to Ashley, not even as a little girl. Perhaps that was why she loved jokes so much— jokes were wordplay, and that felt safe. Dancing was play, sort of. But she hadn't really played pretend as a child. Hadn't had dolls except one giant teddy bear she slept with. Didn't play board games. Didn't play school sports. She liked blocks. And books. She hadn't run around much with the kids in her neighborhood; in fact, her best friend as a girl had been Tica. Ashley had always been uber responsible. Had to be. From practically raising her sister to doing her work with Lift House to committing her time and energy to environmental activism—most of her life was driven by a sense of ensuring survival.

Ashley sighed. *Just play.* It sounded so hard, but what if?

What if she just walked into the other room and was open to whatever happened? What if she engaged in, as the behavioral scientists would say, *autotelic* behavior, letting the present moment unfold without a future goal. What if she just *played*?

It felt like such a risk. What if she couldn't come up with anything? What if he didn't respond? Could she do it wrong? She looked in the mirror and made a goofy face. Rolled her eyes. Took a deep breath. Then said out loud, "Let's play."

It was time to explore.

Luke was standing naked in the middle of the room, his gaze focused on a bird out their window. The room was the perfect temperature for being comfortable in just skin, and Luke owned it. He was so comfortable in his body. Seeing him there, Ashley's heart backflipped. God, he was beautiful, his body the next country she wanted to visit. That gave her an idea.

"Excuse me," she said, her voice low and husky. Luke turned to look at her, his gaze turning appreciative when he saw she wore nothing but a towel.

"You good?"

"Actually, I'd like to apply for a visa."

He gave her a funny look. She almost lost heart.

Just play.

"I, um, I've been traveling and realized there was a place I really want to visit."

The look on Luke's face was slightly baffled but curious. She realized he was taking her seriously because, well, she was usually serious. *Shit.* Her plan, or lack of one, was not going well. How was she supposed to indicate to him that this was a sexual advance? The contour of his body reminded her of what she wanted.

She dropped her towel. His eyes opened wider, taking in her body and her intentions.

"I see." A smile twitched at his lips.

He likes this.

"How can I help you?" His double entendre was not lost on her, and Ashley's fears dissipated in a rush of heat.

"I couldn't help but notice the, um, very fine geography of your, um, country." With both hands, she traced a silhouette of him in the air between them.

"Why, thank you." He grinned. "In fact, we would love for you to visit. It just so happens the borders are open today. There is an entrance fee, though." His whole face was lit up with delight at the whole exchange.

Check that. He loves *this.*

Ashley was feeling increasingly emboldened, almost light-headed, by his immediate willingness to meet her in this co-created playground. "What's the entrance fee?"

"I'll tell you once you get to the border."

She stepped closer, her desire sharpening. "I'm curious, what do people wear there?"

"Oh." His chuckle rumbled low, belying deep satisfaction. "You're wearing the preferred fashion."

She blushed, pleased by how this was going. She could feel the soft peaks of her nipples tightening. "And what is the local currency?"

"Mmm," he murmured, his voice a feather stroking lightly across her nakedness. "We take whatever is offered. We give as much as we can."

Ashley nodded, scrambling to think of other considerations when traveling to a new country. "And what is the voltage there? Will I need an adapter?"

With great humor, he looked down at his stiffening cock that now stood almost fully erect in front of him. "High voltage. High enough to run anything you want."

Ashley couldn't help but laugh at that. "Oooh. Well. I guess the only thing I need before my journey is permission from your customs and border protection to enter."

That was so easy to just ask for consent.

"Oh, yes," he said, very deliberately. "Yes."

And I'm in.

A wild giddiness rose in her. *This is fun!* And she had no idea where things might go next.

She picked up her towel and walked with it to the giant rock in their room, folding it, then placing it on the edge to make padding. She stood back and motioned for Luke to come lean his butt against it.

With an amused and highly aroused look, he did as she bid, leaning against the rock, his hard cock already glistening at the tip. Oh, what that did to her, seeing him posed and ready for her to devour him.

"Now then, about that entrance fee." Luke's voice was barely a growl.

"Yes?"

"I need to see you come. Then I'll know you're ready to enter."

Ashley's eyes grew wide, and she felt his words go straight to the tight bundle of nerves as they all began throbbing at once, as if his words had been a shimmer of hummingbirds all coming to sip nectar from one exquisite spot. She could feel her own wetness already gathering between her thighs. *Oh!* He'd turned the tables.

"Can you pay it?" His voice was charged with erotic challenge.

Instead of answering with words, Ashley walked a few steps to a nearby armchair and deliberately arrayed herself on it, one leg draped over the arm, the other planted on the floor in front of her so that she was spread wide open for Luke's benefit. She smiled as his jaw slackened, the look on his face pure arousal.

She lifted her right hand to her mouth and licked the pad of her middle finger until it was slick, and then she slowly lowered her hand to her mound and pushed the flat of her fingers through the triangle of tight curls before curling her slippery middle finger and gliding it between her folds.

Wet. Oh my gosh. As in dripping.

She exhaled an involuntary moan of relief as the nub of her clit hardened even more beneath her softly stroking finger.

She realized she'd closed her eyes and reopened them to find Luke's gaze intently trained on the place where her hand met her sex. His jaw was rigid now, a slight tick in it, as if in intense concentration. His face flushed with ravenous delight.

Any shame or embarrassment Ashley might have been experiencing was erased by Luke's obvious thrill in watching her touch herself, and she felt herself completely give over to the moment. In fact, she wanted to draw it out. She lifted her glistening finger to the tip of her nose and inhaled. Though her intent had been to tantalize Luke, to her surprise, it excited her, too.

"Mmm-mercy," Luke groaned, his eyes concentrating now on her lips as she slipped her finger in and tasted herself. Musky. Spicy. Surprisingly familiar. She withdrew it from her lips with painstaking leisure.

Luke met her eyes with a penetrating ferocity, his gaze strung somewhere between torture and bliss. She bit her lip, and slowly, she reached down between her legs again, her hand immediately stroking through her center, drawing the slick liquid into circles around the tiny bundle of nerves before plunging one finger into her slippery warmth.

Luke's hands were fisted at his sides as if to keep himself from stroking his cock and pleasing himself as he watched her. She decided to play with him even more. With her free hand, Ashley massaged her breast, teasing and squeezing her bunched nipple, pinching it, twisting it hard, until the sharp pain made her breath hitch.

"Jesus, Ashley." Luke's jaw hung slack, his eyes now fixed on her breasts.

Her hand started moving faster, her strokes flirting longer until finally, she withdrew her finger from her core and quickly worked her swollen clit with three circling fingers. But the orgasm hovered just out of reach. She wanted it, wanted it now, wanted to climax in front of Luke, wanted to see how hard his cock had become, wanted entrance to his body.

"Come," he commanded.

Ashley felt her breath quicken; she whimpered in anticipation until one more stroke caused the orgasm to burst inside her, light spearing through her like shooting stars on a moonless night. Her fingers continued to deliver a slow circling pressure as she jerked violently, the currents of pleasure threatening to sweep her away. It was good, but nowhere near the intensity of the release when Luke was inside her body.

When the trembling finally subsided, she was still panting. Lifting her heavy-lidded gaze, she took in Luke's face: fervor dancing in his eyes, his mouth slightly parted, chest heaving as he, too, struggled to find his breath.

"Damn, woman," he whispered, still staring at the place where her hand now rested lightly, and then he looked up to her eyes in awe. "You are gorgeous."

Suddenly shy, Ashley felt a deep red begin blooming in her chest, then rising toward her face.

"You are perfect."

"Can I enter?"

He gave the slightest nod. She stepped toward him and picked up the towel that had fallen from her hair while her head had been flung back. She loosely folded it, and she set it on the floor in front of Luke, then dropped to her knees, bringing her face to his erection.

She looked up with innocent eyes. "Local delicacy?"

Luke's eyes smoldered, but he chuckled lightly, as if almost incredulous. "Like to try it?"

Ashley answered by putting one hand on his shaft, the other forming a ring at the base. Her palms felt cool against the heat of his cock. Just that touch made Luke groan in immediate approval. His hips thrust forward slightly, as if he couldn't help it. She tightly squeezed his thickness, then pressed the tip of her tongue against his head, licking the glistening bead of precum, relishing the bitter cream of it.

"Ashley," he gasped, and she smiled, loving the almost barbaric power she had right now over his body, loving how much he wanted her.

Ashley angled his cock toward her mouth, licked her lips, opened wide, and took him deep. Above her, she heard a strangled cry from Luke as he flung his head back in instantaneous bliss. She felt triumphant, sucking in his thick shaft from root to tip, gagging a bit as the head of his cock banged the back of her throat. Hot tears prickled in her eyes, and his curses and moans of pleasure gave her a glorious, powerful feeling. She loved him deep in her mouth. She hollowed her cheeks, shielded her teeth, and held him tight at his base to increase the force of her suction as she dragged her mouth back to the tip before deep-throating him again, gagging and clamping around him as he moaned. His hands played in her hair, twisting and twirling the still-damp strands, tugging at her scalp.

Ashley slowed her movements, not wanting him to come just yet, and soon, she felt his hands move beneath her arms, lifting her up, pulling her off him, helping her rise.

"I think I got lost on the way to the capital," she whispered in sultry tones.

Luke wiped her lips clean with his thumb, then kissed her with such savage intensity she lost her breath. He sank his tongue deeply inside her, surely tasting both himself and her, inviting her tongue to play. Every rational thought scattered from her head. When he lifted his mouth, he pierced her with his wild gaze. Then he kissed the fragile skin behind her ear, making her melt. When he felt her acquiescence, he murmured low against her skin, "Everything here is yours."

Ashley tilted her head to scrape the skin of his neck with her teeth, then nibbled and licked and tenderly bit, relishing the salty male taste of him. She was suddenly aware that in fact he was leaving, that soon he'd be back on a plane to Houston, and she'd go back to teaching in Huayllabamba, and a desperation surged through her. Emotion caught in her throat as she rasped, "I never want to leave." As if she might hold him, tethering herself to this moment, she wrapped her arms around his neck and pulled herself up in an unconscious effort to start climbing his sleek, muscled body.

Standing on tiptoe, she wrapped one leg around his waist and felt the hard heat of his cock slip easily back and forth through the soaking valley of her lower lips. For a while, they stood there just like that, Luke rocking his hips slowly against the outside of her sex until he was thoroughly covered in her cream. It was heaven. It was agony. With her bent leg, she pushed up on the rock, trying to get higher on him, and Luke, seeming to understand what she wanted, cupped both his strong hands beneath her round cheeks and lifted her up, then slowly, slowly lowered her until his smooth head was nudging at her entrance.

"Now," she breathed, and they stared at each other in awe as he speared into her wet, most intimate flesh in one swift move, and in unison, they both gasped, their breaths mingling between them. Ashley watched as Luke's face opened into a most beautiful awe, and she writhed to accommodate his plundering shaft, glorying in the feeling of being fully possessed, how she craved it.

They never took their eyes off each other, the room seeming to close in around them. She saw so much love beaconing there in those deep blue orbs, and she knew he must be seeing the same devotion in hers. A fierce joy emblazoned in her until her whole body burned. For a long time, they just stood there like that, joined, mesmerized. She knew from his erratic breathing that Luke was not moving in part to keep himself from finding his release too soon. At the same time, he was letting her sore body grow accustomed again to his glorious intrusion. She flexed her hands around his neck, letting the surfeit energy in her palms find some purpose. Soon, her hips rhythmically rocked as she clenched her thighs around him.

As if that were the sign he'd been waiting for, Luke, too, drove his hips into hers, and she softened around him as her body relaxed to allow for greater penetration. With each deep stroke of his steel-hard cock, the sensitive tips of her breasts brushed lightly against his chest, creating sparks of pleasure until quiet, incoherent sounds filled her throat, and she broke eye contact as her head fell back in pleasure.

Luke took advantage of the new position, exploring the long curve of her neck with wet, sloppy kisses, leaving a glistening trail of devotion everywhere his lips touched. "You belong here with me," he rasped, sinking his teeth into the tender base of her neck. "Oh, you like that, do you?"

Ashley offered him the other side of her neck in response, and a small puff of air met her neck as he laughed; then he licked and nibbled the other side, all the while rocking and pistoning himself into her secret swollen flesh in steady upward drives.

This is my home, she thought, surprising herself with the word. *Home. You are my home.* Her inhales were ragged, urgent.

"Am I hurting you?" Luke asked, pausing his hips and staring at her with concern.

"No, no, don't stop, please."

"Oh, I will keep this going, woman." He picked her up as if she weighed nothing and walked with her wrapped around his sweat-slick body to the bed, where he turned and sat himself down, his cock still buried deep inside her. "Now you are completely in charge," he murmured.

Keeping her eyes on his eyes, she began to rise and lower her sheath on his staff, her ears attuned to the wet sounds of their union. She felt tight around him, and she reveled in the way his thickness dragged against her snug walls, then slipped easily back into her depths.

The friction made her dizzy. Again and again, she rode him, moving until she felt his cock rubbing against that sweet spot inside her. *Oh, yes.* Her lids fell, and she felt the telltale tightening in her sex. Her rhythm faltered, her strength eroding.

"Luke," she gasped. "Are you close?"

"I'm right here with you," he promised, picking up the pace where she had left off, lifting up, thrusting deep, massaging that tenderest spot inside her again and again until Ashley exploded, her body erupting into spasm after delicious spasm, as if millions of tiny crystals were forming inside her, splitting and shining. Her walls rippled around his shaft, and then he, too, was coming, and Ashley watched his face with blurry fascination as he lost all sense of control and surrendered to ecstatic release, his whole body going taut, his expression bathed in elation.

Ashley didn't know how long they sat like that, his heat and strength still buried deep inside of her, her body trembling in tiny aftershocks of pleasure above him. Neither of them said a word. As if they both understood that even the gentlest of whispers would be too crass, too harsh for this transparent moment in which they were so wholly joined. As if, perhaps, if they held still enough, their molten bodies might solidify together into one form, one substance, one irrevocable union.

As if they both knew the next months would do their best to reverse that.

CHAPTER 18

"A H, *PROFESSORA!* KNOCK KNOCK."

Ashley raised her eyebrow at Mayua. His lips curled into an easy smile that reached his eyes. "Yes, Mayu has been teaching me some of your tricks. And you know, this game works in Spanish, too. So come on. Play along. Knock knock."

"Who's there?" Though she said the words, they seemed as hollow as she felt. Since saying goodbye to Luke two days ago, she had felt like a vacant shell of herself.

"Ah, it is as I thought. Perhaps it is not who's *there* but who is *not there* that matters."

Ashley looked at him with eyes full of heartache, not even trying to pretend she was happy. He nodded.

"Yes. I see in your eyes that the rumors were right. It was not my pastries working their magic on you that made you sparkle; it was the magic of love."

Ashley nodded miserably. "Oh, brother." Now that she was speaking of it, even the shell of her was breaking apart. She *missed* Luke.

"Yes, sister, I understand what it is to not be with the one you love. And you saw your love for a short time, and now you miss him even more. Sometimes if you can't eat the whole pastry, taking a small bite is worse than not eating any at all."

It was true. If she had missed Luke before, seeing him here in this small town and being with him here in Peru had somehow ruined her once he left, had ruined how she experienced everything. She felt like a tomato plant that had been transplanted in the shade and was now wilting.

As she slept alone in her twin bed, the loneliness had threatened to swallow her whole. And yesterday, when she'd gone back to school, she must have looked at the doorway ten thousand times as if she expected Luke to come walking through it again. Only he never did. And ten thousand times, her heart had withered when he hadn't appeared.

"Here," Mayua said, handing her an apple pastry across the counter. "Though we have established that a pastry is not as good as love, it does make things just a little bit better."

She managed a weak smile and accepted the sweet. What a gift this man was in her life. His kindness was more important to her now than he could ever understand, for he was, in his wise and goofy way, reminding her she had made strong connections here in Huayllabamba. She had, in fact, been doubting these last two days if she really belonged here at all. Having part of her Houston life resurface made her long for other parts of her Houston life, too—her book club, her mother, her cat, Emilia, her job with STEAMEA, and Luke. He had taken most of her heart with him on Sunday when he'd gotten back on that plane to Houston.

"I can't come back next weekend," Luke had said, "but you could come to Houston. It would just be for a day, but oh, what a day we could have." He'd rubbed small circles with his thumbs on her wrists, causing full-body shivers at the light touch. Even now, she could feel the cool absence where his touch had been.

She'd been so tempted to say *yes, I'll get on a plane*, but in the end, she had declined because she and a friend from her teacher training in Cusco had gotten cheap tickets to fly together to Bolivia that weekend to hang out and see the neighboring country.

"Oh, Bolivia is so beautiful," Luke had gushed. "You'll love it. I was just there last year for work, and I wanted to stay longer and explore it. Someday soon, Ashley, we will go to Bolivia together. We'll go everywhere together."

How her heart had leapt at those words. Not that she wasn't still excited about going to Bolivia with her friend, but she couldn't stop herself from thinking about how wonderful it would be to go there with Luke and explore places she'd read about, places such as Valle de la Luna, a geologic wonder that he would surely make come to life with playful metaphors. The photos were phallic enough—

"I have something interesting to tell you, sister."

Ashley's attention jerked back to the small, sweet-smelling bakery, where she was standing by the counter with a pastry in her hand and her generous friend was trying to cheer her up.

"Someone visited me this weekend when you were gone. I wonder if you can guess who it was?"

"How many guesses do I get?" Ashley honestly had no idea who it might be.

"I will tell you," he said conspiratorially and leaned in. His eyes glimmered. "La Bruja."

"Chaska?" Ashley almost spit out her first bite of pastry.

"All these years, I never knew that she..." His voice trailed off, perhaps not wanting to sound proud or to gossip, but the way his dimples appeared in his cheeks and his eyes flickered with delight told her everything she'd guessed about her landlord's jealousy was true. "She loves me. And Mayu. And I think I love her, too."

"Wow," she said, smiling a real smile for the first time in days.

So that explains why my puma charm for strength and power mysteriously reappeared on my bedside table.

"Something tells me you won't need to worry anymore about the evil eye." He gave her a wink.

"No more guinea pig cleansings?" She nearly laughed just remembering *that*.

"In fact…" Mayua waggled his eyebrows. "She may even make you a spell to strengthen your Americano love."

———

Ashley was shaking with rage, anger blooming through her bloodstream. Her teeth were clenched, and her heart hammered uncomfortably against her chest.

"Can you guess what I saw in Bolivia?" she gritted at Luke through the phone, her voice thick with condemnation. She was pacing on the rooftop of Chaska's house like a caged animal. She hated that she was having this conversation right now. Hated the sharp feeling of betrayal clawing at her from the inside. No *pisco* had been poured for this conversation, though ironically, she had grabbed the puma and was now squeezing it in one hand, its tiny metal legs pricking into her palm, the pain a reminder: *strength and power.*

"Ashley, what—" Luke began.

"Do *you* know what is happening there?" Fury churned in her gut.

"There's a lot to—"

Of course he knows. "Dammit, Luke. How can you possibly live with yourself?"

"Look, Ashley—"

"No, look, Luke." Ashley, who prided herself on staying calm, realized she was rapidly becoming unhinged. She thought back to the pride in the face of one of the men she'd seen in Bolivia, how stoically he'd stood there with his handmade sign as the others marched in a small circle. "I go to another country for a weekend, and what do I see? A protest."

Ashley's trip to Bolivia had been eye-opening, to say the least. She'd gone expecting to relax and explore. Instead, she and her friend had happened upon a vehement and desperate indigenous group who had traveled to the capital to protest a recent accident at an oil extraction site where a forklift had knocked over multiple large drums of chemicals. That was bad enough, but it seemed the company had tried to cover it up, was negligent in their response, and had been dismissive of the magnitude of the spill.

Ashley ranted on, spitting fire. "Of course, I am curious. What are they protesting? And we get closer, Luke, and what are the odds that while I am in *Bolivia*, I see signs protesting Dalton Oil." She remembered one woman dressed in bright skirts and wearing her baby on her back wrapped in a bright red *manta*. Her eyes had been so fierce, so full of purpose, as if she knew that the future health of her child and her child's child depended on her actions now. And staring at the small crowd of indigenous protesters, she knew how futile their efforts were, how easy they would be for a corporation to overlook. And yet here they were, using their voices the only way they knew how, standing up for their land the only way they could. When she talked with them, they told her they couldn't afford to hire a lawyer, and as for any watchdog groups that might have helped them, there were bigger fish to fry. The disparity between their powerlessness and the omnipotence of big oil had inflamed her.

And not just any big oil company. Dalton Fucking Oil.

She was silent for a while, waiting for Luke to respond, but he didn't.

Because I caught you, and you didn't want to get caught.

"It's like something out of FIXX, Luke. We're looking at wildlife loss, soil contamination, possible groundwater pollution, and if it goes on being neglected, then it's in the aquifer, and as you know, it will poison everything in its path for god knows how many years. And although you *know* this, what is Dalton doing?"

Ashley waited a moment for Luke to say something, and he made some vague start, but then all she heard was guilty silence. Some part of Ashley was hoping for a fight. She wanted him to defend Dalton. To say they were working on it. To say that they were sending their best scientists and cleanup equipment, even though it wasn't a major spill. She wanted him to say that there was no spill too small for them to be responsible for and remediate. But he said nothing.

Ashley's voice was cooler now. Factual. "The article I found about it online said *nothing* was being done. That it seemed Dalton Oil was trying to shirk responsibility. And that the reporter had contacted Dalton Oil, and there was no response."

Ashley heard Luke start to say something, but then again, he stopped.

"Luke, please. No response to the reporter and not one to me, either?"

Nothing. *What the hell?* She checked the phone to be sure the connection was not lost. Nope.

Ashley felt herself moving from anger to despair. "I need you to help me understand, Luke. I *know* you are an oil executive for *Dalton*, the company that now needs to be accountable not only to protect the people of the land but the land itself. It's not like I haven't had a hard time reconciling that the man I love runs a company that often makes choices I can't stomach. I *know* you're a good man, I see how you are, and for the last few months, after all your talk about renewables and changing the industry, I managed to set aside most of my concerns about your work. Because you convinced me you *care*. That you *are* doing something to help. But then I see something like this, and I, I can't reconcile it. It doesn't add up between my heart and my head. I can't distinguish between you and your company.

And it's tearing me apart." She took an agonized breath. "Say something."

"I'm trying—"

She waited for him to finish the sentence, then, frustrated, she said in clipped tones, "Try. *Harder.*" But he didn't respond. "Dammit, Luke. Just answer one question. Did you know?"

She heard a deep breath, as if Luke himself was having as hard a time holding it together as she was. As if he were holding back on a tirade of his own.

"Just answer one question. Did. You. Know. Simple yes or no, Luke."

Please say no, please say no. Please say you're not indifferent or, even worse, trying to cover things up.

Luke seemed to hem and haw for some time before he finally, in almost a whisper, said, "Yes."

Shit. Shitty-shit-shit.

Her lungs squeezed, and though she tried to inhale, a tight ball of bitterness and betrayal had stuck in her throat. It took all her energy to swallow. "Then I need some time. Don't call me. Don't email me. Don't text me. I won't answer. I won't read them. And don't come here. If you go anywhere, go to Bolivia. I need some time, Luke, to figure some stuff out. I just don't know how to love you and be so horrified by what you stand for at the same time. I just…*ahhhhh!*" she cried out, utterly crushed.

One. Two. Three. Four. She counted the colorful bulls on the rooftops around her. "I'm not saying we're over; I'm just saying this is too hard to reconcile by phone or text, and I have some serious soul-searching to do. And I need to focus on what I am doing here. I will be home in December. I hope you can wait for me until then, but I understand if you can't."

Luke said nothing, but she could hear his breath.

In a voice so small she could barely hear it herself, she whispered, "Goodbye, Luke."

And she hung up. And lay down on the rooftop for a long time, staring at the sky, too empty to cry.

———

On repeat, Ashley played the memory again:

Luke lifted her book for book club from the table, and a shower of dried rose petals fell like red rain through his fingers to the floor. They'd been from a bouquet he'd sent her. She hadn't been able to help it; she wanted to save them, to preserve the memory of how sweet he was, how thoughtful. He looked up at her and said, "Ashley, I will always send you flowers." But the glimmer in his eyes told her he was tickled she had pressed and saved the petals.

How long ago that shining moment seemed.

Oh, memories. So different from the gray exhaustion and bleakness of this moment. Ashley felt like an old used-up pair of shoes, shabby, down at the heel, barely able to take another step. She felt drained. Depleted. Spent.

In the four days since she'd spoken to Luke, he'd written and texted and called her every day. And just as she'd said she would, she had deleted his every attempt to reach her without reading or listening to his messages. She wasn't even tempted. There was nothing he could say. She couldn't imagine hearing his low, golden voice right now—it always stirred her. How painful that would be. And she didn't want to hear any apologies. She didn't want to be swayed. Nothing he said would make Dalton's lack of response okay. The whole thing felt so irreconcilable.

She felt so heavy. As if her pockets and hems were weighted with stones of sadness. As if there were a mountain range of grief inside a woman's body. How could all the love she felt for him go from feeling like wings that lifted her to a burden she could no longer carry? Her heart was at odds with itself.

Is it worth it to throw away love because of values?

But aren't those values also based on love? Love for the earth, our primary relationship?

But are you really willing to lose him because of your self-righteousness?

But how can I stay with him when I can't respect what he does?

Will I ever feel light again?

She thought about how she was handling this conflict with Luke. In the past, she had chosen flight—just break up and leave. *And you know that doesn't serve you, right, Barris?* She was trying so hard to not make the same mistake twice.

This time, she'd chosen freeze—just put the whole relationship on hold. *Is that realistic? For almost two months?*

What she didn't want to do? Fight. She didn't want to go back and forth debating oil and drilling practices. Especially not on the phone.

What she really wanted to do? Fix. She wanted to fix him, fix his company, fix the world. And fix this ache in her heart when she thought of living without him. Was that too much to ask?

School was a blessing for her—the classroom had always brought out the best in her, and she was so grateful to throw herself into her work. The students gave her purpose, filled her with passion, and reminded her why she was here. But outside of school, she was lost. Today, after the last English class, she'd found herself walking on the path up to the little chapel—more as if she were being walked than doing the walking herself—and now she was surprised to see herself looking down on the little town.

There, in the main square, was the old Pisonay tree with its giant trunk. Ashley had dreamed of kissing Luke against the trunk. Now it seemed a silly romantic fantasy. Any happy memory or hope she had dared to hope served as a battering ram, pummeling her until she felt bruised—not just her heart, but her whole body. And yet she kept reaching for happy memories, no matter how much pain they brought. Or she kept conjuring them *because* of the pain they brought? As if she wanted to confirm the pain? Like putting her tongue on a sore in her mouth just to see if the sore still hurt. And each time she'd touch it, she'd wince and think, "Yeah, it still hurts." But this particular hurt—this was less a sore and more as if her whole being was a giant gaping wound. How long would it take before she always didn't feel so raw, so exposed?

She thought of all the paths she had taken to bring her to this moment right now, some were purposeful, some as unconscious as this walk up toward the chapel.

Where do I belong? Where do I go next?

She didn't really belong here, not for much longer. And what was waiting for her back in Houston. Luke? STEAMEA? She'd have to see him and work with him there. How painful would that be? Luke had become her sense of home. Loneliness consumed her.

She looked out at the cornfields where the kernels had been planted and were about to germinate. If you didn't know that the seeds had been planted, you would think nothing was happening here. The fields certainly looked empty and unproductive, a perfect mirror for her.

Was there something even now growing inside her? Some seed she didn't yet know had been planted? She certainly didn't feel like spring. She felt barren. As if the whole garden of her had been ripped out by its roots and there was nothing left.

She thought of how the people here nurtured their fields in so many ways, not just with fertilizer and water but with rituals for Pachamama. They even chased the irrigation water as it was released into the ditches, throwing petals into the water as it flowed. How was she nurturing her own inner fields?

She thought again of the place in Bolivia where the drums had spilled—how that damage was just as important as any major spill that would garner international attention. She fumed again, thinking of the ruined land there, devastated by Dalton's inaction.

What if I hadn't gone to Bolivia? What if we hadn't turned left on that street in search of coffee and I hadn't seen the protestors?

Then she'd still be fantasizing and dreaming about Luke and all that was possible between them.

How quickly life changes.

Though as she stared out at the cliffs and mountains of the rugged Andes, she thought, too, how little things change. Luke seemed as if he had changed, but when it came down to it, he hadn't. It was just good-sounding talk.

She looked at her wrists and felt the ghost of Luke's fingers tracing lazy circles there. Again. *Damn.* She'd really believed she and Luke could thrive together, believed their love would blossom.

But where the soil is poisoned, the seed won't grow.

———

Ashley's phone vibrated in her pocket, and her heart lurched. *Luke?* She willed herself not to look at it. Ashley hated how her heart rate elevated. *Like a damn Pavlovian lab rat.* But this was no trained response—it was real longing for connection with the man who had her so confused.

After texting and calling her every day for a week and receiving no response, Luke had finally stopped trying to contact her. The last attempt had been just over a week ago. Though Ashley hated to admit it to herself, fickle and contrary as it was, she missed that he was trying to connect. Was he just taking a break for now? Would he be willing to try again when she got home to Houston? He loved her, and he was single focused on getting what he wanted, so either he was trying a new tack or— she shuddered—he had taken her silence to heart.

Ashley waited a few minutes before looking at the phone, giving herself a little pep talk. If it were from Luke, she would delete this message without looking at it, too, just as she had all the other messages. She had set that as a boundary for herself, and she needed this time to think and to focus on her work here. Resolve set in, and she looked at the phone.

Jewel: Call me, Ash

Right away

Please

The last thing Ashley wanted to do was call her sister, who even now, probably *literally*, was in bed with the enemy. But the text sounded urgent. She walked to the rooftop and called.

"Ashley?" Jewel answered the phone, sounding like a little girl.

"Jewel." Ashley's voice was monotone and unamused. Then she realized Jewel was crying. Despite her anger with her sister, the sound of sniffling and irregular breathing between sobs tore at her heart. Had that asshole broken up with her? Of course, it would hurt Jewel terribly, but in the long run, it was for the best. Better now than later.

"Mom is dead."

———

"And then there were two," Jewel said with a sigh the size of Texas, kicking off her heels the instant they stepped into her posh new condo. Ashley would be staying here the next few days while in Houston. "C'mon, sis, let's have a big pour of wine and celebrate our great mama. God, she'll be missed."

While Jewel went into the kitchen in search of glasses, Ashley curled into the corner of the giant sofa. She felt small, displaced, untethered, exhausted. She missed her mom. What had her last conversation been with her mom? Something trivial. What had she left unsaid? Did her mom know how much she loved her? How could she not have known her mother was so close to death? How could Ashley shape her life, now, in service to the memory of her mother? She wanted to hug her mom again. Wanted to smell her, to feel her, to tell her she loved her.

Ashley had given herself over to paperwork, planning the memorial, and the exhaustion of grief. But now, in the quiet, she was finding it hard to believe anything was more important than love. *Luke. Could any argument be worth standing in the way of love?*

A small purr and gentle nudge on her foot caused an instantaneous warmth to spread through her. "Bamba!" she exclaimed, picking up the long-haired black cat. The cat curled in her lap, and she felt a surge of guilt that with all that had been going on, she'd forgotten her beloved pet.

"You knew I needed someone to snuggle with, didn't you?" She stroked the cat beneath its neck. "I missed you," she crooned, loving the connection. And then, with a quick turn of her head, Bamba pushed off from Ashley's lap and raced to the other side of the room, leaving tiny claw marks in her thighs. "Ow!" Ashley rubbed her legs. "Little traitor!"

Ashley was relieved that James wasn't here with them in the opulent condo he'd rented for Jewel. She didn't trust that she could be polite to the unethical sleazebag. *Thank god for small mercies.* The reunion with her sister and her mother's funeral had been emotional enough, and Ashley didn't think she could manage forced small talk with a ruthless oil tyrant on top of it. Apparently, he was off traveling, destroying the world.

"To Mom," Jewel said, handing Ashley a glass, then clinking it with her own.

"To Mom," Ashley echoed, feeling the sharp pang of loss tear through her once again. She took a sip of the dry white wine, but she didn't really taste it. She hadn't tasted much in days. Why was it grief stole your appetite and turned even the best food to cardboard, the best wine to drivel, the best conversation and books to pablum? "I'm glad she was so strict with me," Ashley blurted.

"What?"

"I'm glad Mom made me work hard. I resented her for it when I was a kid. But I'm glad she pushed me." Ashley could easily hear her mother's voice in her mind now saying the same phrase she'd said to her since Ashley was a child: *You were born to change the world, Ashling.*

"You always did go the extra five miles."

"Mom did, too—like how she refused to get on welfare and worked several jobs to support us. She was amazing. Such a good human. Although you know what she told me a couple weeks ago, Jewels?"

"What's that?"

"She said if she had one regret in life, it was that she didn't spend enough time with us and that she didn't ever really learn how to play." The words had hit Ashley extra hard, an unrelenting mirror.

"Good thing one of us in the family knows how to play," Jewel said, kicking up her feet.

"Yeah, I don't know where you got that gene. Maybe Dad." The words sobered her instantly. "Huh. I always wondered if he would just show up at her funeral. I guess now we'll never really know what went down with our father. Or who he is." Ashley thought about telling her sister about the letter she'd written to their father and how she'd found so much release setting it to sail on the river in Huayllabamba, but she didn't. It felt like the kind of experience that would be difficult to explain and would lose some of its magic in the attempt. But the forgiveness she'd felt that day had been enduring. Even now, talking about their father, Ashley wasn't feeling the deep stab of betrayal she usually felt when she thought about him. Her curiosity, however, was still there.

"Actually," Jewel said, arching a brow, "maybe now we *can* know."

"What do you mean?"

"Well, maybe Aunt Jane would tell us something now that…" Jewel's voice trailed off.

Aunt Jane and Uncle Lewis had been there at the funeral. Before she'd left, she'd invited the girls to come visit at her home in Elmsville in the next day or two. Aunt Jane and their mom had been very close, and Ashley's heart pitched, realizing Jewel might be right—Aunt Jane would not only know their father but would also probably know what had happened and just why their mom had always been so tight-lipped about him.

"Huh." She pressed her fingertips to her lips. She had been looking forward to the trip to their mom's hometown anyway, but now the sisters' trip to see Aunt Jane took on new possibility.

Jewel sighed deeply. "The thing I admired most about Mom was how she was grateful for everything. Grateful for that grubby little house. Grateful for her meager paycheck. Mom could be grateful for anything. Running water. Tuesday morning. A bed to sleep in. Even a messed-up younger daughter who never figured out what a work ethic is and dropped out of community college." Jewel took a deep breath. "Mom always, always made me feel loved, even when I was unlovable."

Jewel took a sip of wine and stared at the glass, as if willing herself to appreciate the flavor, the color, the way the golden liquid captured the light. "I wish I could have that same kind of appreciation for the small stuff. But I just can't; I just don't want to live like Mom did, Ashley." She looked around the grand condo they were sitting in even now. "I know that makes me a small person, that I don't want to be poor anymore. But I don't. I like nice things. I like nice clothes and a nice car. I like nice wine.

I like that I feel so safe in this condo with a gate and a security code and a security code and a guard at the door. I like it."

"I get it," Ashley soothed, feeling as if she were taking confession. "I get it, Jewel." Especially the part about feeling safe. Ashley kicked herself again for not being able to save her sister from the rape that still influenced how safe or how not safe Jewel felt in the world.

"I love Jimmy, you know," Jewel asserted. "It's not just about the stuff he buys me." She absentmindedly twirled the diamond bracelet around her wrist. "I love him. And he loves me. I know he does. And we're going to get married, Ash. I know that's hard on you and Luke, but with Mom's death, it's just so clear to me how little time we have. One moment, you're out weeding the yard, and the next, you have a stroke in your sleep and that's it. Whatever time I have left, I want to spend it with Jimmy. Plus, and I know it's TMI, but he is an awesome fuck. I mean *awesome*. And you know, *that's* important to me, too."

Ashley flashed Jewel her palm. "Stop it. That's enough."

Jewel laughed and bit her lip as if she had the most delicious secret she was keeping to herself, then shrugged. "Figured."

As repulsed as Ashley was by any thought of James, clothed or not, she felt herself falling in love again with her sister despite herself. Her crass-talking, bad-ass, pleasure-seeking sister, who did everything she could to hide the vulnerable girl that Ashley had taken care of for so many years. As different as they were, just being with Jewel made Ashley feel a deep centering. Though something about her sister had seemed a little off—she was less strident somehow. More relaxed. Was it Mom's death? Feeling more secure? Ashley wondered if she should ask about it.

"How's Luke?" Jewel asked. "I was surprised he wasn't there with you today."

Doesn't she know? Maybe Luke and his dad were still not on speaking terms after he'd found Jewel in his parents' house.

"We're, um—I stepped away for a while."

"That's what Mom said. I guess I just wondered because of all the flowers he'd sent." In fact, Luke had filled the memorial celebration with flowers. Every surface in the little chapel for her mom's service had been covered with bouquets, over half of them from Luke. In typical Luke fashion, it had been over-the-top generous. Ashley had been grateful for the gesture, but it had also made her unbearably sad. Why couldn't he be just an asshole? It would make it so much easier to not love him, to not be wrestled by right and wrong. Only if he had been an asshole, she would never have fallen for him so hard in the first place. She remembered her mom's joy when Luke had sent her white lilies just a month ago. It was a special man who thought to send flowers to the mom of the woman he loved.

If only things were different. If only he weren't an oilman who didn't clean up after his messes.

But he was.

Everyone had commented on the flowers, of course—every woman in her book club, Emilia, John. All her friends had been there, and they'd all asked about Luke, assuming he must be gone working and that was why he wasn't there. She'd let them think what they wanted, had avoided the subject, which was easy. Everyone was there to talk about her mom, her beautiful mom who had touched so many lives with her humble, happy way of being in the world. So different from the greedy, money-grubbing way of the Daltons. What was that phrase Luke said his dad always said? *We're in it to win it.* That was the antithesis of her mother, who believed in being a player on everyone's team, who believed in working hard so everyone could win.

"I don't want to talk about it, Jewel," Ashley said at last. "But I do want to acknowledge that I have been very angry with you. I'm not sorry for being angry. But I do apologize for cutting you off and not talking to you this last month or so. I apologize for shutting down our communication. It seems to be a pattern of mine, and I'm working on it. I apologize for not being here for you." A surge of guilt rushed through her as she realized just how much she'd hurt them both by refusing to talk to Jewel. Her mom would be so sad if the girls didn't stick together. Hell, *she* would be so sad to lose her sister. "I love you, Jewel. And you are the only family I have now. You're all I have left. Even if I don't always approve of what you do or who you love, I would do anything for you. Anything. You can count on me, Jewel."

"I love you, too, big sis," Jewel said, tears forming in her eyes. "You're the best big sister in the whole world."

And though Ashley had felt disturbingly displaced for many months now, wondering where or what home might be, in that moment sitting on the couch with her sister, she knew she had found it.

———

Ashley had always loved coming to visit Aunt Jane in her two-story Victorian with her huge, abundant gardens surrounding the home. Elmsville was a quiet place with a charming old-town feel just a few hours out of Houston. It seemed to exist in a time warp that kept the whole town center feeling like the 1960s. There were no high-rises, no giant malls, no freeway. There was a big town park and a mom-and-pop pharmacy that had somehow stood up to the pressures of Walmart. There was a Fourth of July parade and, from the looks of it, last week there had been a huge Halloween celebration. Many homes were still decorated to the hilt—giant pumpkins and fake cobwebs and a whole congregation of skeletons filled the yards.

Perhaps Ashley loved coming to Elmsville so much because it was wildly different from her own childhood neighborhood. She'd always felt safe here. And she loved the big yards and the humble but well-cared-for houses. But the main reason she loved it here so much was being with her sassy and sweet Aunt Jane, who even now was standing on the front porch waving her and Jewel in, wearing her big Mama Cass–style shift dress. In fact, Aunt Jane kinda looked like the old Mamas and the Papas singer with her heavyset frame, brown bob, and big smile.

Stepping out of Jewel's car, Ashley was slammed by a wall of autumn heat. "Bless Texas," she said under her breath, almost immediately starting to sweat. She hadn't dressed right for the visit.

"My girls are here!" Aunt Jane shouted, clapping her hands. "Welcome home." Even though her own daughter lived just around the corner, Aunt Jane loved spoiling Ashley and Jewel to the hilt.

"Wow, you sure turned up the heat for us," Jewel said.

"Well, honey girl," Aunt Jane drawled, "you know my secret for staying cool when it's a scorcher. I just don't wear any drawers beneath my thin cotton skirt. I call it a poor woman's air-conditioning."

Ashley and Jewel both laughed and shook their heads in unison. "That's our Aunt Jane," Ashley said, giving the older woman a hug and kiss. "Practical and a whole lotta improper."

"And I smell apple pie!" Jewel squealed.

"Just out of the oven." Aunt Jane pulled Ashley and Jewel into her arms. "I know you both love apple pie, and I would do anything right now to help us all remember just why we're so glad to be alive. Losing your mom can't be easy for you, and god knows it's hell for me. I miss her so much." And though it was hot, they stood there and held each other for a long time before heading in.

After chatting with their uncle, who was busy with a wood-working project in the backyard, the girls came back into the house and settled around the kitchen table for a cup of coffee and a slice of pie with Aunt Jane.

Aunt Jane gaped. "I don't know how you keep that slender figure of yours, Jewel, when you eat pie like a giant weta."

"A giant whatta?"

"A giant weta. It's like a gerbil-sized cricket from New Zealand. We were just watching all about it the other night on The Nature Channel, and it's one of the five hungriest animals on the planet."

"Are you calling me a big bug?" Jewel grimaced, but her fork didn't slow.

"You are the most beautiful hungry bug in the world." Aunt Jane winked at her. "Want another slice?"

Jewel nodded, then flashed her sister a conspiratorial look. "Hey, Aunt Jane? Ashley and I have a serious question for you."

Ashley straightened up and gave her sister an approving nod.

"We hope you'll tell us something about our dad. You know Mom never—"

Aunt Jane interrupted her with a raised hand. "My girls. That man was no father to you. Your mom was right not to talk to you about Wylie." She shuddered. "I don't even like saying his name. That man was no good. And you are lucky that my sweet sister Teresa was able to be both your mother and your father. You are better off not knowing him."

"Why is he such a secret? Did he murder someone? Rob a bank? Is he dead? We can handle it. We want to know."

Aunt Jane put the second slice of pie in front of Jewel. "Look at me. Let it be. He is not worth your time. If he wanted to know you, then he would have come and found you by now. That is painful, I know. It is even more painful for me to have to tell you that the man who hurt your mama is not worth your attention. It's best left alone. Your mama, she knew what she was doing when she cut off all ties with him. Do what your mother did, girls. Look to the future. Don't look back."

Ashley waited for her outspoken sister to argue, but Jewel just took another bite of pie. Ashley stared at these two women she loved and fought the urge to beg for more information. After a moment, she nodded, though inside her, her abandoned little girl stomped her feet. Aunt Jane knew something she wasn't saying. And Ashley wanted to know, too.

CHAPTER 19

ASHLEY FASTENED HER SEAT belt low and tight across her lap and leaned back against the stiff airplane seat. She felt scrunched. At least she got the window. She stared out at the tarmac and let her eyes glaze. Back to Peru. It felt so unreal, so hard to square her life here in Houston with the life she had in Huayllabamba. She felt as if she were floating—a feeling she'd had since her mother died. Actually, it was more as if she were falling without a bottom in sight. Sometimes as she was falling, it seemed as if there were disembodied hands that might be reaching for her to catch her, but she just kept falling and falling and falling. She'd gotten used to it, perhaps. The falling feeling was there when she woke, there as she walked, there as she brushed her teeth, or looked in the mirror, or cooked or packed or conversed. Even now, buckled into her economy seat, she was falling.

She was leaving Houston without seeing Luke. It had been hard not to call him. Hard not to drive to his penthouse and ask his concierge to let her up to see him. Assuming her name was still on his list. Assuming he still *wanted* to see her. Aside from the flowers, there had been no other contact from Luke in two weeks—a dry river. What was he doing? Was he even here in Houston? Was he off planning new oil fields in sensitive areas? Had he given up on their relationship? Had Savannah gotten her evil talons into him again? Was he, too, wondering what it would be like between them when she returned in December?

She closed her eyes and tried to push away the tormenting thoughts. Damn, this was hard. Her gut twisted and pulled. She had no more clarity around her relationship with Luke than when they'd spoken last. She thought of the people in the Bolivian capital, the anguish and dignity in their faces. She thought of Luke drawing words with his finger on her naked back.

At least she and Jewel were back on track. She'd reconnected with a handful of friends, too—she'd seen Meg for coffee. She'd met with the STEAMEA director for tea. She and Emilia had gone out for lunch. *Sweet Emilia.* Knowing things were tough between her and Luke, Emilia had reflected Ashley's own words back to her: *Mistakes can be our best teachers, and everything you learn now will someday make you a better teacher.* Ashley loved that the girl remembered her words, but damn, it was hard to have them turned back on herself.

She hadn't been able to bring herself to go to her mother's house this trip—too painful. That project of packing up her mother's things would have to wait until she came back to Houston near the end of December, another six weeks away.

Her mother. The ache was overwhelming and no less heavy than it had been when she'd first heard. She carried the loss with her everywhere she went like a basket of black stones. She remembered she had saved the small stack of condolence notes for this moment, something to do while waiting for the plane to take off. She'd been looking forward to reading what people might say about her mom. Ashley pulled them out of her bag and looked through them. Most were the same—*So sorry for your loss. Your mother was a wonderful woman. Call me if you need help.* But one began, *Perhaps it feels as if you've swallowed a neutron star.*

Luke. She remembered telling him once that on Earth, a teaspoon of neutron star would weigh six billion tons. That's how she had explained grief to him—like swallowing a neutron star. *And he remembered.*

She read on:

Your mother was an inspiration—so much integrity, so much strength. Those gifts live on in you, and I aspire to her strength and integrity, too. Though these flowers will fade, she will always be alive in your spirit, in your smile.

Luke

Ashley felt an irregular breath escape as she dropped the note on her lap. *Oh, Luke.* Every feeling of love and appreciation and devotion and desire that she'd tried to hold back now crashed through her like a tidal wave crushing a sandcastle wall, and she was swimming with longing, drowning in loss.

I aspire to her strength and integrity, too. What a beautiful way to honor her mother, and she believed the truth of the words. No matter what Luke did or what his company did, she knew that at his core, he, as a human, aspired to strength and integrity. But Bolivia?

She could hear her mother's voice from one of their last conversations: *Ashling. That man loves you. And I have seen how he brings out the very best in you.* Maybe that was true, but there was so much stacked against them when it came to their worldviews. How was she supposed to overcome those differences? Why couldn't Luke be an environmentalist?

And then she thought of something Luke had said to her when they'd met at the museum. *It's not just a job for me. It's how I fill the hole where my brother would be if I hadn't picked up that gun.*

No matter how much she might have wanted him to leave that job, there was so much more at stake for him than just the work he did. It was personal for him, in a deeply ingrained way.

He was such a good person, trying to do his best to reconcile the mistakes of the past.

What am I doing?

Now that the Band-Aid had been ripped off and she'd let Luke's voice into her heart and head again, she was positively rabid for news of him. *Shit.* Why hadn't she tried to reach him while she was here? Why was she so hell-bent on keeping him at a distance, holding his work against him when there was so much at stake beyond his job description? Oh, this situation was so messy when she kept trying to make it cut-and-dried.

What was he doing right now? She felt the burning need to know rush through her, and before she could square what she was doing, she had opened Facebook on her phone and was searching for Savannah's page. She couldn't tell if she hoped more that she would find news of him there or that she wouldn't.

But there he was. *Bingo.*

"Hi," said the woman scooching into the middle seat next to her. She smelled of strong, cheap cologne.

Yikes. This will be a long flight next to the perfume factory.

"Hi," she said, and then she stared again at the photo of Luke and Savannah, a selfie taken…*today. Like ten minutes ago.* And they were surrounded by bookshelves amongst a crowd of other people holding plastic wineglasses. She looked closer at the picture to see that one of Luke's favorite authors was there for a reading and book-signing party.

Savannah: Flipping pages tonight with Lukey at the bookstore.

Ashley startled. *The bookstore? No fucking way.* She read on to see the event was starting soon. A sharp-clawed indignation rose in her, shredding her composure. Jealousy ripped through her.

That's our *special place.*

Ashley almost whimpered as all the knots she had tied on her feelings came unraveled, and the disregarded emotions spilled out with a possessive vengeance. *He's mine,* mine!

But what fueled the possessiveness was love, a love so powerful, so incontestable, so true, and it flooded her, the certainty that any obstacle that came between them must be overcome. And that she had really, really screwed things up by not seeing him now, now when she had the chance. Now, when she could. Her mother had *died* while she was gone. Now was the only time. *Now.* But would he want to see her? He'd stopped sending emails.

With irrational urgency, she reached into her bag for her laptop to search her deleted emails folder, searching Dalton.

"Ladies and gentlemen, we are just waiting for the ground crew to do a final safety check," said the steward's voice through the overhead speaker. "Please—"

She tuned out the steward and found the last email Luke had sent. Subject line: The Truth.

She opened it, and her eyes tried to scan the whole message at once. It was short:

> *Dearest Ashley,*
> *If you are reading this, please call me so I can try to explain everything. The bottom line: You were right. Dalton did try to cover up the spill in Bolivia at first. By the time I found out, critical time had already passed. I have proof, if you need it, that after I learned of the disaster I responded immediately. Help teams were already on their way to the people and land in Bolivia before you even went there. I wanted to respond to you during our call, but I was flustered and unnerved by your pain, and I was stunned. Maybe PTSD? And my childhood stutter came back, and, as you heard, I could barely respond to you. I am embar-*

rassed. I hope you will be able to forgive me, that you will give me the chance to explain what happened in Bolivia and with me. There's so much I have to tell you. You are my everything. My granite. My breath.
Forever yours,
Luke

"Oh my god." Ashley pressed both hands to her chest, her heart hammering in panic. "Oh my god." Horror shook her to the core. She had flustered him to the point of stuttering and then shut him down and out completely? Like an unfeeling monster? He had already addressed the spill when she was reaming him? *She* was the bad guy? Not Luke. *She* was the problem! *Goddammit.*

Luke, will you ever forgive me? She was consumed with a sense of unfathomable doom. *What have I done? What have I done?*

How had she managed to ruin everything? Guilt weighed on her like a leaden dress. A giant hole gaped in her stomach. She felt dizzy. She thought she might throw up.

"The door is closing," announced the steward through the loudspeaker.

"Wait!" Ashley shouted from her seat in row twenty-five. She had to get off this plane. She didn't belong on this flight to Peru. She needed to be on the other side of that door.

She threw her phone and laptop into her bag and bungled past her two seatmates as she juggled her belongings. She wrestled her travel bag out of the overhead bin and ran down the aisle.

"Do you have a checked bag?" asked the steward when she arrived. Though his voice was all business, his eyes were sparkling as if this were not the first time he'd seen a lovestruck woman running madly for the door.

"No!" she confirmed, breathless.

"That's good, honey," he said, and though his posture was professional, his tone was amused. "That means you can go. And good luck."

She flashed him a smile, then headed for the gangplank and began a dead sprint. She had a man to win, if only he would let her in. She ran faster. She *had* to catch him. Now.

To be continued

Grace Woods

Grace Woods is the nom de plume for two female authors brought together by a desire to deliver wildly sensual, unexpected love stories steeped in respect and revelation. They are mentors, mothers, wives, risk takers, businesswomen, avid readers, and lovers of nature. Individually, like the women they write for, they contain multitudes. Together, as Grace Woods, they are a force for telling smart and sexy stories.

For more information, please visit
GraceWoodsRomance.com

Or follow Grace Woods Romance on
Facebook, Instagram and Tik Tok
@gracewoodsromance

Other books by Grace Woods

Printed in Great Britain
by Amazon

29978751R00169